THE MAKING OF A MASTER CRIMINAL

As I approached the front door of the First Bank of Bit O' Heaven, it sensed my presence and swung open with an automatic welcome. I pulled the large handgun from my bag, pointed it at the teller, and growled out my command:

"Your money or your life! Fill this bag with bucks, large denominations, and do it *now!*" As I did this, I managed to hit the alarm button with my elbow. There are some days when you have to do everything for yourself.

By the time the third bag was full, and I was staggering toward the door with my loot, the police began to appear.

"Don't shoot," I squeaked. With real fear because most of them didn't look too bright.

Now you might find all of this a little puzzling—if so, I do not blame you. It is one thing to hold up a bank, another thing still to do it in such a manner that you are sure to be caught. Why, you might ask, be so foolish?

I'll be happy to tell you. To understand my motives, you'll have to understand what life is like on this planet—what *my* life has been like. Let me explain. . . .

A Stainless Steel Rat Is Born

Harry Harrison

BANTAM BOOKS
TORONTO • NEW YORK • LONDON • SYDNEY • AUCKLAND

A STAINLESS STEEL RAT IS BORN

A Bantam Spectra Book / October 1985

ISBN 0-553-24708-5

Published simultaneously in the United States and Canada

Bantam Books are published by Bantam Books, Inc. Its trademark,
consisting of the words "Bantam Books" and the portrayal of a
rooster, is Registered in U.S. Patent and Trademark Office and in
other countries. Marca Registrada. Bantam Books, Inc., 666 Fifth
Avenue, New York, New York 10103.

PRINTED IN THE UNITED STATES OF AMERICA

H   0   9   8   7

CHAPTER ONE

As I approached the front door of The First Bank of Bit O' Heaven, it sensed my presence and swung open with an automatic welcome. I stepped briskly through—and stopped. But I was just far enough inside so that the door was unable to close behind me. While it was sliding shut I took the arc pen from my bag—then spun about just as it had closed completely. I had stopwatched its mechanical reflex time on other trips to the bank, so I knew that I had just 1.67 seconds to do the necessary. Time enough.

The arc buzzed and flared and welded the door securely to its frame. After this all the door could do was buzz helplessly, immobile, until something in the mechanism shorted out and it produced some crackling sparks, then died.

"Destruction of bank property is a crime. You are under arrest."

As it was speaking, the robot bank guard reached out its large padded hands to seize and hold me until the police arrived.

"Not this time, you jangling junkpile," I snarled, and pushed it in the chest with the porcuswine prod. The two metal points produced 300 volts and plenty of amps. Enough to draw the attention of a one ton porcuswine. Enough to short the robot completely. Smoke spurted from all its joints and it hit the floor with a very satisfactory crash.

Behind me. For I had already leapt forward, shouldering aside the old lady who stood at the teller's window. I pulled the large handgun from my bag and pointed it at the teller and growled out my command.

1

"Your money or your life, sister. Fill this bag with bucks."

Very impressive, though my voice did break a bit so the last words came out in a squeak. The teller smiled at this and tried to brazen it out.

"Go home, sonny. This is not . . ."

I pulled the trigger and the .75 recoilless boomed next to her ear; the cloud of smoke blinded her. She wasn't hit but she might just as well have been. Her eyes rolled up in her head and she slid slowly from sight behind the till.

You don't foil Jimmy diGriz that easily! With a single bound I was over the counter and waving the gun at the rest of the wide-eyed employees.

"Step back—all of you! Quick! I want no little pinkies pressing the silent alarm buttons. That's it. You, butter-ball—" I waved over the fat teller who had always ignored me in the past. He was all attention now. "Fill this bag with bucks, large denominations, and do it *now*."

He did it, fumbling and sweating yet working as fast as he could. The customers and staff all stood around in odd poses, apparently paralyzed with fear. The door to the manager's office stayed closed, which meant that he probably wasn't there. Chubby had the bag filled with bills and was holding it out to me. The police had not appeared. There was a good chance I was getting away with it.

I muttered what I hoped was a foul curse under my breath and pointed to one of the sacks that were filled with rolls of coins.

"Dump out the change and fill that too," I ordered, sneering and growling at the same time.

He obeyed with alacrity and soon had this bag stuffed full as well. And still no sign of the police. Could it be that not one of the moronic money employees had pressed the silent alarm button? It could be. Drastic measures would have to be taken.

I reached out and grabbed up another bag of coins. "Fill this one as well," I ordered, slinging it across to him.

As I did this I managed to get the alarm button with my

elbow. There are some days when you have to do everything for yourself.

This had the desired effect. By the time the third bag was full, and I was staggering towards the door with my loot, the police began to appear. One groundcar managed to crash into another (police emergencies are pretty rare around these parts), but eventually they sorted themselves out and lined up outside, guns ready.

"Don't shoot," I squeaked. With real fear, because most of them didn't look too bright. They couldn't hear me through the windows but they could see me. "It's a dummy," I called out. "See!"

I put the muzzle of the gun to the side of my head and pulled the trigger. There was a satisfactory puff of smoke from the smoke generator and the sound effect of the shot was enough to make my ears ring. I dropped behind the counter, away from their horrified gaze. At least there would be no shooting now. I waited patiently while they shouted and cursed and finally broke down the door.

Now, you might find all of this puzzling—if so I do not blame you. It is one thing to hold up a bank, another thing still to do it in such a manner that you are sure to be caught. Why, you might ask, why be so foolish?

I'll be happy to tell you. To understand my motives you have to understand what life is like on this planet—what *my* life has been like. Let me explain.

Bit O' Heaven was founded some thousands of years ago by some exotic religious cult, which has happily since vanished completely. They came here from another planet; some say it was Dirt or Earth, the rumored home of all mankind, but I doubt it. In any case, things didn't work out too well. Maybe the endless labors were too much for them—this was certainly no picnic-world in the early days. As the teachers at school remind us as often as they can, particularly when they tell us how spoiled the young folk are these days. We manage not to tell them that they must be spoiled as well because certainly nothing has changed here in the last thousand years.

In the beginning, sure, it must have been rough. All of

the plantlife was pure poison to human metabolisms and had to be cleared away so edible crops could be grown. The native fauna was just as poisonous, with teeth and claws to match. It was tough. So tough that ordinary cows and sheep had a shockingly short life expectancy. Selective gene manipulation took care of that and the first porcuswine were sent here. Imagine if you can—and you will need a fertile imagination indeed—a one-tonne angry boar hog with sharp tushes and mean disposition. That's bad enough, but picture the creature covered with long quills like an insane porcupine. Odd as it sounds, the plan worked; since the farms are still breeding porcuswine in large numbers it *had* to have worked. Bit O' Heaven Smoked Porcuswine Hams are famed galaxy-wide.

But you won't find the galaxy rushing to visit this piggy planet. I grew up here, I know. This place is so boring even the porcuswine fall asleep.

The funny part is that I seem to be the only one who notices it. They all look at me funny. My Mom always thought that it was just growing pains and burnt porcuswine quills in my bedroom, a folk remedy for same. Dad was always afraid of incipient insanity and used to haul me off to the doctor about once a year. The doctor couldn't find anything wrong and theorized that I might be a throwback to the original settlers, a loser in the Mendelian crapshoot. But that was years ago. I haven't been bothered with parental attention since Dad threw me out of the house when I was fifteen. This was after he had gone through my pockets one night and discovered that I had more money than he did. Mom agreed fervently with him and even opened the door. I think they were glad to see the last of me. I was certainly too much of an irritation in their bovine existence.

What do I think? I think it can be damn lonely at times, being an outcast. But I don't think I would have it any other way. It can have its problems—but problems have solutions.

For example, one problem I licked was getting beat up all the time by the bigger kids. This began happening as soon as I went to school. I made the mistake at first of letting them know I was brighter than they were. Bam, a black eye. The school bullies liked it so much that they had to take turns to beat up on me. I only broke the punishment cycle by bribing a university physical education teacher to give me lessons in unarmed combat. I waited until I was really proficient before fighting back. Then I creamed my would-be creamer and went on to beat up three more of the thugs one after another. I can tell you, all the little kids were my friends after that and never tired of telling me how great it looked to see me chasing six of the worst ruffians down the block. Like I said, from problems come solutions—not to say pleasures.

And where did I get the money to bribe the teacher? Not from Dad, I can tell you. Three bucks a week was my allowance, enough to buy maybe two Gaspo-Fizzes and a small sized Get-Stuffed candy bar. Need, not greed, taught me my first economic lesson. Buy cheap and sell dear and keep the profits for yourself.

Of course there was nothing I could buy, having no capital, so I resorted to not paying at all for the basic product. All kids shoplift. They go through the phase and usually get it beaten out of them when they are detected. I saw the unhappy and tear-stained results of failure and decided to do a market survey as well as a time and motion study before I entered on a career of very petty crime.

Firstly—stay away from the small merchants. They know their stock and have a strong interest in keeping it intact. So do your shopping at the large multis. All you have to worry about then are the store detectives and alarm systems. Then careful study of how they operate will generate techniques to circumvent them.

One of my earliest and most primitive techniques—I blush at revealing its simplicity—I called the book-trap. I constructed a box that looked exactly like a book. Only it had a spring-loaded, hinged bottom. All I needed to do was to push it down on an unsuspecting Get-Stuffed bar to have the candy vanish from sight. This was a crude but workable device that I used for a good length of time. I was about to abandon it for a superior technique when I perceived an opportunity to finish it off in a most positive manner. I was going to take care of Smelly.

His name was Bedford Smillingham but Smelly was the only name we ever called him. As some are born dancers or painters, others are shaped for lesser tasks. Smelly was a born snitch. His only pleasure in life was ratting on his schoolmates. He peeked and watched and snitched. No juvenile peccadillo was too minor for him to note and report to the authorities. They loved him for this—which will tell you a lot about the kind of teachers we had. Nor could he be beatup with impunity. His word was always believed and it was the beater-uppers who suffered the punishment.

Smelly had done me some small ill, I forget exactly what, but it was enough to stir dark and brooding thought, to eventually produce a plan of action. Bragging is a thing all boys enjoy, and I achieved great status by revealing my book-shaped candy bar collector to my peer group. There were oohs and ahhs, made more ooh and ahhish by portioning out some of the loot free for the taking. Not only did this help my juvenile status—but I made sure that it was done where Smelly could eavesdrop. It still feels like yesterday, and I glow warmly with the memory.

"Not only does it work—but I'll show you just how! Come with me to Ming's Multistore!"

"Can we, Jimmy—can we really?"

"You can. But not in a bunch. Drift over there a few at a time and stand where you can watch the Get-Stuffed counter. Be there at 1500 hours and you will really see something!"

Something far better than they could possibly have imagined. I dismissed them and watched the Head's office. As soon as Smelly went through the door I nipped down and broke into his locker.

It worked like a charm. I take some pride in this since it was the first criminal scenario that I prepared for others to take part in. All unsuspecting of course. At the appointed time I drifted up to the candy counter at Ming's, working very hard to ignore the rentaflics, who were working equally hard pretending they weren't watching me. With relaxed motions I placed the book atop the candies and bent to fix my boot fastener.

"Nicked!" the burlier of them shouted, seizing me by the coat collar. "Gotcha!" the other crowed, grabbing up the book.

"What are you doing," I croaked—I had to croak because my coat was now pulled tight about my throat as I hung suspended from it. "Thief—give me back my seven-buck history book that my Mom bought with money earned weaving matts from porcuswine quills!"

"Book?" the great bully sneered. "We know all about this book." He seized the ends and pulled. It opened and the look on his face as the pages flipped over was something sweet to behold."

"I have been framed," I squeaked, opening my coat and dropping free, rubbing at my sore throat. "Framed by the criminal who bragged about using that same technique for his own nefarious ends. He stands there, one Smelly by name. Grab him, guys, before he runs away!"

Smelly could only stand and gape while the ready hands of his peers clutched tight. His schoolbooks fell to the floor and the imitation book burst open and disgorged its contents of Get-Stuffeds upon the floor.

It was beautiful. Tears and recriminations and shouting. A perfect distraction as well. Because this was the day that I field-tested my Mark II Get-Stuffed stuffer. I had worked hard on this device which was built around a silent vacuum pump—with a tube down my sleeve. I brought the tube end close to the candy bars and—zip!—the first of them vanished from sight. It ended up in my trousers, or rather inside the hideous plus-fours we were forced to wear as a school uniform. These bagged out and were secured above the ankle by a sturdy elastic band. The candy bar dropped safely into it, to be followed by another and yet another.

Except I couldn't turn the damn thing off. Thank goodness for Smelly's screaming and struggling. All eyes were on him and not me as I struggled with the switch. Meanwhile the pump still pumped and the Get-Stuffeds shot up my sleeve and into my trousers. I turned it off eventually but if anyone had bothered to look my way, why the empty counter and my bulging-legged form would have been a might suspicious. But thankfully no one did. I exited with a rolling gait, as quickly as I could. As I said, a memory I will always cherish.

Which, of course, does not explain why I have now, on my birthday, made the major decision to hold up a bank. And get caught.

The police had finally broken down the door and were swarming in. I raised my hands over my head and prepared to welcome them with warm smiles.

The birthday, that is the final reason. My seventeenth birthday. Becoming seventeen here on Bit O' Heaven is a very important time in a young man's life.

CHAPTER TWO

The judge leaned forward and looked down at me, not unkindly.

"Now come on, Jimmy, tell me what this tomfoolery is all about."

Judge Nixon had a summer house on the river, not too far from our farm, and I had been there often enough with his youngest son for the judge to get to know me.

"My name is James diGriz, buster. Let us not get too familiar."

This heightened his color a good deal, as you might imagine. His big nose stuck out like a red ski slope and his nostrils flared. "You will have more respect in this courtroom! You are faced with serious charges, my boy, and it might help your case to keep a civil tongue in your mouth. I am appointing Arnold Fortescue, the public defender, as your attorney. . . ."

"I don't need an attorney—and I particularly don't need old Skewey who has been on the sauce so long there isn't a man alive who has seen him sober. . . ."

There was a ripple of laughter from the public seats, which infuriated the judge. "Order in the court!" he bellowed, hammering his gavel so hard that the handle broke. He threw the stub across the room and glared angrily at me. "You are trying the patience of this court. Lawyer Fortescue has been appointed. . . ."

"Not by me he hasn't. Send him back to Mooney's Bar. I plead guilty to all charges and throw myself on the mercy of this merciless court.

He drew in his breath with a shuddering sigh and I

decided to ease off a bit before he had a stroke and collapsed; then there would be a mistrial and more time would be wasted.

"I'm sorry, judge." I hung my head to hide an unrepressed smile. "But I done wrong and I will have to pay the penalty."

"Well, that's more like it, Jimmy. You always were a smart lad and I hate to see all that intelligence going to waste. You will go to Juvenile Correction Hall for a term of not less than—"

"Sorry, your honor," I broke in. "Not possible. Oh, if I only had committed my crimes last week or last month! The law is firm on this and I have no escape. Today is my birthday. My seventeenth birthday.

That slowed him down all right. The guards looked on patiently while he punched for information on his computer terminal. The reporter for the *Bit O' Heaven Bugle* working just as hard on the keys of his own portable terminal at the same time. He was filing quite a story. It didn't take the judge long to come up with the answers. He sighed.

"That is true enough. The records reveal that you are seventeen this day and have achieved your majority. You are no longer a juvenile and must be treated as an adult. This would mean a prison term for certain—if I didn't allow for the circumstances. A first offense, the obvious youth of the defendant, his realization that he has done wrong. It is within the power of this bench to make exceptions, to suspend a sentence and bind a prisoner over. It is my decision . . ."

The last thing I wanted to do was hear his decision now. Things were not going as I had planned, not at all. Action was required. I acted. My scream drowned out the judge's words. Still screaming I dived headlong from the prisoner's dock, shoulder-rolled neatly on the floor, and was across the room before my shocked audience could even consider moving.

"You will write no more scurrilous lies about me, you grubbing hack," I shouted. As I whipped the terminal

from the reporter's hands and crashed it to the floor. Then
stamped the six-hundred-buck machine into worthless junk.
I dodged around him before he could grab me and pelted
towards the door. The policeman there grabbed at me—
then folded when I planted my foot in his stomach.

I could probably have escaped then, but escape at this
point wasn't part of my plan. I fumbled with the door
handle until someone grabbed me, then struggled on until
I was overwhelmed.

This time I was manacled as I stood in the dock and
there was no more Jimmy-my-boy talk from the judge.
Someone had found him a new gavel and he waved it in
my direction, as though wishing to brain me with it. I
growled and tried to look surly.

"James Bolivar diGriz," he intoned. "I sentence you to
the maximum penalty for the crime that you have committed. Hard labor in the city jail until the arrival of the next
League ship, whereupon you will be sent to the nearest
place of correction for criminal therapy." The gavel banged.
"Take him away."

This was more like it. I struggled against my cuffs and
spat curses at him so he wouldn't show any last moment
weaknesses. He didn't. Two burly policemen grabbed me
and hauled me bodily out of the courtroom and jammed
me, not too gently, into the back of the black Maria. Only
after the door had been slammed and sealed did I sit back
and relax—and allow myself a smile of victory.

Yes, victory, I mean that. The whole point of the operation was to get arrested and sent to prison. I needed some
on-the-job training.

There is method in my madness. Very early in life,
probably about the time of my Get-Stuffed successes, I
began to seriously consider a life of crime. For a lot of
reasons—not the least of which was that I *enjoyed* being a
criminal. The financial awards were great; no other job
paid more for less work. And, I must be truthful, I enjoyed the feeling of superiority when I made the rest of
the world look like chumps. Some may say that is a

juvenile emotion. Perhaps—but it sure is a pleasurable one.

About this same time I was faced with a serious problem. How was I to prepare myself for the future? There had to be more to crime than lifting Get-Stuffed bars. Some of the answers I saw clearly. Money was what I wanted. Other people's money. Money is locked away, so the more I knew about locks the more I would be able to get this money. For the first time in school I buckled down to work. My grades soared so high that my teachers began to feel there might be hope for me yet. I did so well that when I elected to study the trade of locksmith they were only too eager to oblige. It was supposed to be a three-year course, but I learned all there was to know in three months. I asked permission to take the final examination. And was refused.

Things were just not done that way, they told me. I would proceed at the same stately pace as the others and in two years and nine months I would get my diploma, leave the school—and enter the ranks of the wage slaves.

Not very likely. I tried to change my course of study and was informed that this was impossible. I had *locksmith* stamped on my forehead, metaphorically speaking of course, and it would remain there for life. They thought.

I began to cut classes and avoid the school for days at a time. There was little they could do about this, other than administer stern lectures, because I showed up for all the examinations and always scored the highest grades. I ought to, since I was making the most of my training in the field. I carefully spread my attentions around so the complacent citizens of the city had no idea they were being taken. A vending machine would yield a few bucks in silver one day, a till at the parking lot the next. Not only did this field work perfect my talents but it paid for my education. Not my school education of course—by law I had to remain there until the age of seventeen—but in my free time.

Since I could find no guidelines to prepare myself for a life of crime, I studied all of the skills that might be of service. I found the word *forgery* in the dictionary, which encouraged me to learn photography and printing. Since unarmed combat had already stood me in good stead, I continued my studies until I earned a Black Belt. Nor was I ignoring the technical side of my chosen career. Before I was sixteen I knew just about all there was to know about computers—while at the same time I had become a skilled microelectronic technician.

All of these were satisfying enough in themselves—but where did I go from there? I really didn't know. That was when I decided to give myself a coming-of-age birthday present. A term in jail.

Crazy? Like a fox! I had to find some criminals—and where better than in jail? A keen line of reasoning, one has to admit. Going to jail would be like coming home, meeting my chosen peer group at last. I would listen and learn and when I felt I had learned enough the lockpick in the sole of my shoe would help me to make my exit. How I smiled and chortled with glee.

More the fool—for it was not to be this way at all.

My hair was shorn, I was bathed in an antiseptic spray, prison clothes and boots were issued—so unprofessionally that I had ample time to transfer the lockpick and my stock of coins—I was thumbprinted and retinapixed, then led to my cell. To behold, to my great joy, that I had a cellmate. My education would begin at last. This was the first day of the rest of my criminal life.

"Good afternoon, sir," I said. "My name is Jim diGriz."

He looked at me and snarled. "Get knotted, kid." He went back to picking his toes, an operation which my entrance had interrupted.

That was my first lesson. The polite linguistic exchanges of life outside were not honored behind these walls. Life was tough—and so was language. I twisted my lips into a sneer and spoke again. In far harsher tones this time.

"Get knotted yourself, toe-cheese. My monicker is Jim. What's yours?"

I wasn't sure about the slang, I had picked it up from

old videos, but I surely had the tone of voice right because I had succeeded in capturing his attention this time. He looked up slowly and there was the glare of cold hatred in his eyes.

"Nobody—and I mean *nobody*—talks to Willy the Blade that way. I'm going to cut you, kid, cut you bad. I'm going to cut my initial into your face. A 'V' for Willy."

"A 'W'," I said. "Willy is spelled with a 'W'."

This upset him even more. "I know how to spell, I ain't no moron!" He was blazing with rage now, digging furiously under the mattress on his bed. He produced a hacksaw blade that I could see had the back edge well sharpened. A deadly little weapon. He bounced it in his hand, sneered one last sneer—then lunged at me.

Well, needless to say, that is not the recommended way to approach a Black Belt. I moved aside, chopped his wrist as he went by—then kicked the back of his ankle so that he ran headfirst into the wall.

He was knocked cold. When he came to I was sitting on my bunk and doing my nails with his knife. "The name is Jim," I said, lip-curled and nasty. "Now you try saying it. Jim."

He stared at me, his face twisted—then began to cry! I was horrified. Could this really be happening?

"They always pick on me. You're no better. Make fun of me. And you took my knife away. I worked a month making that knife, had to pay ten bucks for the broken blade. . . ."

The thought of all of the troubles had started him blubbering again. I saw then that he was only a year or two older than me—and a lot more insecure. So my first introduction to criminal life found me cheering him up, getting a wet towel to wipe his face, giving him back his knife—and even giving him a five-buck goldpiece to stop his crying. I was beginning to feel that a life of crime was not quite what I thought it would be.

It was easy enough to get the story of his life—in fact it was hard to shut him up once he got in full spate. He was filled with self-pity and wallowed in the chance to reveal all to an audience.

Pretty sordid, I thought, but kept silent while his boring reminiscences washed over me. Slow in school, laughed at by the others, the lowest marks. Weak and put upon by the bullies, gaining status only when he discovered—by accident of course with a broken bottle—that he could be a bully too once he had a weapon. The rise in status, if not respect, after that by using threats of violence and more than a little bullying. All of this reinforced by demonstrations of dissections on live birds and other small and harmless creatures. Then his rapid fall after cutting a boy and being caught. Sentenced to Juvenile Hall, released, then more trouble and back to Hall yet again. Until here he was, at the zenith of his career as a knife-carrying punk, imprisoned for extorting money by threat of violence. From a child of course. He was far too insecure to attempt to threaten an adult.

Of course he did not say all this, not at once, but it became obvious after endless rambling complaints. I tuned him out and tuned my inner thoughts in. Bad luck, that was all it was. I had probably been put in with him to keep me from the company of the real hardened criminals who filled this prison.

The lights went out at that moment and I lay back on the bunk. Tomorrow would be my day. I would meet the other inmates, size them up, find the real criminals among them. Befriend them and begin my graduate course in crime. That is surely what I would do.

I went happily to sleep, washed over by a wave of wimpish whining from the adjoining bunk. Just bad luck being stuck in with him. Willy was the exception. I had a roommate who was a loser, that was all. It would all be different in the morning.

I hoped. There was a little nag of worry that kept me awake for a bit, but at last I shrugged it off. Tomorrow would be fine, yes it would be. Fine. No doubt about that, fine. . . .

CHAPTER THREE

Breakfast was no better—and no worse—than the ones I made for myself. I ate automatically, sipping the weak cactus tea and chewing doggedly at the gruel, while I looked around at the other tables. There were about thirty prisoners stuffing their faces in this room, and my gaze went from face to face with a growing feeling of despair.

Firstly, most of them had the same vacuous look of blank stupidity as my cellmate. All right, I could accept that, the criminal classes would of course contain the maladjusted and the mental mud walls. But there had to be more than that! I hoped.

Secondly they were all quite young, none out of their twenties. Weren't there any old criminals? Or was criminality a malfunction of youth that was quickly cured by the social adjustment machines? There had to be more to it than that. There had to be. I took some cheer from this thought. All of these prisoners were losers, that was obvious, losers and incompetents. It was obvious once you thought about it. If they had been any good at their chosen profession they wouldn't be inside! They were of no use to the world or to themselves.

But they were to me. If they couldn't supply the illegal facts that I needed, they would surely be able to put me in touch with those who did. From them I would get leads to the criminals on the outside, the professionals still uncaught. That was what I had to do. Befriend them and extract the information that I needed. All was not lost yet.

It didn't take long for me to discover the best of this despicable lot. A little group was gathered around a hulking young man who sported a broken nose and a scarred face. Even the guards seemed to avoid him. He strutted a good deal and the others made room around him when he walked in the exercise yard after lunch.

"Who is that?" I asked Willy, who huddled on the bench next to me, industriously picking his nose. He blinked rapidly until he finally made out the subject of my attentions, then waved his hands with despair.

"Watch out for him, stay away, he's bad medicine. Stinger is a killer, that's what I heard, and I believe it too. And he's a champ at mudslugging. You don't want to know him."

This was intriguing indeed. I had heard of mudslugging, but I had always lived too close to the city to have seen it in action. There was never any of it taking place near enough for me to hear about, not with the police all around. Mudslugging was a crude sport—and illegal—that was enjoyed in the outlying farm towns. In the winter, with the porcuswine in their sties and the crops in the barns, time would hang heavy on their agrarian hands. That was when the mudslugging would begin. A stranger would appear and challenge the local champion, usually some overmuscled ploughboy. A clandestine engagement would be arranged in some remote barn, the women dismissed, moonshine sureptitiously brought in plastic bottles, bets made—and the barefisted fight begun. To end when one of the combatants could not get off the ground. Not a sport for the squeamish, or the sober. Good, hearty, drunken masculine fun. And Stinger was one of this stalwart band. I must get to know Stinger better.

This was easily enough done. I suppose I could have just walked over and spoken to him, but my thought patterns were still warped by all of the bad videos I had watched for most of my life. Plenty of these were about criminals getting their just deserts in prison; which is probably where I originated the idea of this present escapade. Never matter, the idea was still a sound one. I could prove that by talking to Stinger.

To do this I walked, whistling, about the yard until I

was close to him and his followers. One of them scowled at me and I scuttled away. Only to return as soon as his back was turned, to sidle up beside the head villain.

"Are you Stinger?" I whispered out of the side of my mouth, head turned away from him. He must have seen the same videos because he answered in the same way.

"Yeah. So who wants to know?"

"Me. I just got into this joint. I got a message for you from the outside."

"So tell."

"Not where these dummies can hear. We gotta be alone."

He gave me a most suspicious look from under his beetling brows. But I had succeeded in capturing his curiosity. He muttered something to his followers, then strolled away. They remained behind but flashed murderous looks at me when I strolled in the same direction. He went across the yard towards a bench—the two men already there fleeing as he approached. I sat down next to him and he looked me up and down with disdain.

"Say what you gotta say, kid—and it better be good."

"This is for you," I said, sliding a twenty-buck coin along the bench towards him. "The message is from me and from no one else. I need some help and am willing to pay for it. Here is a down payment. There is plenty more where this came from."

He sniffed disdainfully—but his thick fingers scraped up the coin and slipped it into his pocket. "I ain't in the charity business, kid. The only geezer I help is myself. Now, shove off—"

"Listen to what I have to say first. What I need is someone to break out of prison with me. One week from today. Are you interested?"

I had caught his attention this time. He turned and looked me square in the eye, cold and assured. "I don't like jokes," he said—and his hand grabbed my wrist and twisted. It hurt. I could have broken the grip easily, but I did not. If this little bit of bullying was important to him, then bully away.

"It's no joke. Eight days from now I'll be on the outside. You can be there too if you want to be. It's your decision."

He glared at me some more—then let go of my wrist. I rubbed at it and waited for his response. I could see him chewing over my words, trying to make up his mind. "Do you know why I'm inside?" he finally asked.

"I heard rumors."

"If the rumor was that I killed a geezer, then the rumor was right. It was an accident. He had a soft head. It broke when I knocked him down. They was going to pass it off as a farm accident but another geezer lost a bundle to me on the match. He was going to pay me next day but he went to the police instead because that was a lot cheaper. Now they are going to take me to a League hospital and do my head. The shrinker here says I won't want to fight again after that. I won't like that."

The big fists opened and closed when he talked and I had the sudden understanding that fighting was his life, the one thing that he could do well. Something that other men admired and praised him for. If that ability were taken away—why they might just as well take away his life at the same time. I felt a sudden spurt of sympathy but did not let the feeling show.

"You can get me out of here?" The question was a serious one.

"I can."

"Then I'm your man. You want something out of me, I know that, no one does nothing for nothing in this world. I'll do what you want, kid. They'll get me in the end, there is no place to hide anywhere when they are really looking for you. But I'm going to get mine. I'm going to get the geezer what put me in here. Get him proper. One last fight. Kill him the way he killed me."

I could not help shivering at his words because it was obvious that he meant them. That was painfully clear. "I'll get you out," I said. But to this I added the unspoken promise that I would see to it that he got nowhere near the object of his revenge. I was not going to start my new criminal career as an accomplice to murder.

Stinger took me under his protective wing at once. He shook my hand, crushing my fingers with that deadly grip, then led me over to his followers.

"This is Jim," he said. "Treat him well. Anyone causes him trouble got trouble with me." They were all insincere smiles and promises of affection—but at least they wouldn't bother me. I had the protection of those mighty fists. One of them rested on my shoulder as we strolled away. "How you going to do it?" he asked.

"I'll tell you in the morning. I'm making the last arrangements now," I lied. "See you then." I strolled off on an inspection tour, almost as eager to be out of this sordid place as he was. For a different reason. His was revenge—mine was depression. They were losers in here, all losers, and I like to think of myself as a winner. I wanted to be well away from them all and back in the fresh air.

I spent the next twenty-four hours finding the best way out of the prison. I could open all of the mechanical locks inside the prison easily enough; my lockpick worked fine on our cell door. The only problem was the electronic gate that opened out into the outer courtyard. Given time—and the right equipment—I could have opened that too. But not under the eyes of guards stationed in the observation booth above it right around the clock. That was the obvious way out, so it was the route to be avoided. I needed a better idea of the layout of the prison—so a reconnoiter was very much in order.

It was after midnight when I eased out of my bed. No shoes, I had to be as quiet as possible, so three pairs of socks should do the job. Working silently, I stuffed extra clothing under the blankets so the bed would look occupied if one of the guards should look in through the barred door. Willy was snoring lustily when I clicked the lock open and slipped out into the corridor. He wasn't the only one enjoying his sacktime and the walls echoed with *zzzz*ing and gronking. The nightlights were on and I was alone on the landing. I looked over the edge carefully and saw that the guard on the floor below was working on his racing form. Wonderful, I hoped that he had a winner. Silent as a shadow I went to the stairs and up them to the floor above.

Which was depressingly identical to the one below; nothing but cells. As was the next floor and the one above that. Which was the top floor so I could go no higher. I was about to retrace my steps when my eye caught a glint of metal in the shadows at the far end. Nothing ventured, as the expression goes. I scuttled past the barred doors, and the—hopefully—sleeping inmates, to the distant wall.

Well, well, what did we have here! Iron rungs in the wall—vanishing up into the darkness. I grabbed onto the first one and vanished up with them. The last rung was just below the ceiling. It was also just under a trapdoor that was let into the ceiling above. Metal, with a metal frame—and locked securely as I discovered when I pushed up against it. There had to be a lock, but it was invisible in the darkness. And I had to find it. Looping one arm through the iron rung I began to run my fingertips over the surface of the door in what I hoped was a regular pattern.

There was nothing there. I tried again, changing hands because my arm felt like it was being dragged from its socket—with the same result. But there *had* to be a lock. I was panicking and not using my brain. I fought back my rising fears and stirred up my brain cells. There must be a lock or seal of some kind. And it was not on the trapdoor. So—it had to be on the frame. I reached out slowly, ran my fingers along the sides of the frame. And found it at once.

How simple the answers are when you ask the right questions! I eased the lockpick from my pocket and slipped it into the lock. Within seconds it had clicked open. Seconds after that I had pushed the trapdoor up, climbed through, closed it behind me—and sniffed appreciatively of the cool night air.

I was out of prison! Standing on the roof, yes, of course, but free in spirit at least. The stars were bright above and shed enough light so I could see across the dark surface. It was flat and broad, bordered with a knee-high parapet and studded with vents and pipes. Something large and bulky occluded the sky, and when I worked my way close to it I heard the dripping of water. The water tank, fine, now what was visible below?

To the front I looked down into the well-lit courtyard, guarded and secure. But what was the back like?

Far more interesting, I assure you. There was a straight drop of five stories to a rear yard, which was feebly illuminated by a single bulb. There were waste bins there, and barrels, and a heavy gate in the outer wall. Locked, undoubtedly. But what man had locked man could unlock. Or rather I could. This was the way out.

Of course there was the five-story drop, but something could be worked there. Or perhaps I could find another way into the backyard. Plenty of time to run through the permutations of escape, six days yet. My feet were getting cold and I yawned and shivered. I had done enough for one night. My hard prison bunk seemed very attractive at this moment.

Carefully and silently I retraced my steps. Eased the trapdoor shut above me, checked to see that it was locked, went down the ladder and the stairs to my floor. . . .

And heard the voices ahead. Loud and clear. The loudest of all being my dear cellmate Willy. I took one horrified look at the open door of my cell, at the heavy boots of the guards there, then pulled myself back and ran up the stairs again. With Willy's words ringing like a tocsin of doom in my ears.

"I woke and he was gone! I was alone! Monsters ate him or something! That's when I started shouting. Save me, please! Whatever got him came right through the locked door. It's gonna get me next!"

CHAPTER FOUR

Anger at my cretinous cellmate warmed me; the imminence of my capture instantly chilled me again. I fled unthinkingly, away from the voices and commotion. Back up the stairs, one flight, another—

Then all the lights came on and the sirens began to wail. The prisoners stirred and called out to one another. In a few moments they would be at the cell doors, would see me, would cry out, guards would appear. There was no escape. I knew this, yet all I could do was run. To the top floor—then past the cells there. All of which were now brightly lit. I would be seen by the prisoners as I went by them, and I knew for certain that I would be ratted on by whichever juvenile delinquent spotted me. It was all over.

Head high, I walked past the first cell and glanced in as I passed.

It was empty. As were all of the other cells on this floor. I still had a chance! Like a demented ape I swarmed up the iron rungs and fumbled my lockpick into the lock. There were voices below me, getting louder, and footsteps as well as two of the guards ascended the stairs that faced away from me. But all that one of them had to do was turn his head. And when they reached the floor I would be seen at once.

The lock clicked open and I pushed and swarmed up through the opening. Flat on the roof I eased the door down. Seeing two fat guards through the opening just turning my way as it shut.

Had they seen it closing? My heart thudded like an

insane drum and I gasped for air and waited for the shouts of alarm.

They did not come. I was still free.

Some freedom! Depression instantly clutched and shook me. Free to lie on the roof, to shiver violently as the perspiration began to dry, free to huddle up here until I was found.

So I huddled and shivered and generally felt sorry for myself for about a minute. Then I stood and shook myself like a dog and felt the anger begin to rise.

"Big criminal," I whispered aloud, just to make sure that I heard. "Life of crime. And on your first big job you let yourself be trapped by a knife-wielding moron. You've learned a lesson, Jim. May you someday be free to put it into practice. Always guard your flanks and your rear. Consider all the possibilities. Consider the fact that the cretin might have woken up. So you should have coshed him or something to make certain of his sound sleep. Which is certainly water over the dam. Remember the lesson well, but look around now and try to make the best of this rapidly disintegrating escape."

My options were limited. If the guards opened the trapdoor and came up to the roof they would find me. Was there any place to hide? The top of the water tank might offer a temporary refuge, but if they came this far they would certainly look there as well. But with no way to get down the sheer walls it offered the only feeble hope. Get up there.

It wasn't easy. It was made of smooth metal and the top was just beyond my reach. But I had to do it. I stepped back and took a run, leaped, and felt my fingers just grasp the edge. I scrabbled for a hold but they pulled loose and I dropped heavily back to the roof. Anyone below would have certainly heard that. I hoped I was over an empty cell and not the hall.

"Enough hoping and not enough trying, Jim," I said, and added a few curses in the hope of building my morale. I had to get up there!

This time I retreated to the far edge, the backs of my

knees against the parapet, taking breath after deep breath.
Go!

Run up, fast, the right spot—jump!

My right hand slapped against the edge. I grabbed and
heaved. Got my other hand up there and pulled mightily,
scraping and bruising myself on the rough metal, hauling
myself up onto the top of the tank.

To lie there breathing heavily, looking at a dead bird
not a foot from my face, vacant eyes staring into mine. I
started to pull away when I heard the trapdoor slam
heavily back onto the roof.

"Give me a push up, will you? I'm stuck!"

By the wheezing and grunting that followed I was sure
that this had to be one of the fat guards that I had seen on
the floor below. More gasping and puffing heralded the
arrival of his adipose companion.

"I don't know what we're doing up here," the first
arrival whined.

"I do," his companion said quite firmly. "We're obeying
orders, which never did no one no harm."

"But the hatch was locked."

"So was the cell door he went through. Look around."

The heavy footsteps circled the roof, then returned.

"Not here. No place to hide. Not even hanging over the
edge because I looked."

"There is one place, one place we haven't looked."

I could feel the eyes burning towards me through the
solid metal. My heart had started the drumbeat thing
again. I clutched at the rusty metal and felt only despair as
the footsteps crunched close.

"He could never climb up there. Too high. I can't even
reach the top."

"You can't even reach your shoelaces when you bend
over. Come on, give me a lift up. If you boost my foot I
can reach up and grab on. All I got to do is take a look."

How right he was. Just one look. And there was nothing
I could do about it. With the lethargy of defeat possessing
me. I lay there, hearing the scratching and the curses, the
overweight puffing and scrabbling. The scratching grew

close and not a foot before my face a large hand appeared, groping over the edge.

My subconscious must have done it because I swear there was no logical thought involved. My hand shot out and pushed the dead bird forward, to the very edge, below the fingers—which descended and closed on it.

The results were eminently satisfying. The bird vanished, as did the hand, followed by screams and shouts, scrabblings, and two large thuds.

"Why did you do that—?"

"I grabbed it, uggh—oww! My ankle is broke."

"See if you can stand on it. Here, hold my shoulder. Hop along on the other foot, this way. . . ."

There was plenty of shouting back and forth through the trapdoor while I hugged myself with relief and pleasure. They might be back soon, there was that chance, but at least the first round was mine.

As the seconds, then the minutes, moved slowly by I realized that I had won the second round as well. The search had moved away from the roof. For the moment. The sirens cut off and the bustle moved down to the ground below. There were shouts and the slamming of doors, racing of engines as cars moved out into the night. Not soon after—wonder of wonders—the lights began to go out. The first search was over. I started to doze—then jerked myself awake.

"Dummy! You are still in the soup. The search has been made, but this joint is still sealed tight. And you can bet your last buck that starting at first light they will go through every nook and corner. And will be up here with a ladder this time. So with that in mind it is time to move."

And I knew just where I was moving to. The last place they would look for me this night.

Through the trapdoor one last time, and down the darkened corridor. Some of the inmates were still muttering about the events of the night, but all of them appeared to be back in their bunks. Silently I slipped down the stairs and up to cell 567B. Opening it in absolute silence and

closing it behind me the same way. Past my stripped bunk
to the other bunk where my fink friend Willy slept the
sleep of the unjust.

My hand clamped his mouth shut, his eyes sprang open,
and I exacted primal and sadistic pleasure by whispering
in his ear.

"You are dead, you rat, dead. You called the guards and
now you are going to get what you deserve. . . ."

His body gave one gigantic heave then went limp. The
eyes were closed. Had I killed him? At once I regretted
the bad taste of my little joke. No, not dead, passed out,
his breathing light and slow. I went to get a towel, soaked
it in cold water—then let him have it right in the mush.

His scream turned to a gurgle as I stuffed the towel into
his mouth.

"I'm a generous man, Willy, that's how lucky you are.
I'm not going to kill you." My whispered words seemed to
reassure him because I felt the tremble in his body sub-
side. "You are going to help me. If you do that you will
come to no harm. You have my word. Now prepare to
answer my question. Think carefully about this. You are
going to whisper just one thing. You are going to tell me
the number of the cell that Stinger is in. Nod your head if
you are ready. Good. I'm taking the towel away. But if you try
any tricks or say anything—*anything*—else, why then you
are dead. Here goes."

". . . *231B* . . ."

This same floor, good. The towel went right back in.
Then I pressed hard behind his right ear, applying continous
pressure to the blood vessel that leads to the brain. Six
seconds unconsciousness, ten seconds death. He thrashed
then went limp again. I released my thumb on the count
of seven. I do have a forgiving nature.

I used the towel to clean my face and hands, then
groped for my shoes and put them on. Along with another
shirt and my jacket. After that I gurgled down at least a
litre of water and was ready to face the world again. I
stripped the blankets from the beds, bundled them under
my arm—then left.

On tiptoe, as silently as I could, I slipped down to Stinger's cell. I felt immune, impervious. I realized that this was both foolish and dangerous. But after the traumatic events of the evening I seemed to have run out of fear. The cell door opened beneath my delicate touch and Stinger's eyes opened as well when I pushed his shoulder.

"Get dressed," I said quietly. "We're getting out now."

I'll give him this much—he didn't bother asking questions. Just pulled his clothes on while I took the blankets from his bunk. "We need at least two more," I said.

"I'll get Eddie's."

"He'll wake up."

"I'll see he goes back to sleep."

There was a murmured question—followed by a solid thud. Eddie went back to sleep and Stinger brought over the blankets.

"Here's what we do," I told him. "I found the way up to the roof. We go there and knot these blankets together. Then we climb down them and get away. Okay?"

Okay! I had never heard a more insane plan in my life. But not Stinger.

"Okay! Let's go!"

Once more up the stairs—I was really getting pretty tired of this—and tired all over as well. I climbed the rungs, opened the trapdoor, and pushed the blankets through onto the roof when he passed them up to me. He didn't say a word until I had closed and sealed the door again.

"What happened? I heard you got away and I was going to kill you if they ever brought you back."

"It's not that simple. I'll tell you when we get clear. Now let's start tying. Opposite corners lengthwise; we need all the length we can get. Use a square knot like you learned in the Boy Sprouts. Like this."

We knotted and tied like crazy until they were all connected, then took the ends and pulled and grunted and that was that. I tied one end to a solid-looking pipe and threw the bundle of blankets over the side.

"At least twenty feet short," Stinger said, scowling down

at the ground. "You go first because you're lighter. If it breaks with me at least you got a chance. Get moving."

The logic of this could not be argued with. I climbed up on the parapet and seized the top blanket. Stinger squeezed my arm with an unexpected show of emotion. Then I was climbing down.

It was not easy. My hands were tired and the blanket fabric hard to grip. I went down as quickly as I could because I knew that my strength was running out.

Then my legs scrabbled at empty air and I had reached the end. The hard floor of the courtyard appeared to be very far below. It was difficult to let go—or rather really very easy. I could hold on no longer. My fingers opened and I fell—

—hit and rolled and sat on the ground gasping for breath. I had done it. High above I could see the dark figure of Stinger swarming down the rope, hand over hand. Within seconds he was on the ground, landing light as a cat beside me, helping me to my feet. Half-supporting me as I stumbled to the gate.

My fingers were trembling and I couldn't get the lock open. We were painfully visible here under the light and if any of the guards glanced out of a window above we were trapped. . . .

I took in a long, shuddering breath—then inserted the picklock once again. Slowly and carefully feeling the grooves on the interior, turning and pushing.

It clicked open and we hurled ourselves through. Stinger pushed it silently shut, then turned and ran out into the night with me right at his heels.

We were free!

CHAPTER FIVE

"Wait!" I called after Stinger as he pelted down the road. "Not that way. I've got a better plan. I worked it out before I was sent up."

He slowed to a halt and thought about this and slowly made up his mind. "You called the shots OK so far. So what we gonna do?"

"For openers—leave a trail that they can follow with sniffer robots. This way."

We left the road and cut through the grass and down to the nearby stream. It was shallow but cold and I could not suppress a shiver as we waded across. The main highway ran close by and we headed that way. Crouching low as a heavy transporter thundered by. For the moment there was no other traffic in sight.

"Now!" I called out. "Straight up to the road—then right back down walking in your own footprints."

Stinger did what he was told, backtracking with me to the stream and into the frigid water again.

"That's smart," he said. "The sniffers find where we went into the water, where we came out—and follow us to the road. Then they think that a groundcar maybe picked us up. So what comes next?"

"We go upstream—staying in the water—to the nearest farm. Which happens to be a porcuswine farm. . . ."

"No way! I hate them mothers. Got bit by one when I was a kid."

"We have no other choice. Anything else we do the fuzz will pick us up at daybreak. I can't say I love the porkers either. But I grew up on a farm and I know how to get along with them. Now let's move before my legs freeze off at the ankles."

It was a long, cold slog and I could not stop the trembling once it began. But there was absolutely nothing else to do except push on. My teeth were rattling in my head like castanets before we came to the brook that bubbled down through the fields to join the stream that we were wading in. The stars were beginning to fade; dawn was not too far away.

"This is it," I said. "The stream that we want. That chopped tree is my landmark. Stay right behind me—we're very close now." I reached up and broke off a dead branch that overhung the stream, then led the way. We waded along until we reached a tall, electrified fence that spanned the stream. It could be clearly seen in the growing light. I used the branch to lift the bottom of the fence so Stinger could crawl under; then he did the same for me. As I stood up I heard the familiar rustle of large quills from the oak grove nearby. A large, dark form separated itself from the trees and moved towards us. I grabbed the branch from Stinger and called out softly.

"Sooo-ee, sooo-ee . . . here swine, swine, swine."

There was a bubbling grunt from the boar as it approached. Stinger was muttering under his breath, curses or prayers—or both—as he stood behind me. I called again and the great creature came close. A real beauty, a tonne at least, looking at me with its small red eyes. I stepped forward and raised the branch slowly—and heard Stinger moan behind me. The boar never moved as I poked the stick behind its ear, parted the long quills—and began to scratch its hide industriously.

"What are you doing? It'll kill us!" Stinger wailed.

"Of course not," I said, scratching harder. "Listen to it?" The porcuswine's eyes were half-closed with pleasure and it was burbling happily. "I know these big porkers well. They get vermin under their quills and can't get at them. They love a good scratch. Let me do the other ear—there are nice itchy patches behind the ears—then we can go on."

I scratched, the boar moaned happily, and dawn crept up on us. A light came on in the farmhouse and we knelt down behind the porcuswine. The door opened, someone threw out a basin of water, then it closed again.

"Let's get to the barn," I said. "This way."

The boar grumbled when I stopped scratching, then trotted along behind us, hoping for more, as we skulked across the farm. Which was a good thing since there were plenty more of the spiky porkers on all sides. But they moved aside when the king-pig approached and we proceeded in stately parade to the barn.

"So long, big feller," I said, giving a last good scratch. "Been nice knowing you." Stinger had the barn door open and we slipped inside. We had just slid the bolt again when the heavy wood trembled as our overweight companion leaned against it and snorted.

"You saved my life," Stinger gasped. "I'll never forget that."

"Just skill," I said humbly. "After all, you are good with fists—"

"And you're great with pigs!"

"I wouldn't have phrased it *exactly* that way," I muttered. "Now let's get up into the hayloft where it is warm—and where we won't be seen. There is a long day ahead of us and I want to spend as much of it as I can sleeping."

It had been quite a night. I burrowed into the hay, sneezed twice as the dust got into my nose—then must have fallen instantly asleep.

The next thing I knew Stinger was shaking me by the shoulder and sunlight was streaming between the boards in the wall. "Cops is here," he whispered.

I blinked the sleep from my eyes and looked through the crack. A green and white police floater was hovering outside the farmhouse door and two uniformed pug-uglies were showing a sheet to the farmer. He shook his head and his voice was clear above the farmyard sounds.

"Nope. Never seen neither of them. Never seen a soul in a week if you want to know. Fact is, kind of nice to talk to you fellers. These guys really look nasty, criminals you say . . ."

"Pops, we ain't got all day. If you didn't see them they could still be hiding on your farm. Maybe in your barn?"

"No way they could do that. Them's *porcuswine* out there. Most ornery critters in creation."

"We still got to look. Orders are to search every building in the vicinity."

The policemen started our way and there was a screech like an insane siren and the thud of sharp hooves. Around the corner of the barn—quills rattling with anger—came our friend of the night before. He charged and the police dived for their floater. The angry boar crashed into it, sending it rocking across the yard with a great dent in its side. The farmer nodded happily.

"Told you weren't no one in the barn. Little Larry here, he don't cotton onto strangers. But drop by anytime you're in the neighborhood, fellers. . . ."

He had to shout the last words because the floater was heading west with Little Larry in snorting pursuit.

"Now that is what I call beautiful," Stinger said, awe in his voice. I nodded silent agreement. Even the dullest of lives contain moments of pure glory.

Enough fun; time to work. I chewed on a straw and stretched out on the warm hay. "Porcuswine are nice when you know them."

"The police don't seem to think so," he said.

"Guess not. That was the best thing I ever saw. I don't exactly get along with the police."

"Who does? What you got sent up for, Jimmy?"

"Bank robbery. Did you ever hold up a bank?"

He whistled appreciation and shook his head *no*. "Not my style. I wouldn't know what to do first. Mudslugging's my style. Ain't been beat in nine years."

"Knocking around the way you do you must meet a lot of people. Did you ever meet Smelly Schmuck?" I extemporized rapidly. "He and I did some banks in Graham State."

"Never met him. Never even heard of him. You're the first bank robber I ever met."

"Really? Well, I guess there aren't that many of us these days. But you must know some safecrackers. Or groundcar thieves?"

All I got for my efforts was another shake of the head. "The only time I ever meet guys like you is in jail. I know some gamblers; they go around the mudslugging fights. But they're all two-buckers, losers. I did know one once who swore he knew The Bishop, long time ago."

"The Bishop?" I said, blinking rapidly, trying to sum up what little I knew of the ecclesiastical hierarchy. "I don't go to church much these days. . . ."

"Not that kind of bishop. I mean The Bishop, the geezer used to clean out banks and things. Thought you would have heard of him."

"Before my time, I guess."

"Before everyone's time. This was years ago. Cops never got him, I hear. This two-bucker bragged he knew The Bishop, said that he had retired and was lying low. He must of been lying, two-bucker like him."

Stinger knew no more than this and I hesitated to pump him too hard. Our conversation died away and we both dozed on and off until dark. We were thirsty and hungry, but knew that we had to remain undercover during daylight. I chewed on my straw and tried not to think of large beers and bottles of cold water, but thought about The Bishop instead. It was a thin lead, but was all that I had. By the time the sun went down I was hungry and thirsty and thoroughly depressed. My prison escapade had turned out to be a dangerous fiasco. Jails were for losers—that's about all I had found out. And in order to discover this fact I had risked life and limb. Never again. I took a silent oath to stay away from prison and the minions of the law in the future. Good criminals don't get caught. Like The Bishop, whoever he might be.

When the last trace of light was gone from the sky we eased the barn door open. A bubbling grunt reached our ears and a great form blocked our exit. Stinger gasped and I grabbed him before he could flee.

"Grab a stick and make yourself useful," I said. "I'll teach you a new skill."

So we scratched like crazy under the creature's quills while it grunted with pleasure. Trotting behind us like a pet dog when we finally left. "We got a friend for life," I said as we slipped out the gate and I waved goodbye to our porcine pal.

"Those kind of friends I can live without forever. You figure out what we do next?"

"Absolutely. Advance planning, that's my middle name. There is a siding down this way where they transship from the linears to trucks. We stay away from it because the police are sure to be there. But all the trucks take the same road to the highway where there is a traffic control light. They have to stop until the highway computers see them and let them on. We go there—"

"And break into the back of one of the trucks!"

"You're learning. Only we get one in the right lane going west. Otherwise we end up back in the fine city of Pearly Gates and right after that in the prison we worked so hard to get out of."

"Lead the way, Jim. You are the brainiest kid I ever met. You're going to go far."

That was my expressed wish and I nodded quick agreement. I was just sorry that he wasn't going too. But I didn't want to live with some far-off yokel's life on my conscience—as much as he might deserve a little agro. But Stinger planned far more than that. I could not be party to a killing.

We found the road and waited in the bushes beside it. Two trucks rumbled up together—with the lights of another one following. We stayed out of sight. First one, then the second pulled out and headed east. When the third slowed down to stop for his turn, lights came on. West!

We ran. I was fumbling with the locking bar when Stinger shouldered me aside. He hauled down and the door swung open. The truck started forward and he pushed me up into it. He had to run as it started its turn—but grabbed the sill and pulled himself up with a single heave of those mighty arms. Between us we got the door closed but not sealed.

"We done it!" he said triumphantly.

"We certainly did. This truck is going in the right direction for you—but I have to get back to Pearly Gates as soon as the heat dies down. In about an hour we'll be passing through Billville. I'll leave you there."

It was a quick trip. I swung down at the first stop for a light and he gripped my hand. "Good luck, kid," he called out as the truck pulled away. I couldn't wish him the same.

I dug out a buck coin as the truck rumbled way. And made a mental note of its registration number. As soon as it was out of sight I headed towards the lights of a phonebox. I felt like a rat as I punched the buttons for the police.

But, really, I had no choice.

CHAPTER SIX

Unlike the hapless Stinger, I had a careful escape plan worked out. Part of it was a literal misdirection for my late partner. He was not really stupid, so it shouldn't take him very long to figure out who had blown the whistle on him. If he talked and told the police that I had returned to the fine city of Pearly Gates—why that would be all for the better. I had no intention of leaving Billville, not for quite a while.

The office had been rented through an agency and all transactions had been done by computer. I had visited it before my hopeless bank job, and at that time had left some supplies there. They would come in very handy right now. I would enter through the service door of the fully automated building—after turning off the alarms by using a concealed switch I had been prudent enough to install there. It had a timer built into it, so I had ten lazy minutes to get to the office. I yawned as I picked the lock, sealed the door behind me, then trudged up three flights of stairs. Past the dull eyes of the deactivated cameras and through the invisible—and inoperative—infrared beams. I picked the lock of the office door with two minutes to spare. I blanked the windows, turned on the lights—then headed for the bar.

Cold beer has never tasted better. The first one never even touched the sides of my throat and sizzled when it hit my stomach. I sipped the second as I tore the tab on a dinpac of barbecued ribs of porcuswine. As soon as the steam whistled through the venthole I ripped open the lid of the stretched pack and pulled out a rib the length of my arm. Yum!

Showered, dipilated and wrapped around a third beer, I began to feel much better. "On," I told the terminal, then punched into the comnet. My instructions were simple; all newspaper records on the planet for the last fifty years, all references to a criminal named The Bishop, check for redundancies around the same date and don't give me any duplicates. Print.

Before I had picked up my beer again the first sheets were sliding out of the fax. The top sheet was the most recent—and it was ten years old. A not too interesting item from a city on the other side of the planet, Decalogg. The police had picked up an elderly citizen in a low bar who claimed that he was The Bishop. However it had turned out to be a case of senile dementia and the suspect had been ushered back to the retirement home from which he had taken a walk. I picked up the next item.

I tired towards morning and took a nap in the filing cabinet which turned into a bed when ordered to do so. In the gray light of dawn, helped by a large black coffee, I finished placing the last sheet into the pattern that spread across the floor. Rosy sunlight washed across it. I turned off the lights and tapped the stylo against my teeth while I studied the pattern.

Interesting. A criminal who brags about his crimes. Who leaves a little drawing of a bishop behind after scarpering with his loot. A simple design—easy enough to copy. Which I did. I held it out at arm's length and admired it.

The first bishop had been found in the empty till of an automated liquor store sixty-eight years ago. If The Bishop had started his career of crime as a teenager, as I have done, that would put him in his eighties now. A comfortable age to be, since life expectancy has now been pushed up to a century and a half. But what had happened to him to explain the long silence? Over fifteen years had passed since he had left his last calling card. I numbered off the possibilities on my fingers.

"Number one, and a chance always to be considered, is that he has snuffed it. In which case I can do nothing so let us forget about that.

"Two—he could have gone offplanet and be pursuing his life of crime among the stars. If so, forget it like number one. I need a lot more golden bucks, and experience, before I try my hand on other worlds.

"Three, he has gone into retirement to spend his ill-gotten gains—in which case more power to him. Or four, he has changed rackets and stopped leaving his spoor at every job."

I sat back smugly and sipped the coffee. If it were three or four I had a chance of finding him. He had certainly had a busy career before the years of silence; I looked at the list with appreciation. Plane theft, car theft, cash theft, bank emptying. And more and more. All of the crimes involving moving bucks from someone else's pockets to his pockets. Or real property that could be sold quickly, with forged identification, for more bucks. And he had never been caught, that was the best part of it. Here was the man who could be my mentor, my tutor, my university of crime—who would one day issue a diploma of deviltry that would eventually admit me to the golden acres I so coveted.

But how could I find him if the united police forces of an entire world, over a period of decades, had never been able to lay a finger on him? An interesting question.

So interesting that I could see no easy answer. I decided to let my subconscious work on this problem for a bit, so I pushed some synapses aside and let the whole thing slip down into my cerebellum. The street outside was beginning to fill up with shoppers and I thought that might be a good idea for me as well. All the rations I had here were either frozen or packaged, and after the sludgy prison food I felt the urge for things that crackled and crunched. I opened the makeup cabinet and began to prepare my public persona.

Adults don't realize—or remember—how hard it is to be a teenager. They forget that this is the halfway house of maturity. The untroubled joys of childhood are behind one, the mature satisfactions of adulthood still ahead. Aside from the rush of blood to the head, as well as other places, when thoughts of the opposite sex intrude, there are real difficulties. The hapless teenager is expected to act like an adult—yet has none of the privileges of that exalted state. For my part I had escaped the tedious tyranny of teendom by skipping over it completely. When not lolling about in school or trading lies with my age group, I became an adult. Since I was far more intelligent than most of them—or at least I thought that I was—adults that is, I had only to assume the physical role.

First an application of crowsfooter around my eyes and on my forehead. As soon as this colorless liquid was applied wrinkles appeared and the calendar of my age rushed forward a number years. A few wattles under my chin blended in well with the wrinkles, while the final touch was a nasty little moustache. When I pulled on my shapeless under-office clerk jacket, my own mother would not have recognized me if she had passed me in the street. In fact this had happened about a year ago and I had asked her the time and even then no spark of recognition had brought a glint to her bovine eyes. Taking an umbrella from the closet, since there was absolutely no possibility of rain, I stepped from the office and proceeded to the nearest shopping mall.

I must say, my subconscious was really working fast this day, as I shortly found out. Even after all the beers I still had a thirst. That dry stay in the barn had left its mark. Therefore I turned smartly under the platinum arches of Macswineys and marched up to the serving robot that was built into the counter. The plastic head had a permanent grin painted on it and the voice was syrupy and sexy.

"How can I be of service, sir or madam?" They could have spent a few bucks on a sex-recognition program I thought as I scanned the list of TUM-CHILLER YUMMY DRINKS on the wall.

"Let me have a double-cherry oozer with lots of ice."

"On the way, sir or madam. That will be three bucks, if you please."

I dropped the coins in the hopper and the serving hatch flipped open and my drink appeared. While I reached for it I had to listen to a robotic sales pitch.

"Macswineys is happy to serve you today. With the drink of your choice I am sure you would like a barbecued porcuswineburger with yummy topsecret sauce garnished with sugarfried spamyams. . . ."

The voice faded away from my attention as my subconscious heaved up the answer to my little problem. A really simple and obvious answer that was transparent in its clarity, pristine pure and simple. . . .

"Come on, buster. Order or split, you can't stand there all day."

The voice graveled in my ear and I muttered some excuse and shuffled off to the nearest booth and dropped into it. I knew now what had to be done.

Simply stand the problem on its head. Instead of me looking for The Bishop I would have to make him look for me.

I drank my drink until my sinuses hurt, staring unseeingly into space as the pieces of the plan clicked into place. There was absolutely no chance of my finding The Bishop on my own—it would be foolish to even waste my time trying. So what I had to do was commit a crime so outrageous and munificent that it would be on all the news channels right around the planet. It had to be so exotic that not a person alive with the ability to read—or with a single finger left to punch in a news channel—would be unaware of it. The entire world would know what had happened. And they would know as well that The Bishop had done it because I would leave his calling card on the spot.

The last traces of drink slurped up my straw and my eyes unfocused and I slowly returned to the garish reality of Macswineys. And before my eyes was a poster. I had been staring at it, without seeing it, for some time. Now it registered. Laughing clowns and screaming children. All rapt with joy in slightly faulty 3D. While above their heads the simple message was spelled out in glowing letters.

SAVE YOUR COUPONS!!
GET THEM WITH EVERY PURCHASE!!
FREE ADMISSION TO LOONA PARK!!!

I had visited this site of plastic joys some years before—and had disliked it even as a child. Horrifying rides that frightened only the simple. Rotating up-and-down rides only for the strong of stomach; round-and-round and throw up. Junk food, sweet candy, drunk clowns, all the heady joy to please the very easily pleasable. Thousands attended Loona Park every day and more thousands flooded in on weekends—bringing even more thousands of bucks with them.

Bucks galore! All I had to do was clean them out—in such a very interesting way that it would make the top news story right around the planet.

But how would I do it? By going there, of course, and taking a good hard look at their security arrangements. It was about time that I had a day off.

CHAPTER SEVEN

For this little reconnaissance trip it would be far wiser for me to act my age—or less. With all the makeup removed I was a fresh-faced seventeen again. I should be able to improve upon that; after all I had taken an expensive correspondence course in theatrical makeup. Pads in my cheeks made me look more cherubic, particularly when touched up with a bit of rouge. I put on a pair of sunglasses decorated with plastic flowers—that squirted water when I pressed the bulb in my pocket. A laugh a second! Styles in dress had changed, which meant that plus-fours for boys had gone out of fashion, thank goodness, but shorts were back. Or rather a reprehensible style called short-longs which had one leg cut above the knee, the other below. I had purchased a pair of these done in repulsive purple corduroy tastefully decorated with shocking-pink patches. I could scarcely dare look at myself in the mirror. What looked back at me I hesitate to describe, except that it looked very little like an escaped bank robber. Around my neck I slung a cheap disposable camera that was anything but cheap, disposable—or only a camera.

At the station I found myself lost in a sea of lookalikes as we boarded the Loona Special. Screaming and laughing hysterically and spraying each other with our plastic flowers helped to while away the time. Or stretch it to eternity in at least one case. When the doors finally opened I let the multichrome crowd thunder out, then strolled wearily after them. Now to work.

Go where the money was. My memories of my first visit

43

were most dim—thank goodness!—but I did remember that one paid for the various rides and diversions by inserting plastic tokens. My father had furnished a limited and begrudging number of these, which had been used up within minutes, and of course no more had been forthcoming. My first assignment then was to find the font of these tokens.

Easily enough done, for this building was the target of every prepubescent visitor. It was a pointed structure like an inverted icecream cone, bedecked with flags and mechanical clowns, topped with a golden calliope that played ear-destroying music. Surrounding it at ground level and fixed to its base was a ring of plastic clown torsos, rocking and laughing and grimacing. Repellent as they were, they provided the vital function of separating the customers from their money. Eager juvenile hands pushed buck bills into the grasping palms of the plastic punchinellos. The hand would close, the money vanish—and from the clown's mouth a torrent of plastic tokens would be vomited into the waiting receptacle. Disgusting—but I was obviously the only one who thought so.

The money went into the building. Now I must find where it came out. I strolled about the base and discovered that the regurgitating dispensers did not quite girdle it. To the rear, behind the concealment of trees and shrubs, a small building snuggled up to the base. I pushed my way under the shrubs and found myself facing a private policeman stationed beside an unmarked door.

"Get lost, kid," he said sweetly. "Employees only."

I dodged around him and pushed against the door—and managed to photograph it at the same time. "I gotta go to the bathroom," I said crossleggedly. "They said the bathroom was here."

A hard hand pulled me away and propelled me back to the shrubbery. "Not here. Out. Back the way you came."

I went. Very interesting. No electronic alarms and the lock was a Glubb—reliable but old. I was beginning to like Loona Park after all.

It was an excruciating wait until dark when the park

closed down. Out of boredom I sampled the Glacier Ride where one hurtled through mock ice caverns with Things frozen into the ice on all sides—though they occasionally lunged out at the screeching riders. Rocjet Rovers was equally bad, and in the name of good taste I will draw the curtain down over the heady joys of Candyland and the Swamp Monster. Suffice to say that the time did arrive at last. The token dispenser closed down an hour before the park shut. From a nearby vantage point I watched with avid interest as an armored van took away a great number of solid containers. Even more interesting was the fact that when the money went—so did the security. I imagine that the logic behind this was that no one in their right mind would want to break in and steal the tokens.

So I wasn't in my right mind. As darkness fell I joined the exhausted celebrants as they staggered towards the exits. Except that I didn't get that far. A locked door at the rear of Vampire Mountain unlocked easily under my gentle ministrations. I slipped into the darkness of the service area. High above me, pale fangs shone and fake blood dripped; I felt very comfortable indeed tucked in behind a coffin filled with dirt.

I let an hour go by, no more. This should clear the employees out of the way but still leave enough revelers in the streets outside the park so that my disgusting outfit would not be noticed when I finally made my exit.

There were guards about, but they were easily avoided. As I had expected, the Glubb opened easily and I slipped quickly inside. The room proved to be windowless, which was fine since my light would then not be seen. I switched it on and admired the machinery.

A simple and clean design—I appreciate that in machinery. The dispensers were ringed about the walls. Silent now, but still obvious in their operation. When coins or bills were inserted they were counted and passed on. Machines above released the measured amount of tokens into the delivery chutes. Beside them pipes sprang out of the floor and terminated in a bin above—undoubtedly they were filled from underground conveyors that returned the tokens ready for redispensing. The bucks, untouched by human hands, were being conveyed through sealed and transparent tubes to the collection station, where the coins fell into locked boxes. They were not for me since they were too bulky to move easily. But, ahh, the bills, they were far lighter and worth far more. They slipped along the chutes until they dropped gracefully through an opening in the top of a safe. An operation that appeared to be relatively secure from light-fingered employees.

Wonderful. I admired the machinery and thought about it, then made notes. The dispensers had been manufactured by a firm by the name of Ex-changers, and I took pix of their trademark on the machines. The safe was a secure and reliable brand that easily yielded to my ministrations. It was empty of course, but I had expected that. I made a note of the combination, then opened and closed it a number of times until I could do it with my eyes closed. A plan was taking shape in my head and this was to be an integral part of it.

Finished at last, I slipped from the building without being seen, and with little more effort escaped from the park to join the frolicking throngs. They were less boisterous on the return journey and I only had to use my spray-glasses twice. I cannot describe the relief I felt when I finally staggered through the office door, stripped off the outlandish garb, then buried my nose in a beer. Then, metaphorically of course, I put my thinking cap on.

The next weeks were busy ones. While I worked at the equipment I needed for my operation I followed the news accounts closely. One of the prison escapers, after a fierce struggle, had been recaptured. His companion had not been found, despite the help rendered by the one who had been caught. Poor Stinger; life wouldn't be the same for him once the will to fight was taken from him. However life would still be the same for the man he had planned to kill so I did not feel too sorry for Stinger. And I had work to do. Two things to do in tandem; plan the robbery—and lay the trap for The Bishop. I am proud to say that I accomplished both with some ease. After this I waited until there was a dark and stormy night to visit Loona Park again. I was in and out as quickly as I could, which was some hours since there was a good deal of work to be done.

After that it was only a matter of waiting for the right time. A weekend would be best, with the tills overflowing. As part of my plans I had rented the garage quite legally, but had stolen the small van most illegally. I used the waiting time to repaint it—a better job than the original if I must say so—to add new identification numbers, and to fix nameplates to the doors. At last Saturday came and I had to work hard to control my impatience. To pass the time, moustached and crowfooted, I enjoyed a good and leisurely lunch, for I had to wait until late afternoon, when the coffers would be full. The drive into the countryside was pleasant, and I reached my appointed spot at the appointed time. Close to the service entrance to the park. I had some apprehension as I pulled on the skintight and transparent gloves—but the feeling of anticipation was far greater. With a smile on my lips I reached out and switched on the apparatus fixed underneath the dash before me.

An invisible radio signal winged out and I tried to visualize with my mind's eye what happened next. Fast as light to the receiver, down the wires to its target—which was a tiny charge of explosive. Not much, just a carefully measured amount that would destroy the latch on one of the token dispensers without rupturing the tube at the same time. With the latch destroyed, a steady stream of colored plastic wafers should now be rattling down into the dispenser, filling it and flowing over—gushing on in a never-ending stream. What a benefactor I was! How the children would bless me had they but known my identity.

But that wasn't all that was going to happen. For every minute now another radio signal pulsed out of my transmitter, another latch was destroyed, another gusher of tokens spouting forth each time that this happened. Another and then another. At the proper moment I started the van's engine and drove to the service gate of Loona

Park, opened the window, and leaned out above the sign on the door that read EX-CHANGERS DISPENSING MACHINES.

"Got a radio call," I said to the guard there. "You got some kind of problem here?"

"No problem," the guard said, heaving the gate open. "More like a riot. You know where the building is?"

"Sure do. Help is on the way!"

Though I had visualized the effects of my unexpected largesse, I quickly discovered that reality far surpassed my wildest expectations. Screaming, cheering kiddies rushed about laden with tokens, while others fought for places around the gushing dispensers. Their happy cries were ear-splitting and the attendants and guards could do nothing to stop their wave of exuberance. It was slightly less crowded on the service road, but I still had to drive slowly, hand on the horn, to make my way through the stragglers. Two guards were pushing kids back through the shrubs when I drove up.

"Got some trouble with the dispensers?" I asked sweetly. The guard's snarled response was lost in childish cries of delight, which was probably all for the best. He unlocked the door and all but pushed me and my toolbox through.

There were four people there, struggling ineffectually with the machines. They could not be cut off since I had taken the liberty of shorting the switchbox. A bald-headed man was working on an armored cable with a hacksaw and I made tsk-tsking sounds. "That is a recipe for suicide," I said. "You got a four-hundred-volt line in there."

"Can you do anything better, buster," he snarled. "They're your damned machines. Go to work."

"I shall—and here is the cure."

I opened the sizeable toolbox, which contained only a shining metal tube, and took it out. "This will do the job," I said, turning the valve at the top and hurling it from me. The last thing I saw were their eye-popping expressions as the black smoke billowed out and filled the room—blocking out all vision completely.

I had been expecting it; they had not. The toolbox was in my arms as I took four measured paces in the darkness and fetched up against the side of the safe. Any noises I made were drowned by their shouts and screams and the constant chugging of the token dispensers. The safe opened easily, the lid of the toolbox fit neatly against the lower edge. I leaned in, felt the mounds of bills, then swept them forward into the waiting container. It was quickly filled and I snapped it shut. My next task was to make sure that the right person took responsibility for this crime. The card with its inscription was in my top pocket. I slipped it out and laid it carefully in the safe, which I then locked again to make absolutely sure that my message would be received and not lost in all the excitement. Only then did I pick up the now-heavy toolbox and stand with my back to the safe, turning and orientating myself.

I knew that the exit was there in the darkness, nine easy paces away. I had taken five when I bumped into someone and strong hands grabbed me while a hoarse voice shouted in my ear.

"I got him! Help me!"

I dropped the box and gave him exactly the help he needed, running my hands up his body to his neck and doing all the right things there. He grunted and slid away. I groped for the box—for a panicky moment I couldn't find it. Then I did, clutched the handle, and seized it up and stood. . . .

And realized I had lost all sense of direction during the fracas.

My panic was as dark as the smoke, and I shook so hard that I almost dropped the case. Seventeen years old and very much alone—with the unknown world of adults closing in upon me. It was over, all over.

I don't know how long this crisis lasted, probably only seconds, although it seemed infinitely longer than that. Then I grabbed myself by the metaphorical neck and shook myself quite hard.

"You wanted it this way—remember? Alone with everyone's hand turned against you. So give in to them—or start thinking. Fast!"

I thought. The people screaming and banging all about

me were no help or threat—they were as confused as I
was. All right, hand outstretched, go forward. Any direction. Reach something that could be identified by touch.
Once this was done I should be able to work out where I
was. I heard a thudding ahead, it had to be one of the
dispensers, then I bumped into it.

While at the same moment a draft of air touched my
face and a familiar voice called out close by.

"What's going on in here?"

The guard! And he had opened the door. How very nice
of him. I moved along the wall, avoiding him easily since
he was still shouting in the darkness, then followed the
billowing smoke out into the light of day. Blinking at the
brightness and at the other guard who was stationed just
before me, grabbing me.

"Just hold it right there. You ain't going nowhere."

He could not have been much wronger, I mean grabbing onto a Black Belt like that. I eased him to the ground
so he wouldn't hurt himself when he fell, threw the box
into the van, looked around to see that I was totally
unobserved, closed the door, started the engine, then
drove slowly and carefully away from fun-filled Loona
Park.

CHAPTER EIGHT

"All fixed, everything just fine back there," I called out to the guard and he nodded while he pulled the gate open. I drove off in the direction the city, slowly around a bend—then turned sharply inland on an unpaved road.

My escape had been as carefully planned as the theft. Stealing money is one thing; keeping it is another altogether. In this age of electronic communication a description of me and the van would be flashed around the planet in microseconds. Every police car would have a printout and every patrolman verbal warning. So how much time did I have? Both guards were unconscious. But they could be revived, could pass on the information, a phone call would be made, warning given. I calculated that this would take at least five minutes. Which was fine since I only needed three.

The road wound up through the trees, made a final turn—and ended in the abandoned quarry. My heart was thudding a bit since I had to take one chance in this operation. And it had worked—the rental car was still here, just where I had left it the day before! Of course I had removed some vital parts from the engine, but a determined thief could have towed it away. Thank goodness that there was only one determined thief around.

I unlocked the car and took out the box of groceries, then carried it to the van. The side of the box swung down—revealing an empty box. The protruding tops of packets and containers, just the glued-together tops of packets and containers. Very ingenious, if I say so myself. Which I have to, since no one else knows about this

operation. Money into box, close box, put in car. Take off
work clothes, shiver in the cool breeze as I throw them
into the truck. Along with moustache. Pull on sports outfit, actuate timer on thermite charges, lock van, get in car.
Simply drive away. I had not been observed so there was
no reason at all now why I shouldn't get away with my
little adventure. I stopped at the main road and waited for
a clutch of police cars to go roaring by in the direction of
Loona Park. My, but they were in a hurry. I turned onto
the road and drove slowly and carefully back to Billville.

By this time the van would be burning merrily and
melting down to a pool of slag. No clues there! The van
was insured by law so the owner would be reimbursed.
The fire would not spread—not from the heart of the stone
quarry—and no one had been injured. It had all worked
well, very well.

Back in the office I heaved a sigh of relief, opened a
beer and drank deep—then took the bottle of whiskey
from the bar and poured a stiff shot. I sipped it, wrinkled
my nose at the awful flavor, then poured the rest of the
drink into the sink. What filthy stuff. I suppose if I kept
trying I would get used to it someday, but it scarcely
seemed worth the effort.

By now enough time should surely have elapsed for the
press to have reached the scene of the crime. "On," I
called out to my computer, then, "Print the latest edition
of the newspaper."

The fax hummed silkily and the paper slid into the tray.
With a color pic of the money fountain operating at full
blast on the front page. I read the report with a glow of
pleasure, turned the page, and saw the drawing. There it
was, just as they had found it when they had finally
opened the safe. A drawing of a bishop with a line of chess
notation written below it.

R—Kt 4 X B

Which means in chess notation Rook to square Knight 4
takes Bishop.

When I read it the warm glow of pleasure was replaced

by a chill of worry. Had I given myself away to the police? Would they analyze the clue and be waiting for me?

"No!" I cried aloud. "The police are lazy and relaxed with little crime to keep them on their toes. They may puzzle over it—but they will never understand it until it is too late. But The Bishop should be able to work it out. He will know that it is a message for him and will labor over it. I hope."

I sipped at my beer and had a good worry. It had taken me tedious hours to work out this little mind-twister. The fact that The Bishop used a chess bishop as his calling card had led me to the chess books. I assumed that he—or she, I don't believe that anyone had ever determined The Bishop's sex, although it was assumed the criminal was male—cared about chess. If more knowledge was needed he could consult the same books that I had. With very little effort it could be discovered that there are two different ways of noting chess moves. The oldest of them, the one that I had used, named the squares of the file after the piece that sat at the end of the file. (If you must know, "ranks" are the rows of squares that stretch from side to side of a chessboard. "Files" are the rows that stretch between the players. So the square on which the White King sits is King 1. King 2 would be the next one up. If you think that this is complicated don't play chess—because this is the easiest part! However there is a second form of chess notation that assigns a number to each of the 64 squares on the board. So Knight 4 can be either 21, 8, 22, or 45.

Confusing? I hope so. I hope the police never think it is a code and get around to cracking it. Because if they do I am cracked as well. This little bit of chess movement contains the date of my next crime, when I am going to "take bishop," meaning take The Bishop card to a crime. Meaning also I am going to take credit for being The Bishop. Also meaning I am taking The Bishop to the cleaners.

I have the scenario clear in my mind. The police puzzle over the chess move—then discard it. Not so The Bishop in his luxury hideout. He is going to be angry. A crime has been committed and he has been blamed. Money has been taken—and he doesn't have it! My hope is that he will worry over this chess move, see it as a clue, scribble away at it, and eventually solve it.

By thinking about the fact that Knight is a homonym for night. Night three—what can that mean? The third night of what? The third night of the Modern Music Festival in the city of Pearly Gates, that is what. And this third night is also the forty-fifth day of the year, which is—that's correct—also known as Knight 3 in one of its four permutations. With this added verification The Bishop would be sure that some crime would take place on the third night of the Festival. A crime involving money of course. My mental fingers were crossed in the hope that he would be more interested in me than in informing the police in advance about the crime.

I hoped that I had struck the right balance. Too complex for the police, but capable of solution by The Bishop. And he had exactly one week to solve it and come to the Festival.

Which also meant that I had one week to hype myself up and depress myself down, get too much sleep—then not enough sleep. And take pleasure only in the construction of plans and apparatus for this bold foray into the pockets of the public.

On the night in question it was raining heavily—which suited me perfectly. I turned up the collar of my black coat, jammed my black hat down on my head, then seized up the black case that held the musical instrument. A horn of some kind. This was made obvious by the swollen shape at one end, where the case swelled out to accommodate the bell. It might be a crumpaphone or even a dagennet. Public transportation took me close to the stage entrance to the theater. As I walked the rest of the way I soon found myself braving the elements among other black-garbed, instrument-bearing musicians. I had my pass ready, but the doorman just waved us through and out of the rain. There was little chance that anyone would question my identity because I was only one of 230. For tonight was the premier of what was sure to be a head-destroying piece of so-called music modestly entitled *Collision of Galaxies*, scored for 201 brass instruments and 29 percussion. The composer, Moi-Woofter Geeyoh, was not known for the delicate disonances of her compositions. The choice of this piece of music had also made this the night of my choice; even reading the score gave one a headache.

There was a shortage of dressing rooms for the musical multitude and they were milling about all over the place emitting lost noises. No one noticed when I slipped away, drifted up a back staircase—and let myself into a janitorial broomcloset. The service staff had long departed so I would not be disturbed—other than by the music. Nevertheless I locked the door from the inside. When I heard the sounds of tuning up I took out my copy of the score of *Collision*.

It started out calmly enough—after all, the galaxies had to get on stage before they could collide. I followed the score with my finger until it reached the red mark I had placed there. The score folded neatly into my pocket as I carefully unsealed the door and looked out. Corridor empty, as it should be. With steady tread I walked down the corridor, the floor of which was already beginning to throb with impending galactic destruction.

The door was labeled PRIVATE—KEEP OUT. I took the black mask from one pocket, removed my hat and pulled the mask on, extracted the key to the door from another. I did not want to waste time with lockpicks, so had made this key when I had scouted this location. I hummed along with the music—if that could be said to be possible—with the key in the lock. At the correct destructive crash I opened the door and stepped into the office.

My entrance had of course been unheard, but my movements caught the older man's eye. He turned and stared and the pen he had been using dropped from his limp fingers. His hands reached towards the ceiling when I drew the impressive—and fake—gun from my inside pocket. The other and younger man could not be threatened and dived to the attack. And continued to dive unconscious to the floor, knocking over and breaking a chair on the way.

None of this made a sound. Or rather it made a lot of sound, none of which could be heard over the music that was now rapidly working itself up to a crescendo that would drown out the crack of doom. I moved fast because the really loud parts were coming close.

I took two pairs of handcuffs from a coat pocket and locked the older man's ankle to his desk, then pulled his arms down before they got tired. I next secured the sleeping dreamer the same way. Almost time. I took the plastic explosive from another pocket—yes, there *were* a lot of pockets in this garment, and not by chance either—and slapped it to the front of the safe. Right over the time lock. They must have felt very secure here with their careful arrangements. All the night's ample receipts had been locked away in the safe in the presence of armed guards. To remain locked and secure until the morning when other armed guards would be present when it opened. I pushed the radio fuse into the explosive, then retreated across the room until I was out of line of fire along with the others.

Every loose object in the room was bouncing in time with the music now while dust rained down from the ceiling. It still wasn't time. I used the opportunity to rip out the phones by their roots. Not that anyone would be talking on a phone until after the concert.

There it was—almost there! I had the musical score in my mind's eye and at the instant when the galaxies finally impacted I pressed the radio actuator.

The front of the safe blew off in silent motion. I was stunned by the musical catastrophe way up here in the office—not by the explosion—and I wondered how many of the audience had gone deaf in the name of art. My wondering didn't stop me from shoveling all the buck bills from the safe into my instrument case. When it was filled I tipped my hat to my prisoners, one wide-eyed, one unconscious, and let myself out. The black mask went back into its pocket and I went out of the theater by an unwatched emergency exit.

It was a brisk two-block walk to the underpass entrance and I was just one other figure hurrying through the rain. Down the steps and along the corridor, to take the turning that led to the station. The commuter trains had left and the corridor was deserted. I stepped into the phone booth and made my unobserved identity change in exactly twenty-two seconds, precisely the rehearsed time. The black covering of the case stripped away to reveal the white covering of the case inside. The flared bell-shape went too. That had been shaped from thin plastic that crunched and went into a pocket with the black cover. My hat turned inside out and became white, my black moustache and beard disappeared into their appointed pocket so that I could shed the coat and turn it inside out so that it too, that's right, became white. Thus garbed, I strolled into the station and out the exit along with the other arriving passengers, to the cab rank. It was a short wait; the cab rolled up and the door opened. I climbed in and smiled appreciatively at the shining skull of the robot driver.

"Mah good man, tay-ake me to thu Arbolast Hotel," I said in my best imitation Thuringian accent—since the Thuringar train had arrived at the same time I had.

"Message not understood," the thing intoned.

"Ar-bo-last Ho-tel, you metallic moron!" I shouted. "Ar-bowb-bo-last!"

"Understood," it said, and the cab started forward.

Just perfect. All conversations were stored in a molecular recorder for one month in these cabs. If I were ever checked on, the record would reveal this conversation. And my hotel reservation had been made from a terminal in Thuringia. Perhaps I was being too cautious—but my motto was that this was an impossibility. Being too cautious, I mean.

The hotel was an expensive one and tastefully decorated with mock arbolasts in every corridor and room. I was obsequiously guided to mine—where the arbolast served as a floor lamp—and the robot porter glided away smarmily with a five buck coin in his tip slot.

I put the bag in the bedroom, took off the wet coat, extracted a beer from the cooler—and there was a knock on the door.

So soon! If that was The Bishop he was a good tail, because I had not been aware of being followed. But who else could it be? I hesitated, then realized that there was one certain way to find out. With smile on face, in case it was The Bishop, I opened the door. The smile vanished instantly.

"You are under the arrest," the plainclothes detective said, holding out his jeweled badge. His companion pointed a large gun at me just to make sure that I understood.

CHAPTER NINE

"What . . . what . . ." I said, or something very like this. The arresting officer was not impressed by my ready wit.

"Put on your coat. You are coming with us."

In a daze I stumbled across the room and did just as he commanded. I should leave the coat here, I knew that, but I had no will to resist. When they searched it they would find the mask and key, everything else that would betray me. And what about the money? They hadn't mentioned the bag.

As soon as my arm was through the sleeve the policeman snapped a handcuff on my wrist and clicked the other end to his own wrist. I was going nowhere without them. There was little or nothing I could do—not with the gun wielder three steps behind us.

Out the door we went and along the corridor, to the elevator, then down to the lobby. At least the detective had the courtesy to stand close to me so the handcuffs were not obvious. A large black and ominous groundcar was parked in the middle of the no-parking zone. The driver didn't even bother to glance in our direction. Though as soon as we had climbed in and the door closed, he pulled away.

I could think of nothing to say—nor were my companions in a conversational mood. In silence we rolled through the rainy streets, past police headquarters which was unexpected, to stop before the Bit O' Heaven Federal Building. The Feds! My heart dropped. I had been correct in assuming that breaking the clues and catching me had certainly been beyond the intelligence of the local police.

But I had not reckoned upon the planetary investigation agencies. By hindsight—which is not very satisfying—I saw my error. After years of absence The Bishop strikes again. Why? And what does the bit of chesswackery mean? Put the cryptologists on it. Oho, a bit of bragging, scene and date of the next crime revealed. Keep it Federal and out of the hands of the local and incompetent police. Watch the cash with the most modern of electronic surveillance techniques. Track the criminal to see if others are involved. Then pounce.

My state of black depression was so great that I could scarcely walk. I swayed when our little procession stopped before a heavy door labeled FEDERAL BUREAU OF INVESTIGATION, with DIRECTOR FLYNN in smaller gold letters beneath it. My captors knocked politely and the doorlock buzzed and opened. We filed in.

"Here he is, sir."

"Fine. Secure him to the chair and I'll take over from here on out."

The speaker sat massively behind the massive desk. A big man with sleek black hair, who was made even bigger by the enormous quantity of fat that he was carrying around. His chin, or chins, hung down onto the swelling volume of his chest. The size of his stomach kept him well back from the desk, upon which the fingers of his clasped hands rested like a bundle of stout sausages. He returned my shifty gaze with his steady and steely one. I made no protest as I was guided to the chair, dropped into it, felt the handcuffs being secured to it, heard footsteps recede and the door slam.

"You are in very big trouble," he intoned.

"I don't know what you mean," I said, the impact of my innocence lessened by the squeak and tremor of my voice.

"You know full well what I mean. You have committed the crime of theft tonight, purloining the public purse donated by stone-deaf music lovers. But that is the least of your folly, young man. By your age I can tell that you have also purloined the good name of another. The Bishop.

You are pretending to be something that you are not. Here, take these."

Purloined a good name? What in the galaxy was he talking about? I snatched the keys out of the air by reflex. Gaped at them—then gaped even more broadly at him as I tremblingly unlocked the cuffs.

"You are not . . ." I gurgled. "I mean, the arrest, this office, the police . . . You are . . ."

He calmly waited for my next words, a beatific smile on his face.

"You are . . .The Bishop!"

"The same. My understanding of the message concealed by your feeble code was that you wanted to meet me. Why?"

I started to rise and an immense gun appeared in his hand, aimed between my eyes. I dropped back into the chair. The smile was gone, as was all warmth from his voice.

"I don't like to be imitated, nor do I like to be played with. I am displeased. You now have three minutes to explain this matter before I kill you, then proceed to your hotel room to retrieve the money you stole this evening. Now the first thing that you will reveal is the location of the rest of the money stolen in my name. Speak!"

I spoke—or rather I tried to speak but could only sputter helplessly. This had a sobering affect. He might kill me—but he was not going to reduce me to helpless jelly first. I coughed to clear my throat, then spoke.

"I don't think that you are in too much of a hurry to kill me—nor do I believe in your three-minute time limit. If you will cease in your attempts to bully me I shall try to tell you carefully and clearly my motives in this matter. Agreed?"

Speaking like this was a calculated risk—but The Bishop was a game player, I knew that now. His expression did not change, but he nodded slightly as though conceding a Pawn move—knowing that he still had my King well in check.

"Thank you. I never thought of you as a cruel man. In

fact, when I discovered your existence, I used you as a career model. What you have done, what you have accomplished, is without equal in the history of this world. If I offended you by stealing money in your name I am sorry. I will turn all the money from that robbery over to you at once. But if you will stop to think—it is the only thing that I could do. I had no way of finding you. So I had to arrange things so that you could find me. As you have. I counted upon your curiosity—if not your mercy—not to reveal my identity to the police before you had met me yourself."

Another nod granted me another Pawn move. The unwavering barrel of the gun informed me that I was still in check.

"You are the only person alive who knows my identity," he said. "You will now tell me why I should not kill you. Why did you want to contact me?"

"I told you—out of admiration. I have decided on a life of crime as the only career open to one of my talents. But I am self-trained and vulnerable. It is my wish to be your acolyte. To study at your knee. To enter the academy of advanced crime in the wilderness of life with you on one end of the log and me on the other. I will pay whatever price you require for this privilege, though I may need a little time to raise more money since I am turning the receipts of my last two operations over to you. There it is. That is who I am. And, if I work hard enough, you are whom I wish to be."

The softening gaze, the thoughtful fingers raised to chin meant I was out of check for the moment. But the game wasn't won yet—nor did I wish it to be. I wanted only a draw.

"Why should I believe a word of this?" he asked at last.

"Why should you doubt it? What other possible reason could I have?"

"It is not your motives that disturb me. I am thinking about the possibility of someone else's, someone in a position of police responsibility who is using you as a pawn to find me. The man who arrests The Bishop will rise to the top of his chosen profession."

I nodded agreement as I thought furiously. Then smiled and relaxed. "Very true—and that must have been the very first thing to come to your mind. Your office in this building either means that you are high in the ranks of law enforcement, so high that you could easily find out if this had been the plan. Or—even more proof of your genius— you have ways and means of penetrating the police at any level, to fool them and use them to actually arrest me. My congratulations, sir! I knew that you were a genius of crime—but to have done this, why it borders on the fantastic!"

He nodded his head slowly, accepting his due. Did I see the muzzle of the gun lowered ever so slightly? Was a drawn game possibly in sight? I rushed on.

"My name is James Bolivar diGriz and I was born a little over seventeen years ago in this very city in the Mother Machree Maternity Hospital for Unemployed Porcuswineherders. The terminal I see before you must access official files at every level. Bring up mine! See for yourself if what I have told you is not the truth."

I settled back into the chair while he tapped commands on the keyboard. I did nothing to distract him or draw his attention while he read. I was still nervous but worked to affect a surface calm.

Then he was done. He leaned back and looked at me calmly. I didn't see his hands move—but the gun vanished from sight. Drawn game! But the pieces were still on the board and a new game was beginning.

"I believe you, Jim, and thank you for the kind words. But I work alone and wish no disciples. I was prepared to kill you to preserve the secret of my identity. Now I do not think that will be necessary. I will take your word that you will not look for me again—or use my identity for any more crimes."

"I grant your requests instantly. I only became The Bishop to draw your attention. But reconsider, I beg of you, my application for membership in your academy of advanced crime!"

"There is no such insitution," he said, hauling himself to his feet. "Applications are closed."

"Then let me rephrase my request," I said hurriedly, knowing my remaining time was brief. "Let me be personal, if I can, and forgive any distress I may cause. I am young, not yet twenty, and you have been on this planet for over eighty years. I have been only a few years at my chosen work. And, in this brief time, I have discovered that I am truly alone. What I do I must do for myself and by myself. There is no comradeship of crime because all of the criminals I have seen are incompetents. Therefore I must go it alone. If I am lonely—then dare I even guess at the loneliness of your life?"

He stood stock-still, one hand resting on the desk, staring at the blank wall, as through a window, at something I could not see. Then he sighed, and with the sound, as though it had released some power that kept him erect, he slumped back into the chair."

"You speak the truth, my boy, and only the truth. I do not wish to discuss the matter, but your barb has been driven well home. Nevertheless what is, will be. I am too old a dog to change his ways. I bid you farewell, and thank you for a most interesting week. Been a bit like old times."

"Reconsider, please!"

"I cannot."

"Give me your address—I must send you the money."

"Keep it, you earned it. Though in the future earn it under a different identity. Let The Bishop enjoy his retirement. I will add only one thing, a bit of advice. Reconsider your career ambitions. Put your great talents to work in a more sociably acceptable manner. In that way you will avoid the vast loneliness you have already noted."

"Never!" I cried aloud. "Never. I would rather rot in jail for the rest of my life than accept a role in the society I have so overwhelmingly rejected."

"You may change your mind."

"There is no chance of that," I said to the empty room. The door had closed behind him and he was gone.

CHAPTER TEN

Well, that was that. There is nothing like an overwhelming depression to bring one down from the heights of elation. I had done exactly what I had set out to do. My complex plan had worked perfectly. I had unearthed The Bishop from his secret lair and had made him an offer he couldn't refuse.

Except he had. Even the pleasure of having pulled off the successful robbery now meant nothing. The bucks were like ashes in my hand. I sat in my room at the hotel and looked into the future and could see only a vast vacuity. I counted the money over and over until the sums were meaningless. In making my plans I had considered all of the possibilities but one—that The Bishop would turn me down. It was kind of hard to take.

By the time I got back to Billville the next day I was wallowing in a dark depression and thoroughly enjoying the bath of self-pity. Which I normally cannot stand. Nor could I this time. I looked in the mirror at the hollow-eyed and woebegone face and stuck my tongue out at it.

"Sissy!" I said. "Momma's boy, whiner, self-indulgent wimp," and added whatever other insults I could think of. Having cleansed the air a bit, I made a sandwich and a pot of coffee—no alcohol to clog the synapses!—and sat down to munch and guzzle and think about the future. What next?

Nothing. At least nothing constructive that I could think of at this moment. All of my plans had ended at a blank wall and I could see no way around or over it. I slumped back and snapped my fingers at the 3V. A commercial channel came on and before I could change channels the announcer appeared in glorious three dimension and color. I didn't switch because the announcer was a she and wearing only the flimsiest of swim suits.

"Come where the balmy breezes blow," she cajoled. "Come join me on the silver sands of beautiful Vaticano Beach, where the sun and waves will refresh your soul. . . ."

I turned the thing off. My soul was in fine shape and the fine shape of the announcer only gave me more problems to think about. Future first, heterosexual love later. But the commercial had at least given me the beginning of an idea.

A holiday? Take a break? Why not—lately I had been working harder than any of the businessmen I so badly did not want to become. Crime had paid, and paid nicely, so why didn't I spend some of the hard-earned loot? I probably wouldn't be able to escape from my problems. I had learned by experience that physical displacement was never a solution. My troubles always went with me, as ever-present and nagging as a toothache. But I could take them with me to someplace where I might find the leisure and opportunity to sort them out.

Where? I punched up a holiday guide from the database and flipped through it. Nothing seemed to appeal. The beach? Only if I could meet the girl from the commercial, which seemed far from likely. Posh hotels, expensive cruises, museum tours, all of them seemed about as exciting as a weekend on a porcuswine ranch. Maybe that was it—I needed a breath of fresh air. As a farm boy I had seen enough of the great outdoors, usually over the top of a pile of porcuswine you-know-what. With that sort of background I had welcomed my move to the city with open arms—and hadn't ventured out since.

That might be the very answer. Not back to the farm but into the wilderness. To get away from people and things, to do a little chatting with mother nature. The more I thought of it the better it sounded. And I knew just where I wanted to go, an ambition I had had since I was knee-high to a porcuswinelet. The Cathedral Mountains. Those snow-covered peaks, pointing towards the sky like giant church towers, how they used to fill my childish dreams. Well, why not? About time to make a few dreams come true.

Shopping for backpack, sleeping bag, thermal tent, cooking pots, lights—all the gear needed—was half the fun. Once outfitted, I couldn't waste time on the linear but took the plane to Rafael instead. I bulged my eyes at the mountains as we came in to land and snapped my fingers and fidgeted while I waited for the luggage. I had studied the maps and knew that the Cathedral Trail crossed the road in the foothills north of the airport. I should have taken the connecting bus like the others instead of being conspicuous in a taxi, but I was in too much of a rush.

"Pretty dangerous, kid, I mean walking the trail alone." The elderly driver smacked his lips as he launched into a litany of doom. "Get lost easily enough. Get eaten by direwolves. Landslides and avalanches. And . . ."

"And I'm meeting friends. Twenty of them. The Boy Sprouts Hiking Team of Lower Armmpitt. We're gonna have fun," I invented rapidly.

"Didn't see no Boy Sprouts out here lately," he muttered with senile suspicion.

"Nor would you," I extemporized, bent over in the back seat and flipping through the maps quickly. "Because they took the train to Boskone, got off there, right at the station close to where the trail crosses the tracks. They'll be waiting for me, troop leader and all. I would be afraid to be alone in the mountains, sir."

He muttered some more, muttered even louder when I forgot to tip him, then chuckled in his gray whiskers as he drove away because, childishly, I had then overtipped him. While resisting strongly the impulse to slip him a phoney five buck coin. The sound of the motor died away and I looked at the well-marked trail as it wound up the valley—and realized that this had been a very good idea indeed.

There is no point in waxing enthusiastic about the joys of the Great Outdoors. Like skiing, you do it and enjoy it, but don't talk about it. All the usual things happened. My nose got sunburned, ants got into my bacon. The stars were incredibly clear and close at night, while the clean air did good things to my lungs. I walked and climbed, froze myself in mountain streams—and managed to forget my troubles completely. They seemed very out of place in this outdoor world. Refreshed, cleansed, tired but happy, and a good deal thinner, I emerged from the mountains ten days later and stumbled through the door of the lodge where I had made reservations. The hot bath was a blessing, and the cold beer no less. I turned on the 3V and got the tailend of the news, slumped down and listened with half an ear, too lazy to change channels.

". . . reports a rise in ham exports exceeding the four percent growth predicted at the first of the year. The market for porcuswine quills is slipping however, and the government is faced with a quill mountain that is already drawing criticism.

"Closer to home, the computer criminal who broke into Federal Files goes on trial tomorrow. Federal prosecutors treat this as a most serious crime and want the death penalty reestablished. However . . ."

His voice faded from my attention as his smarmy face vanished from the screen to be replaced by the computer criminal himself being led away by a squad of police. He was a big man, and very fat, with a mane of white hair. I felt a clutch in my chest just near the place I imagined my heart to be. Wrong color hair—but wigs would take care of that. There was no mistaking him.

It was The Bishop!

I was out of the tub and across the room and hitting the frame freeze controls. It is a wonder I did not electrocute myself. Shivering with cold, and scarcely aware of it, I flipped back, then zoomed for detail. Enlarged the frame when he looked back over his shoulder for an instant. It was he—without a doubt.

By the time I had wiped off the suds and dressed, the general shape of my plans was clear. I had to get back to the city, to find out what had happened to him, to see what I could do to help. I punched up flight information; there was a mail flight just after midnight. I booked a seat, had a meal and a rest, paid my bill, and was the first passenger aboard.

It was just dawn when I entered my office in Billville. While the computer was printing out all the news items on the arrest, I made a pot of coffee. Sipping and reading, my spirits sank like a rock in a pond. It was indeed the man I knew as The Bishop, although he went under the name of Bill Vathis. And he had been apprehended leaving the Federal Building, where he had installed a computer tap which he had been using to access Top Secret files. All of this had happened the day after I left on my escapist holiday.

I had the sudden realization of what this meant. Guilt assailed me because I was the one who had put him into jail. If I had not started my mad plan, he would never have bothered with the Federal files. He had only done that to see if the robberies had been part of a police operation.

"I put him in jail—so I will get him out!" I shouted, leaping to my feet and spilling coffee across the floor. As I mopped it up I cooled down a bit. Yes, I would *like* to get him out of jail. But could I do it? Why not? I had some experience now in jail-breaking. It should be easier to get from the outside in than it had been doing it the other way. And, after further thought, I realized that perhaps I would not have to go near the jail. Let the police get him out for me. He would have to be taken to court, so would be in transit in various vehicles.

I soon discovered that it was not going to be that easy. This was the first major criminal that had been caught in years and everyone was making a big fuss over it. Instead of being taken to the city or state jail, The Bishop was being held in a cell inside the Federal Building itself. I could get nowhere near it. And the security measures when he was taken to the courthouse were unbelievable. Armed vans, guards, moncycles, police hovercraft and copters. I was not going to get to him that way either. Which meant I was baffled for the moment. Interestingly enough, so were the police—but for very different reasons.

They had discovered, after endless search, that the real

Bill Vathis had left the planet twenty years before. All of the records of this fact had vanished from the computer files—and it was only a note written by the real Vathis to a relative that had established the disappearance of the original. Well—if their prisoner wasn't Vathis. Who was he?

When their captive was questioned, according to the report released to the press, "He answered the question only with silence and a distant smile." The prisoner was now referred to as Mr. X. No one knew who he was—and he chose not to speak on the matter. A date was fixed for the trial, not eight days away. This was made possible by the fact that Mr. X refused to plead neither innocent nor guilty, would not defend himself—and had refused the services of a state-appointed attorney. The prosecution, greedy for a conviction, stated that their case was complete and asked for an early trial. The judge, eager as well to be in the limelight, agreed to their request and the date was set for the following week.

I could do nothing! Back to the wall, I admitted defeat—for the moment. I would wait until after the trial. Then The Bishop would simply be one more prisoner and would have to be taken from the Federal Building at last. When he was safely in jail I would arrange his escape. Well before the arrival of the next spacer that would take him away for brain-cleansing and purifying. They would use all of the miracles of modern science to turn him into an honest citizen and, knowing him, I was sure that he would rather die than have that happen. I must intervene.

But they were not making it easy for me. I could not find a way to be in the courtroom when the trial began. So I, along with every other inhabitant of the planet as far as could be determined, watched the trial on TV when it began.

And ended with suspicious speed. All of the first morning was taken with recitals of the well-documented account of what the defendant had done. It was pretty damning. Computer malfeasance, memory bank barratry, CPU violation, terminal treachery, dropping solder on classified documents—it was terrible. Witness after witness read out their statements, all of which were instantly accepted and entered into the evidence. Through all this The Bishop neither watched nor listened. His stare was into the distance, as though he were looking at much more interesting things than the simple operation of the court. When the evidence had been given, the judge banged his gavel and ordered a break for lunch.

When the court reconvened—after a break long enough for a seventeen-course banquet with dancing girls for afters—the judge was in a jovial mood. Particularly after the prosecution had done a damning summoning up. He nodded agreement most of the time and thanked all the smarmy ambulance chasers for the excellent job that they had done. Then he looked his most pontifical and spoke in pregnant periods for the records.

"This case is so clear that it is transparent. The state has brought charges so damning that no defense could possibly stand before them. That no defense was offered is even greater evidence of the truth. The truth is that the defendant did wilfully, with malice and forethought commit all of the crimes for which he stands accused. There can be no doubt about that. The case is an open and shut one. Nevertheless I shall deliberate the rest of this day and far into the night. He will have his chance of justice that he rejected. I will not find him guilty until tomorrow morning when this court resumes. At that time I will pass sentence. Justice will be done and will be seen to be done."

Some justice, I muttered through my teeth and started to switch off the set. But the judge wasn't through.

"I have been informed that the Galactic League is very interested in this case. A spacer has been dispatched and will be here within two days. The prisoner will then be taken from our custody and we will, if you will excuse and understand my emotions, be well rid of him."

My jaw dropped and I stared moronically at the screen. It was over. Just two days. What could I do in two days? Was this to be the end of The Bishop—and the end of my scarcely launched career in crime?

CHAPTER ELEVEN

I was not going to give up. I had to at least try, even if I failed and were caught myself. It was my fault that he had gotten into this position. I owed him at least an attempt at a rescue. But what could I do? I couldn't get near him in the Federal Building, approach him in transit, or even see him in court.

Court. Court? Court. Court! Court—why did I keep thinking about the court? What was there about it that tickled my interest, that scratched at my medulla oblongata with an idea trying to get in?

Of course! "Yippee!!" I enthused and ran around in small circles waving my arms and gurgling out loud my best imitation—they used to love it at parties—of a rutting porcuswine.

"What about the court?" I asked myself, and was ready with the snappy answer. "I'll tell you about the court. It is in an old building, an Ancient Artifact under preservation order. It probably has some old records in the basement and undoubtedly bats in the attic. During the day it is guarded like the mint—but it is empty at night!"

I dived for my equipment cabinet and began hurling various necessities to the floor. Toolkit, lockpicks, lights, wires, bugs—all the apparatus I would need for the job.

Now a car—or rather a van—was very much in order since I would hopefully need transportation for two. I took care of that next. I had a number of sites that I had noted in case of need—and now I needed. Although it was still daylight, the trucks and vans of the Crumb-ee Bakery were back in their lot being readied for their pre-dawn tasks of

72

the following day. A few vans were being taken into the garage for servicing and one of them happened to go a bit farther. Right onto the road and towards the city limits. I was on a countryside road by dusk, in Pearly Gates soon after dark, and letting myself into a back door to the courthouse not long after that.

The burglar alarms were antiques, meant to keep out children or mental defectives—since there was obviously nothing in the building worth stealing. That's what they thought! Armed with pix I had made myself of the courtroom during the trial, I went directly to it. Courtroom six. I stood in the doorway and looked about the darkened room. The lights from the street outside cast an orange glow through the high windows. I walked silently inside, sat down in the judge's chair, then looked into the witness box. In the end I found the chair in which The Bishop had sat during his lightning trial, where he would sit on the morrow. This is where he would sit—and this is where he would stand when he rose to hear his sentence. Those great hands would grasp the rail here. Just here.

I looked down at the wooden floor and smiled grimly. Then knelt and tapped on it. Then took out a drill as the various parts of my plan began to fall into place.

Oh, but this was a busy night! I had to clear boxes from the cellar beneath the courtroom, saw and hammer and sweat, and even slip out of the courthouse long enough to find a sports supply store and break into it. And, most critical of all, I had to work out a route of escape. The escape itself would not have to be rushed—but it would have to be secure. If I had had the time a bit of tunneling would have been in order. But I had no time. Therefore ingenuity would have to replace manual labor. As I cogitated in a comfortable position I found myself nodding off. Never! I made my way from the building yet again, found an all-night restaurant staffed by surly robot machines, and drank two large coffees with extra caffeine. This worked, producing ideas as well as instant heartburn. I staggered off and broke into a clothing store. By the time I reached the courthouse again I really was staggering with fatigue.

With fumbling fingers I resealed all of the doors, removed all traces of my passage. The first light of dawn was graying the windows before I was done. I fumbled with tired fingers as I sealed the cellar from the inside, stumbled across the room, sat down on the canvas, set my alarm watch—and lay down to instant slumber.

It was pitch dark when the mosquito whine of the alarm irritated me awake. I had a moment of panic until I remembered that the cellar was windowless. It should be full daylight outside by now. I would see. I turned on a worklight, made adjustments—then turned on the TV monitor. Perfect! A color picture of the courtroom above filled the screen, transmitted from the optical bug I had planted the night before. Some ancient employees were dusting the furniture and sweeping the floor. The session would begin in an hour. I left the set running while I made a last check of my labors of the previous night. All working, all in order . . . so all I had to do was wait.

That was what I did. Sipping at the cold coffee and chewing painfully on a stale sandwich from the previous day's supplies. The suspense ended when the courtroom doors were thrown open and the lucky spectators and the press came in. I could see them imaged clearly on the screen, hear the shuffle of their footsteps overhead. The sound of their voices murmured from the speaker, quieting only when they were silenced for the arrival of the judge. All eyes were on him, all ears twitching attentively when he cleared his throat and began to speak.

First he bored everyone into a state of stupefaction by going over the previous day's evidence in detail, then adding his obvious agreement to each summation and observation. I let his voice drone on while I looked at The Bishop, zooming in on his face.

He gave them nothing. His features were set, he looked almost bored. But there was a glint to his eyes that was almost hatred, nearer contempt. A giant pulled down by ants. The set of his jaw indicated that they may have imprisoned his body, but his soul was still free. But not for long if the judge had his way!

Now something in the judge's voice caught my attention. He had finished his preamble at last. He cleared his throat and pointed at The Bishop.

"Defendant will stand for sentencing."

All eyes were on the prisoner. He sat stolidly, unmoving. There was a growing rustle and murmur. The judge began to turn red and he hammered with the gavel.

"I will be obeyed in this court," he thundered. "The defendant will rise or will be forced to do so. Is that understood?"

Now I was sweating. If only I could have told him not to cause any difficulties. What would I do if he were held up by great ugly policemen? Two of them had already started forward at the judge's signal. It was then that The Bishop slowly raised his eyes. The look of withering contempt he directed at the judge would have deterred anyone not as dense as his honor; it was a glare of repulsion that might have destroyed minor life forms.

But he was standing! The police halted as the large hands went out and seized the solid railing. It creaked as he tugged on it and heaved his giant form up, to stand erect. His head was high as he released the rail and his arms dropped to his sides. . . .

Now! I stabbed down on the button. The explosions were not loud—but their effect was dramatic. They severed the two bolts that held the edge of the trapdoor into place. Under the great weight of The Bishop the door swung wide and he plunged down like a missile. I rushed up the ladder as he fell past me—but had time for a last glimpse of the courtroom on the screen.

There was silence as he vanished from sight. The springs slammed the trapdoor up into position and I pushed the heavy steel sealing bolts into place beneath it. This happened so fast that the horizontal form of The Bishop was still bouncing up and down on the trampoline when I turned to look. I scurried down the ladder to his side as he finally came to rest, looking up at me with stolid gaze as he spoke.

"Ah, Jim my boy. How nice to see you again." He took

my proffered hand and I helped him down to the floor. Above us there was pandemonium, shouting and screaming that could be clearly heard though the floor. I permitted myself one glorious look at the screen, at the pop-eyed judge, the scurrying policemen.

"Very impressive, Jim, very," The Bishop said, admiring the scene on the screen as well.

"Right!" I ordered. "Look at it as you strip off your outer clothing. Very little time, explanations will follow."

He hesitated not a millisecond but was hurling clothing from him even as the words were clearing my lips. The great rotund form emerged, clothed in tasteful purple undergarments, and he raised his hands above his head at my shouted command. Standing on the ladder I pulled the immense dress down over him.

"Here is the coat," I said. "Put that on next. Dress touches the ground, so don't remove shoes. Large hat next, that's it, mirror and lipstick while I unbolt the door.

He did what I said without a murmur of protest. The Bishop had vanished from sight and a lady of truly heroic proportions now emerged. There was a hammering above his head which he completely ignored.

"Let's go!" I called out, and he minced across the room in a most feminine fashion. I kept the door closed until he reached me and I used those few seconds to fill him in. "They'll be at the cellar stairs by now—but they are blocked. We go the other way." I pulled on the policeman's helmet to go with the uniform I was wearing. "You are a prisoner in my custody. We are leaving—now!"

I took him by the arm and we turned left down the dusty corridor. Behind us there was much crashing and shouting from the blocked stairwell. We hurried on, to the boiler room, and through that to the set of short stairs that rose up to the heavy exit door. With its hinges now greased and lock well oiled. It opened at a touch and we stepped out into the alleyway.

Not an arm's length from the back of a policeman who was standing guard there. He was the only one.

It took only an instant to examine the scene. The narrow alley was open at the far end. There was a dead end behind us. People—and safety—were in the street beyond the police guard. Then The Bishop climbed up beside me and something grated under his foot. The policeman turned his head to look.

I could see his eyes widen—as well they might, for the lady beside me was an impressive sight. I took advantage of his diverted attention to jump forward and reach out to keep his head turning even more in the same direction. He seized me in strong hands—which quickly went limp since the Tongoese neck twist produces instant unconsciousness when the rotation reaches 46 degrees from full front. I eased him to the ground, then stopped The Bishop from striding forward with my raised palm.

"Not that way."

The door on the building across the alley said SERVICE ENTRANCE and was locked. It opened to my ready key. As I waved my portly companion inside I took off my cap and threw it beside the policeman. I closed the door from the inside and dropped my uniform jacket as I did. The necktie went next as we strolled into the department store, until I was dressed simply in slacks and shirt. I put my moustache into my pocket and we joined the other customers. Occasionally looking at a display as we passed, but certainly never dawdling. There were a few amazed looks at my companion, but this was a very proper store and no one was so rude as to stare. I went first through the exit, holding the door, then led by a few paces as we joined the passing throng. Behind us, getting weaker as we went, were shouts and cries and the sound of alarm bells and sirens. I permitted myself a small smile. When I glanced back I saw that my companion had permitted herself one as well. She even had the nerve to let me have a brief wink. I turned back quickly—I couldn't encourage this sort of thing—then turned the corner into the side street, where the bread truck awaited.

"Stand here and look into your mirror," I said, unlocking the rear door. I busied myself inside, then barely had time to move aside as a great form hurtled by.

"No one looking . . ." he gasped.

"Perfect."

I climbed out, secured the door, went to the driver's side, climbed in, and started the engine. The van rumbled forward, slowly forcing its way through the pedestrians at the corner, then waited for a break in traffic.

I had considered driving back and past the courthouse, but that would have been dangerous braggadocio. Better to simply slip away.

When the street was empty I turned in the opposite direction and drove carefully towards the city limits. I knew all the back roads so we would be away well before they could be blocked.

We were not out of danger yet—but I still felt smug satisfaction. And why not! I had done it! Committed the escape of the century to save the criminal of the century. Nothing could stop us now!

CHAPTER TWELVE

I drove, slowly but steadily, for the rest of the morning and into the afternoon. Avoiding all of the major highways by staying with the secondary roads. Though my route, by necessity, had to vary in direction, I nevertheless moved steadily south. Doing my best to add real feeling and emotion to Pi-r squared. Sounds familiar? It should be since it is probably the single geometry theorem that anyone ever remembers. The area of a circle is equal to its radius times the value of Pi—squared. So each roll of the wheels of the bread van added an ever-increasing area that must be searched to find the escaping prisoner.

Four hours of this should put us well ahead of the police. The fact had to be considered as well that The Bishop had been locked in the back of the van for all of this time and knew nothing of my plans for the future. Explanations were in order—as was some food. I was getting hungry and, considering his girth, he would surely be feeling the same. With this in mind I pulled into the next suburban shopping center, checked the quick-food restaurants as I drove by, then parked at the far end of the lot. Backed up close to a blank wall. The Bishop blinked benevolently when I opened the rear door admitting light and fresh air.

"Time for lunch," I said. "Would you like . . ."

I lapsed into silence as he raised his hand in a gesture of silence.

"Permit me, Jim, to say something first. Thank you. From the bottom of my heart I thank you for what you have done. I owe you my life, no less. Thank you."

I stood with lowered eyes—I swear I was blushing like a girl!—and twisting my toe around and around on the ground. Then I coughed and found my voice.

"I did what had to be done. But—could we talk of this later?" He sensed my embarrassment and nodded, a regal figure despite the absurd garb he was still wearing. I pointed to the box on which he had been sitting. "There are clothes in there. While you change I'll get some food. You don't mind junk food from Macswineys?"

"Mind? After the loathsome sludge of the prison food, one of their Barbecued Porcuswineburgers would be unto paradise. With a large portion of sugarfried spamyams, if you please."

"Coming up!"

I closed the van door with a feeling of relief and trotted off towards the beckoning platinum arches. The Bishop's enthusiasm for fast food was most encouraging in a way that he could not suspect yet.

Loud munching and rustling sounded from the tables on all sides as I passed and made my way up to the serving counter. I reeled off my order to the plastic-headed robotic attendant, stuffed bills into the hopper—then grabbed the bag of food and drink as it slid out of the gate.

We sat on the boxes in the back of the van and ate and drank with enthusiasm. I had left the rear door open a crack, which gave us more than enough light. During my absence The Bishop had discarded his dress and was now wearing more masculine garb—the largest size I could find. He wolfed down half of his sandwich, nibbled a few spamyams to hold it in place, then smiled over at me.

"Your plan of escape was pure genius, my boy. I noticed the change in the flooring when I first sat down in the chair in the courtroom and pondered long over its significance. I hoped it was what I thought it might be, and can truthfully say that when the ground opened under my feet, so to speak, I felt a feeling of pleasure such as I had never experienced before. The sight of that despicable judge's face disappearing from my sight is a memory I shall always treasure."

Smiling broadly he finished the rest of the sandwich, then wiped his lips delicately before speaking again.

"Since I do not wish to cause you greater embarrassment with more fulsome praise, perhaps I should ask you what plans you have made to keep me safe from the hands of the law? Because, knowing you as I do now, I am secure in the belief that you have planned ahead in precise detail."

Praise from The Bishop was praise indeed and I basked in the warmth of it for a few moments while I worried out a bit of swinish gristle from between my teeth. "I have done that, thank you. The bread truck is our vehicle of invisibility, for it and its brothers trundle the highways and byways of this country daily." For some reason I found myself sounding more and more like The Bishop when I spoke. "We will stay in it until nightfall, slowly approaching our destination all of the while."

"And of course casual police patrols will not bother us, since the identifying numbers on this vehicle are not the ones that were on it before it came into your possession."

"Precisely. The theft will have been reported and local police informed. But the search will not widen, for this vehicle will be found not far from its depot in Billville in the morning. The new numbers, soluable in paint thinner, will have been removed, the odometer turned back to show only a brief joy ride by the thieves. If a van like this were seen and noted in the distant city of Bit O' Heaven, there will be nothing to connect that bread van with this one. That trail will run cold as will all the others."

He digested this bit of information, along with the last of the spamyams, then licked his fingers ruminatingly. "Capital. I could not have done better myself. Since further movement will be dangerous—the police will soon have a net over the entire country—I presume that Billville is our destination?"

"It is. I have my establishment there. Also your place of security. When I asked about your food tastes I had that in mind. You are going to take up residence in an automated Macswineys until the heat of the chase dies down."

His eyebrows climbed up to his forehead and I saw him glance with some apprehension at the discarded wrappings, but he was kind enough not to speak his doubts aloud. I hurried to reassure him.

"I have done it myself—so don't worry. There are some slight discomforts. . . ."

"But none to equal that of Federal prison! I apologize for an unseemly thought. No offense given."

"Or taken. It all came about by accident one evening when the police were a little close behind me for comfort. I picked the lock on the service entrance of the local Macswineys, the very one that you will be visiting, and my pursuers lost my trail. While I waited for a safe period I examined the premises. Amazing! Operating at high speed all around me was the solution to the single problem that faces all fast-food chains. The cost of keeping even the highly underpaid and unskilled employees. Human beings are both intelligent and greedy. They tend to become skilled, then want more money for their work. The answer is to do away with human beings completely."

"Admirable solution. If you are finished with your crumplumps I just might nibble one or two while I listen to your fascinating documentary."

I passed the greasy bag to him and went on. "Everything is mechanized. As the customer speaks his order the required item of food is ejected from the deep-frozen store into a super-voltage radar oven where it is instantly blasted to steamingly edible temperature. These ovens are so powerful that an entire frozen porcuswine can be exploded into steam and greasy particles in twelve microseconds."

"Amazing!"

"Beverages are dispensed with the same lightning speed. By the time a customer has finished speaking, his entire order is waiting. Behind a steel door, of course, until he has paid. The machinery is fully automatic and reliable and rarely touched by human hands. It is inspected weekly, while the frozen food store is replenished weekly as well. But not on the same day so that the vehicles don't get in each other's way."

"Crystal clear!" he cried aloud. "One makes one's home, so to speak, in the machinery chamber. When the frozen store is replenished, access to it will be from outside the building and the living chamber will not be entered. On the day the machinery is inspected the occupant rests comfortably in the freezing room until the technicians leave. I assume there is a connecting door, easily found. Ahh, yes, the freezer—that explains the large and warm garment I found packed in with my clothes. But should there be an equipment failure . . . ?"

"The alarm sounds in the central repair depot and a mechanic is dispatched. I have also arranged for it to sound in the room as well to allow enough time to slip away. I have also made provision for unexpected visits by the engineering staff. An alarm sounds if a key is placed in the outer lock, which then jams for precisely sixty seconds. Any questions?"

He laughed and reached out and patted my shoulder. "How could there be? You have thought of everything. Might I ask about reading matter and, how shall I phrase it delicately, sanitary facilities?"

"Portable viewscope and library with your bedroll. All needed facilities already plumbed in for visiting technicians."

"I could ask for no more."

"But . . . I could." I lowered my gaze—then raised it and steeled myself to speak. "You once told me that you were not in the acolyte-seeking business. Dare I ask you if you still feel that way? Or would you consider dallying the hours away with some lessons in criminal lore? Just to pass the time, so to speak."

Now it was his turn to lower his eyes. He sighed, then spoke. "I had good reasons to reject your request. Good at the time, or so I believed. I have changed my mind. In gratitude for my rescue I would enroll you in my school of Alternate Life-styles for a decade or more. But I don't believe you would like mere gratitude. That would not wear well, unless I have misread your character. I don't believe you rescued me just to gain my gratitude. So I therefore tell you, in all truth, that I look forward to passing on the few things I have learned down through the years. I look forward to our continuing friendship as well."

I was overwhelmed. We were on our feet at the same time and shaking hands, laughing. His grip was like steel but I didn't mind at all. It was I who turned away first, then looked at my watch.

"We have been here too long already and must not draw any attention. I shall drive on now—and the next stop will be the last one, for we will have arrived. Please exit quickly, enter the service door at once, and close it behind you. I'll be back as soon as this van has been disposed of, so the next person to open the door will be me."

"At your orders, Jim. But speak—and I shall obey."

It was a boring drive but a necessary one. But bored I was not, for I was filled with plans and thoughts of the future. I drove through street after street, stopping only once to charge the batteries at an automated service station. Then onward again, doomed forever to rumble through the back roads of Bit O' Heaven, watching the sun creep towards the horizon. To at last pull into the service road of the Billville shopping center, now empty of traffic until morning.

No one in sight. The Bishop passed me with a swish and the door slammed. The operation was still going well and I was in a hurry to finish, but knew better than to rush now. No one saw me when I carried the boxes and equipment into the building and dumped them in my office. It was taking a chance, but it had to be done. The chances that the van would be noticed and remembered were slim. Before I drove away I sprayed the interior of the van with print-go, a solvent that destroys fingerprints and should be in common use by all criminals. Even bread-van thieves.

This was it. I could do no more. I parked the van at the end of a quiet suburban street and walked back into town. It was a warm night and I enjoyed the exercise. When I passed the pond in Billville Park I heard a water bird calling out sleepily. I sat on the bench and looked out at the still surface of the pond. And thought about the future and my destiny.

Had I really succeeded in breaking free with my old life? Was I to succeed in the life of crime that I so much wanted? The Bishop had promised to help me—and he was the only person on the planet who could.

I whistled as I walked towards the shopping center. Looking forward to a brilliant and exciting future. So involved in my thoughts that I ignored the occasional surface car that passed, barely aware of one stopping behind me.

"You there, kid, just a minute."

Without thinking I turned about, so distracted that I didn't notice until too late that I was standing under the street light. The policeman sat in the car staring at me. I'll never know why he stopped, what he wanted to talk to me about, because that thought fled his mind instantly. I could see recognition there as his eyes widened.

In my concern over The Bishop I had forgotten completely that I was still a wanted criminal and jail-breaker, that all the police had my photograph and description. And here I was strolling the streets bereft of any disguise or attempt at security. All these thoughts passed through my head and out my ear in the instant that he recognized me. Nor did I even have time for any mental kicks in the seat of my trousers.

"You're Jimmy diGriz!"

He seemed as surprised as I was. But not surprised enough to slow down his reflexes. Mine were still getting into gear by the time his were all through operating. He must have practiced that draw in the mirror every day because he was fast. Too fast.

As I was turning to run, the muzzle of his recoilless .75 appeared in the open window.

"Gotcha!" he said. With a dirty, wide, evil law-enforcing smile.

CHAPTER THIRTEEN

"Not me—someone else—mistaken identity!" I gasped, but shoved my hands into the air at the same time. "Would you shoot a hapless child just on suspicion?"

The gun never wavered, but I did. Shuffling sideways towards the front of the car.

"Stop that and get back here," he shouted, but I kept the nervous shuffling going. I doubted, or hoped, that he wouldn't shoot me in cold blood. As I remember, that is against the law. I wanted him to come after me, because in order to do that he would have to take the gun out of the window. There was no way that he could point it at me and open the door at the same time.

The gun vanished—and so did I! The instant he lowered it I turned and ran, head down and pumping as fast as I could. He shouted after me—and fired!

The gun boomed like a cannon and the slug zipped past my ear and slammed into a tree. I spun about and stopped. This cop was insane.

"That's better," he called out, resting the gun on top of the open door and aiming it at me with both hands. "I fired to miss. Just once. Next time I hit. I got the gold medal for shooting this piece. So don't make me show you how good I am with it."

"You are mad, do you know that?" I said, all too aware of the quaver in my voice. "You just can't shoot people on suspicion."

"Yes I can," he said, walking up to me with the gun still pointed steady as a rock. "This ain't suspicion but identification. I know just who you are. A wanted criminal. You know what I'll say? I'll say this criminal grabbed my gun and it went off and he got shot. How does that sound? Want to grab my gun?"

He was a nutter all right, and a police nutter at that. I could see that he really wanted me to make a break so he could fire off his cannon. How he had escaped all the tests that were supposed to keep his kind out of law enforcement I will never know. But he had done it. He was licensed to carry a gun and was looking for an excuse to use it. That excuse I was not giving him. I extended my arms slowly before me, wrists together.

"I'm not resisting, officer, see. You are making a mistake, but I am going quietly. Put on the cuffs and take me in."

He looked downright unhappy at this, and frowned at me. But I made no more moves and in the end he scowled, pulled the handcuffs from his belt, and tossed them over to me. The gun never wavered.

"Put them on."

I locked them on one wrist, very loosely so I could slip my hand out of them, then on the other. I was looking down when I did this and I did not see him move. Until he had me by both wrists and had squeezed both cuffs until they had locked hard deep into my skin. He smiled down at me, twisting the metal into my flesh with sadistic glee.

"Gotcha now, diGriz. You are under arrest."

I looked up at him, he was a head taller than me and maybe twice my weight—and I burst out laughing. He had put the gun back in its holster in order to grab me—that's what he had done. The big man had grabbed the little kid. He couldn't understand why I was laughing and I gave him no opportunity to find out. I did the easiest, best, and fastest thing possible under the circumstances. Also the dirtiest.

My knee came up hard into his groin and he let go of my wrists at the impact and bent double. I did him a favor, the poor man must have been in some pain, and got him in the side of the neck with my joined hands as he went by. He was unconscious before he hit the ground. I knelt and started to go through his pockets for the keys to the handcuffs.

"What's happening there?" a voice called out as a light came on over the door of the nearest house. The sound of that shot would bring the whole street out soon. I would worry about the cuffs later. Right now I had to make tracks.

"Man's been hurt!" I shouted. "I'm going for help." This last was called over my shoulder as I trotted off down the street and around the corner. A woman appeared in the doorway and called after me but I wasn't staying around to listen. I had to keep moving, get away from this place before the alarm was called in and the search began. Things were coming apart. And my wrists hurt. I looked at them when I passed the next street light and saw that my hands were white, and were getting numb as well. The cuffs were so tight they were cutting off all the blood circulation. Any slight guilt I may have had over the dirty fighting vanished on the instant. I had to get these things off—and fast. My office, the only place.

I got there, avoiding the main streets and staying away from people. But when I reached the back door of the building my fingers were numb and stiff. I could feel nothing.

It took an intolerably long time to fish the keys out of my pocket. When I succeeded I instantly dropped them. Nor could I pick them up again. My fingers would not close. I could only drag my lifeless hands over the keys.

There are low moments in life—and I believe that this was the lowest one that I had ever experienced. I just could not do what had to be done. I was finished, licked, through. I couldn't get into the building. I couldn't help myself. It didn't take a medical degree to figure out that if I didn't get the cuffs off soon I was going to go through life with plastic hands. This was it.

"This is not it!" I heard myself snarling. "Kick the door open, do something, unlock it with your toes."

No, not my toes! I fumbled the keys about on the

ground with my dead fingers until I had separated out the correct key. Then bent my body over it and touched it with my tongue, feeling its position, ignoring the filth and dirt that I licked up along with it. Then I pulled back my lips and seized the key with my teeth. Good so far!

If you should ever be tempted to unlock a door with a key in your teeth while wearing handcuffs I have only a single word of advice. Don't. You see, you have to turn your head sideways to get the key into the keyhole. Then roll your head to turn the key, then butt the door with your head to get it open. . . .

It worked at last and I fell face first onto the floor inside. With the knowledge that I would have to do the whole thing all over again upstairs. That I did do it, and finally slid through into the office, owes more to persistence, stubbornness and brute force than to intelligence. I was too exhausted to think. I could only react.

I elbowed the door shut and stumbled to my workbench, hurled my toolbox to the floor, and kicked its contents about until I found the vibrosaw. I picked this up with my teeth and managed to wedge into an open desk drawer, holding it in place as I closed the drawer with my elbow. Closing it on my lip as well, which brought forth a nice gusher of blood. Which I ignored. My wrists were on fire—but my hands were past feeling. White and dead-looking. I had run out of time. I used my elbow to turn on the saw. Then pushed the handcuffs towards the blade, pulling my arms apart hard to stretch the chain. The blade buzzed shrilly and the chain was cut and my arms flew wide.

Next came the more exacting job of cutting the cuffs off without cutting my flesh. Too much.

There was blood everywhere before I was done. But the cuffs were off and I could see the flesh turn pink as circulation was restored.

After this, all I was up to was collapsing into a chair and watching the blood drip. I sat like this for about a minute when the numbness ended and the pain began. With an effort I stumbled to my feet and dragged over to the medical locker. Getting this good and bloody as well while I shook the pain capsules out and managed to swallow two of them. Since I was already there I pulled out the antiseptic and bandages and cleaned up the cuts. They were more messy than dangerous and none were very deep. I bandaged them, then looked into the mirror and shuddered and did something about the lip.

A police siren wailed by in the street outside—and I realized that the time had come to do some furious thinking and planning.

I was in trouble. Billville wasn't very big, and all exits would be sealed by now. That's what I would have done first, if I were looking for a fugitive. And even the dimmest of policemen would have figured this one out as well. Barricades on all the roads, copters out with nightscopes to watch the open fields, police at the linear station. All holes plugged. Trapped like a rat. What else? The streets would be patrolled too, easy enough to do by groundcar. And the later it got the fewer people there would be about and the more dangerous it would be to wander around.

Then, in the morning, what then? I knew what then. A search of every room in every building until I was found. I felt the perspiration bead my forehead at the thought. Was I trapped?

"No surrender!" I shouted aloud, then jumped to my feet and paced back and forth. "Jimmy diGriz is too slippery to be caught by the ham-handed minions of the local law. Look how I slipped away from that homicidal copper. Slippery Jim diGriz, that's who I am. And I am about to slip away from them again. But how?"

How indeed. I cracked open a beer, drank deep, then slumped back into the chair. Then looked at my watch. It was already getting too late to risk my presence on the street. The restaurants would be emptying, the feely and stinky cinemas disgorging their customers, couples marching homeward two by two. Any single individual drawing the instant attention of the law.

It had to be the morning then. I would have to venture forth in the light of day—or the rain! I punched up the weather report as quickly as I could, then slumped back once again. 99% chance of sunshine. I might as easily wish for an earthquake as a storm.

The office was a mess; it looked like the aftermath of an explosion in the slaughterhouse. I would have to clean it up. . . .

"No, Jim, you will not have to clean it up. Because the police are going to find it sooner or later, and probably sooner. Your fingerprints are everywhere and they know your blood type. They'll have a really good time trying to figure out what happened to you."

It would give them something to think about at least. And maybe cause a little trouble for one sadistic copper. I wheeled the chair over to the terminal and typed out the message. The printer whistled and I took the sheet of paper from the hopper. Wonderful!

TO THE POLICE. I WAS SHOT DEAD BY YOUR MURDERING POLICE OFFICER YOU FOUND UNCONSCIOUS. HE GOT ME. I AM BLEEDING INTERNALLY AND WILL DIE SOON. GOOD-BYE CRUEL WORLD. I NOW GO TO THROW MYSELF INTO THE RIVER.

I doubted very much if the ruse would work, but it might at least get that gun-crazy cop in trouble. And keep the rest of them busy dredging the river. There was some blood on the note and I smeared more on from the bandages. Then laid it carefully on the table.

This bit of tomfoolery had cheered me a bit. I sat back and finished the beer and made plans. Was I leaving anything important behind? No, there were no records kept here that I would need in the future. I found my doomsday key and unlocked the destruct switch, then pressed it. A single click from the memory banks was the only evidence that all of the computer's memory had just turned into random electrons. Everything else—tools, equipment, machinery—was expendable, could be replaced when needed. But I was not leaving the money.

All this was pretty tiring—but I couldn't afford to rest until all arrangements were complete. I pulled a pair of thin plastic gloves over the blood and bandages and set to work. The money was in the safe, since I robbed banks and did not believe in supporting them by opening an account. I put it all into a businessman's carrybag. It was only half full, so I added all the microtools that would fit. In the space that was left I stuffed in as much clothing as I could, then stood on the thing until I got it closed and locked.

New clothes and a disguise next. A black four-piece business suit, the fabric enriched by a pattern of tiny white buck bills. An orange rollneck, just what all the young bankers were wearing, along with trendy porcuswineherd boots with builtup heels. Add some to my height—that would help. When I left I would wear the moustache and goldrimmed glasses. What I could do now was darken my hair with dye and add to my fading tan. Preparations done, woozy with beer, fatigue, and pain pills, I opened the file cabinet bed, set the alarm, and dropped into oblivion.

There were giant mosquitoes circling my head, more and more of them, after my blood, mosquitoes . . .

I opened my eyes and blinked away the dream. My alarm watch, since I hadn't turned it off, had raised the volume on the mosquito buzzing, louder and louder until it sounded like a squadron of them diving to the attack. I pushed the button, smacked by gummy lips together, then stumbled over for a glass of water. It was full daylight outside and the early risers were just appearing.

Preparations made, I washed and dressed with care. Nifty orange gloves that matched the shirt hid my bandaged hands. When the streets were at their rush-hour busiest I seized up the carrybag, then checked carefully to make sure that the hall outside was empty. Stepped out and closed the door without looking back. This part of my life was over with. Today was the first day of my new life.

I hoped. I walked to the stairs with what I hoped was a very sincere, businessman-type walk, down past the first arrivals, and into the street.

To see the policeman on the corner looking closely at every passerby.

I did not look at him, but found an attractive girl walking ahead of me with very neat legs indeed. I watched their twinkling advance and tried to forget the nearby minion of the law. Came towards him, passed him, walked away from him. Waiting for the cry of recognition . . .

It never came. Maybe he was looking at the girl too. One down—but how many more to go?

This was the longest walk that I had ever taken in my life. Or at least it seemed that way. Not too fast, not too slow. I struggled to be part of the crowd, just another wage-slave going to work, thinking only of profit and loss and debenture bonds. Whatever debenture bonds were. One more street—safe so far. There's the corner. The service road behind the shopping center. No place for a businessman like you. So look sharp and don't hang about. Around the corner to safety.

Safety? I staggered as though I had been struck.

The Macswineys service van was outside the door and a hulking brute of a mechanic was just going inside.

CHAPTER FOURTEEN

I looked at my watch, snapped my fingers, then turned away from the service road in case my actions were being observed. And marched on smartly until I came to the first Speedydine. Just to make my day complete there were two policemen sitting in the first booth. Looking at me, of course. I marched past, eyes front, and found the seat farthest from them. There was an itching between my shoulder blades that I didn't dare scratch. I couldn't see them—but I knew what they were doing. They were looking at me, then talking to each other, deciding I was not quite what I looked like. Better investigate. Stand, walk my way, lean over my booth . . .

I saw the blue-trousered legs out of the corner of my eye and my heart instantly began hammering so loudly I was sure the whole restaurant could hear it. I waited for the accusing words. Waited . . . let my eyes travel up the blue-clad legs . . .

To see a uniformed linear driver sitting down across from me. "Coffee," he said into the microphone, shook his newspaper open, and began to read.

My heart slowed to something resembling normal and I silently cursed myself for suspicion and cowardice. Then spoke aloud into my own microphone in the deepest voice I could sum up.

"Black coffee and mulligatawny dumplings."

"Deposit six bucks, if you please."

I inserted the coins. There was a rumble of machinery at my elbow and my breakfast slid out onto the table. I ate slowly, then glanced at my watch, then went back to sipping my coffee. As I well knew from the earlier occasion when I had nipped into the freezer, when I had been hiding out there, thirty minutes was the minimum service time for a Macswineys mechanic. I allowed forty before I slid out of the booth. I tried not to think about what I would find when I finally got into the back of the fastfood parlor. I remembered my parting words only too well, I would be the next person through the door. Ho-ho. The next person had been the mechanic. Had he caught The Bishop? I sweated at the thought. I would find out soon enough. I passed the booth where the police had been. They were gone—out searching some other part of the city for me I hoped—and I headed back to the shopping center. To be greeted by the glorious sight of the Macswineys van drawing out into the road ahead of me.

The key was ready in my hand as I approached the door. The road ahead was empty—then I heard the footsteps coming up behind me. The police? With boring repetition my heart started the thudding routine again. I walked slower as I came close to the door. Then stopped and bent over and slipped the palmed key into my hand as though I had just picked it up. I examined it closely as someone came up, then passed me. A young man who showed not the slightest interest in my existence. He went on and turned into the back entrance to the market.

I took one look over my shoulder—then jumped for the door before anything else happened. Turned the key, pushed—and of course it didn't open.

The delay mechanism I had installed was working fine. It would unlock in one minute. Sixty short seconds.

Sixty incredibly crawling seconds. I stood there in my fine business outfit, as out of place in this alley as teats on a boar porcuswine, as we used to say back on the ranch. Stood there and sweated and waited for police or passersby to appear. Waited and suffered.

Until the key turned, the door opened—and I fell through.

Empty! On the far wall the automatic machinery clattered and whirred. The drink dispenser gurgled and a filled container whistled down its track and vanished. To be followed by the steaming bulk of a burger. Night and day this went on. But among all this mechanical motion no human form appeared. They had captured him—the police had The Bishop. And they would capture me next. . . .

"Ahh, my boy, I thought it might be you this time."

The Bishop emerged from the freezer, immense in his insulated gear, his sleeping roll and carryall tucked under his arm. He slammed the door behind him and the strength went out of me with a woosh and I slumped down with my back to the wall.

"Are you all right?" he asked, concern in his voice. I waved a weak hand.

"Fine, fine—just let me catch my breath. I was afraid they had you."

"You shouldn't have worried. When you did not reappear within a reasonable time I assumed there had been some hitch in your plans. So I rehearsed my evacuation moves just in case the legitimate users appeared today. And they did. It is really quite cold in there. I wasn't sure how long they would be, but I was sure you had installed some way of discovering when they left. . . ."

"I meant to tell you!"

"No need. I found the hidden speaker and switch and listened to someone who mutters profanities while he works. After some time the slam of the door and silence were welcome information indeed. Now about yourself. There were problems?"

"Problems!" I burst out laughing with relief. Then stopped when I heard a hysterical edge to the sound. I told him, omitting some of the more gruesome details. He made appropriate noises at the right places and listened attentively until the bitter end.

"You are being too harsh on yourself, Jim. A single lapse after all the tension of the day is not to be unexpected."

"But not to be allowed! Because I was stupid I almost had both of us caught. It won't happen again."

"There is where you are wrong," he said, shaking a thick admonitory finger. "It could happen at any time—

until you have trained yourself in your work. But you will be trained and trained efficiently . . ."

"Of course!"

". . . until a lapse like this one will be impossible. You have done incredibly well, for one of your inexperience. Now you can only improve."

"And you will teach me how—how to be a successful crook like you!"

His brow furrowed at my words and his expression was grave. What had I said that was wrong? I chewed my sore lip with worry as he unrolled his bedroll in silence, spread it out then sat upon it crosslegged. When at last he spoke I hung upon his every word.

"Now your first lesson, Jim. I am not a crook. You are not a crook. We do not want to be criminals for they are all individuals who are stupid and inefficient. It is important to comprehend and appreciate that we stand outside of society and follow strict rules of our own, some of them even stricter than those of the society that we have rejected. It can be a lonely life—but it is a life you must choose with your eyes open. And once the choice has been made you must abide by it. You must be more moral than they are because you will be living by a stricter moral code. And this code does not contain the word 'crook.' That is their word for what you are and you must reject it."

"But I want to be a criminal. . . ."

"Abandon the thought—and the title. It is, and you must excuse me saying it, a juvenile ambition. It is only your emotional striking out at the world you dislike and cannot be considered a reasoned decision. You have rejected them—but at the same time accepted their description of what you are. A crook. You are not a crook, I am not a crook."

"Then—what are we?" I asked, all eagerness. The Bishop steepled his fingers as he intoned the answer.

"We are Citizens of the Outside. We have rejected the simplistic, boring, regimented, bureaucratic, moral, and ethical scriptures by which they live. In their place we have substituted our own far superior ones. We may physically move among them—but we are not of them. Where they are lazy, we are industrious. Where they are immoral, we are moral. Where they are liars, we are the Truth. We are probably the greatest power for good to the society that we have discarded."

I blinked rather rapidly at that one, but waited patiently because I knew that he would soon make all clear. He did.

"What kind of a galaxy do we live in? Look around you. The citizens of this planet, and of every other planet in the loose organization known as the Galactic League, are citizens of a fat, rich union of worlds that has almost forgotten the real meaning of the word crime. You have been in prison, you have seen the dismal rejects whom they consider criminals. And this is what is called a frontier world! On the other settled planets there are few malcontents and even fewer who are socially maladjusted. Out there the handful who are still being born, in spite of centuries of genetic control, are caught early and their aberrations quickly adjusted. I made one single trip offplanet in my life, a tour of the nearest worlds. It was terrible! Life on those planets has all the color and wonder of a piece of wet cardboard. I hurried back to Bit O' Heaven for, loathsome as it can be at times, it is still a bit o' heaven compared to the others."

"Someday—I would like to see these other worlds."

"And so you shall, dear boy, a worthy ambition. But learn your way around this one first. And be thankful they don't have complete genetic control here yet—or the machines to mentally adjust those who struggle against society. On other planets the children are all the same. Meek, mild, and socially adjusted. Of course some do not show their genetic weakness—or strength as we call it—until they are adults. These are the poor displaced ones who try their hands at petty crimes—burglary, shoplifting, rustling and the like. They may get away with it for a week or two or a month or two, depending on their degree of native intelligence. But as sure as atomic decay, as sure as the fall of leaves in the autumn—and just as predestined—the police will eventually reach out and pull them in."

I digested this information, then asked the obvious question.

"But if that is all there is to crime, or rebellion against the system—where does that leave you and me?"

"I thought you would never ask. These dropouts I have described, whom you have associated with in prison, comprise ninety-nine point nine percent of crime in our organized and dandified society. It is the last and vital one-tenth of one percent that we represent that is so vital to the fabric of this same society. Without us the heat death of the universe would begin. Without us the lives of all the sheep-like citizenry would be so empty that mass suicide to escape it would be the only answer. Instead of pursuing us and calling us criminals they should honor us as first among them!"

There were sparks in his eyes and thunder in his voice when he spoke. I did not want to interrupt his fulminatory speech, but there were questions to be asked.

"Please excuse me—but would you be so kind as to point out just why this is so?"

"It is so because we give the police something to do, someone to chase, some reason for rushing about in their expensive machines. And the public—how they watch the news and listen for the latest reports on our exploits, how they talk to each other about it and relish every detail! And what is the cost of all this entertainment and social good? Nothing. The service is free, even though we risk life, limb, and liberty to provide it. What do we take from them? Nothing. Just money, paper, and metal symbols. All of it insured. If we clean out a bank, the money is returned by the insurance company who, at the end of the year, may reduce their annual dividend by a microscopic amount. Each shareholder will receive a millionth of a buck less. No sacrifice, no sacrifice at all. Benefactors, my boy, we are nothing less than benefactors.

"But in order for us to accomplish all this good for them we must operate outside their barriers and well outside of their rules. We must be as stealthy as rats in the wainscoting of their society. It was easier in the old days of course, and society had more rats when the rules were looser, just as old wooden buildings have more rats than concrete buildings. But there are rats in the buildings now as well. Now that society is all ferroconcrete and stainless steel there are fewer gaps between the joints. It takes a very smart rat indeed to find these openings. Only a stainless steel rat can be at home in this environment."

I broke into spontaneous applause, clapping until my hands hurt, and he nodded his head with gracious acceptance of the tribute.

"That is what we are," I enthused. "Stainless steel rats! It is a proud and lonely thing to be a stainless steel rat!"

He lowered his head in acknowledgment, then spoke. "I agree. Now—my throat is dry from all this talking and I wonder if you could aid me with the complex devices about us. Is there any way you might extract a double-cherry oozer from them?"

I turned to the maze of thudding and whirring machinery that covered the inner wall.

"There is indeed, and I shall be happy to show you how. Each of these machines has a testing switch. This, if you will look close, is the one on the drink dispenser. First you must turn it to on, then you can actuate the dispenser, which will deliver the drink here instead of to a customer on the other side. Each is labeled—see, this is the cherry oozer. A mere touch and . . . there!"

With a whistling thud it dropped into place and The Bishop seized it up. As he began to drink he froze, then whispered out of the corner of his mouth.

"I just realized, there is a window here and a young lady is staring in at me!"

"Fear not," I reassured him. "It is made of one-way glass. She is just admiring her face. It is the inspection port to look at the customers."

"Indeed? Ahh, yes, I can see now. They are indeed a ravenous lot. All that mastication causes a rumble in my own tum, I am forced to admit."

"No trouble at all. These are the food controls. That nearest one is for the Macbunnyburger, if you happen to like them."

"Love them until my nose crinkles."

"Then here."

He seized up the steaming package, traditionally decorated with beady eyes and tufted tail of course, and munched away. It was a pleasure to watch him eat. But I tore myself away before I forgot and pushed coins into the slot on back of the armored coinbox.

The Bishop's eyes widened with astonishment. As soon as he swallowed he spoke.

"You are paying! I thought that we were safely ensconced in a gustatorial paradise with free food and drink at our beck and call, night and day?"

"We are—for all of this money is stolen and I am just putting it back into circulation to keep the economy healthy. But there is no slack in the Macswineys operation. Every morsel of porcine tissue, every splinter of ice is accounted for. When the mechanic tests the machines he is responsible for every item delivered. The shop's computer keeps track of every sale so that the frozen supplies are filled exactly to the top each time they are replenished. All of the money collected is taken away each day from the safe on the outer wall—which is automated as well. An armored van backs over it just as the time lock disengages. A code is keyed in and the money disgorged. So if we simply helped ourselves, the records would reveal the theft. Prompt investigation would follow. We must pay for what we use, precisely the correct amount. But, since we won't be coming back here, we will steal all the money on the day we leave."

"Fine, my boy, fine. You had me worried there for a minute with your bit of forced honesty. Since you are close to the controls, please trigger another delicious morsel of Lepus Cuniculus while I pay."

CHAPTER FIFTEEN

I suppose that there have been stranger places to go to school, but I can't think of any. At certain times of day it was hard to be heard above the rattle, hiss, and roar of the dispensing machinery. Lunch and dinner were the busiest times, but there was another peak when the schools got out. We would eat then as well, since it was so hard to talk, working our way through the entire Macswineys inventory. Countless Macbunnyburgers hopped down our throats, and many a Frozen Fomey followed. I liked Dobbindogs until one too many cantered past my gums, and switched to jellied porcuswinetrotters, then to feline-fritters. The Bishop was very catholic in his tastes and liked everything on the menu. Then, once the crowds had gone, after we had patted the last trace of gravy from our lips, we would loll back at our ease and my studies would continue. When we started on computer crime I discovered what The Bishop had been up to for the past couple of decades.

"Give me a terminal and I can rule the world," he said, and such was the authority of his voice that I believed he could. "When I was young I delighted in all manner of operations to please the citizens of this planet. It was quite a thrill to intercept cash shipments while en route, then substitute my calling card for the bundles of bills. They never did find out how I did it. . . ."

"How did you?"

"We were talking about computers."

"Digress just this once, I beg of you. I promise to put

the technique to good use. Perhaps, with your permission, even leave one of your cards."

"That sounds an excellent idea. Baffle the current crop of coppers as thoroughly as I did their predecessors. I'll describe what happens—and perhaps you can discover for yourself how it was done. In the Central Mint, a well-guarded and ancient building with stone walls two meters thick, are located the giant safes filled with billions of bucks. When a shipment is to be made, guards and officials fill a bullion box, which is then locked and sealed while all present look on. Outside the building waits a convoy of coppers all guarding a single armored car. At a given signal the car backs up against the armor-plated delivery door. Inside the building the steel inner door is opened, the box placed inside the armored chamber. This door is sealed before the outer one can be opened. The box then travels in the armored car to the linear train, where an armored wagon receives it. This has but the single door, which is locked and sealed and wired with countless alarms. Guards ride in a special chamber of each car as it shuttles through the linear network to the city needing the bucks. Here another armored car awaits, the box is removed—still sealed—placed in the car, and taken to the bank. Where it is opened—and found to contain only my card."

"Marvelous!"

"Care to explain how it was done?"

"You were one of the guards on the train . . ."

"No."

"Or drove the armored car . . ."

"No."

I racked my brains this way for an hour before he relented and explained. "All your suggestions have merit, but all are dangerous. You are far more physical than I ever was. In my operations I always preferred brains to brawn. The reason that I never had to break into the box and extract the money is that the box was empty when it left the building. Or rather it was weighted with bricks as well as my card. Can you guess now how it was done?"

"Never left the building," I muttered, trying to stir my

brain to life. "But it was loaded into the box, the box put into the truck . . ."

"You are forgetting something."

I snapped my fingers and leapt to my feet. "The wall, of course it had to be the wall. You gave me all the clues, I was just being dense. Old, made of stone, two meters thick!"

"Exactly so. It took me four months to break in, I wore out three robots doing it, but I won out in the end. First I bought the building across the road from the mint and we tunneled under it. With pick and shovel. Very slow, very silent. Up through the foundations of the building and inside the wall. Which proved to have an outer and inner stone wall, and as is the building custom, it was filled with rubble in between. Our diamond saws were never heard when we opened the side of the armored vault connecting the inside of the mint with the outside. The mechanism I installed could change boxes in one point oh five seconds. When the inner door was closed, the lock had to be thrown before the outer door could be opened. That was enough time, almost three seconds, to allow for the switch. They never did find out how I did it. The mechanism is still in place. But the operation was basically misdirection, along with a lot of digging. Computer crime is something else altogether. Basically it is an intellectual exercise."

"But isn't computer theft almost impossible these days, with codes and interlocks?"

"What man can code or lock, man can decode and unlock. Without leaving any trace. I will give you some examples. Let us begin with the rounding-off caper, also called the salami. Here is how it works. Let us say that you have 8,000 bucks in the bank, in a savings account that earns eight percent a year. Your bank compounds your account weekly in order to get your business. Which means at the end of the first week your bank multiplies your balance by .0015384 percent and adds this sum to your balance. Your balance has increased by 12.30 bucks. Is that correct? Check it on your calculator."

I punched away at the sum and came up with the same

answer. "Exactly twelve bucks and thirty centimes interest," I said proudly.

"Wrong," he said deflatingly. "The interest was 12.3072, wasn't it?"

"Well, yes, but you can't add seventy-two-hundredths of a centime to someone's account, can you?"

"Not easily, since financial accounts are kept to two decimal places. Yet it is at this precise moment in the calculations that the bank has a choice. It can round all decimals above .005 up to the nearest centime, all those below .0049 down to zero. At the end of a day's trading the rounding-ups and rounding-downs will average out very close to zero so the bank will not be out of pocket. Or, and this is the accepted practice, the bank can throw away all decimal places after the first two, thereby making a small but consistent profit. Small on banking terms—but very large as far as an individual is concerned. If the bank's computer is rigged so that all the rounding-downs are deposited to a single account, why at the end of the day the computer will show the correct balance in the bank's account and in the client's accounts. Everyone will be quite pleased."

I was punching like fury into my calculator, then chuckled with glee at the results. "Exactly so. All are pleased—including the holder of that account that now holds the round-downs. For if only a half a centime is whipped from ten-thousand accounts, the profit is a round fifty bucks!"

"Exactly. But a large bank will have a hundred times that number of accounts. Which is, as I know from happy experience, a weekly income of five-thousand bucks for whoever sets up this scam."

"And this, this is your smallest and simplest bit of computer tomfoolery?" I asked in a hushed voice.

"It is. When one begins to access large corporative computers, the sums become unbelievable. It is such a pleasure to operate at these levels. Because if one is careful and leaves no traces, the corporations have no idea that they have even been fiddled! They don't want to know about it, don't even believe it when faced with the evidence. It is very hard to get convicted of computer crime. It is a fine hobby for one of my mature years. It keeps me busily engaged and filthy rich. I have never been caught. Ahh, yes, except once. . . ."

He sighed heavily and I felt mortified.

"My fault!" I cried. "If I had not tried to contact you, why you would never have got involved with the Feds."

"No guilt, Jim, feel no guilt over that. I misjudged their security controls, far more rigid than the ones I had been dealing with. It was my mistake—and I certainly paid for it. Am still paying. I am not decrying the safety of our refuge here, but this junk food begins to wear on one after a bit. Or perhaps you haven't noticed?"

"This is the staff of life of my generation."

"Of course. I had not thought of that. The horse tires not of hay, the porcuswine will snuffle up his swill greedily unto eternity."

"And you could probably tuck into lobster and champagne for the next century."

"Well-observed and correct, my boy. How long do you think that we shall be here?" he asked, pushing away half of an unconsumed portion of crumptumps.

"I would say a minimum of two weeks more." A shudder shivered his frame.

"It will be a good opportunity for me to reduce."

"By that time the heat of the chase will have died down considerably. We will still have to avoid public transportation for a good while after that. However I have prepared an escape route that should be secure fairly soon."

"Dare I ask what it is?"

"A boat, rather a cabin cruiser on the Sticks River. I bought it some time ago, in a corporative name, and it is at the marina just outside Billville."

"Excellent!" He rubbed his hands with glee. "The end of summer, a cruise south, fried catfish in the evening, bottles of wine cooling in the stream, steaks at riverside restaurants."

"And a sex change for me."

He blinked rapidly at that, then sighed with relief when

I explained. "I'll wear girl's clothes when I'm aboard and can be seen from the shore, at least until we are well away from here."

"Capital. I shall lose some weight—there will be no difficulty dieting here. Raise a moustache, then a beard, die my hair black again. It is something to look forward to. But shall we say one month instead of two weeks? I could last that amount of time incarcerated in this gustatorial ghetto as long as I would not be eating. My figure will be the better for the extra weeks, my hair and moustache longer."

"I can do it if you can."

"Then it is agreed. And we shall make the most of the time now by forwarding your education? RAM, ROM, and PROM will be the order of the day."

I was too busy with my studies to be bothered by the omnipresent odor of barbecued porcuswineburgers. Besides that, I could still eat them. So as my comprehension grew of all the varied possibilities of illegality in our society, so did my companion's figure fade. I wanted to leave earlier, but The Bishop, having made up his mind, would not be swayed.

"Once a plan is made it must always be followed to the letter. It should only be changed if outside circumstances change. Man is a rationalizing animal and needs training in order to become a rational one. Reasons can always be found for altering an operation." He shuddered as the machines speeded up with a roar; school was out, then crossed off one more day on his calendar. "An operation well-planned will work. Meddle with it and you destroy it. Ours is a good plan. We will stay with it."

He was far leaner and harder when the day of our exodus finally arrived. He had been tried in the gustatory furnace and had been tempered by it. I had put on weight. Our plans were made, our few belongings packed, the safe cleaned out of all of its bucks—and all trace of our presence eliminated. In the end we could only sit in silence, looking again and again at our watches.

When the alarm sounded we were on our feet, smiling with pleasure.

I turned off the alarm as The Bishop opened the door of the freezer room. As the key turned in the outer lock we closed the door behind us. Stood and shivered in Macswineys' mausoleum while we listened to the mechanic enter the room we had so recently left.

"Hear that?" I asked. "He's adjusting the icer on the cherry oozer dispenser. I thought it sounded funny."

"I prefer not to discuss the contents of the ghastly gourmet gallery. Is it time to go yet?"

"Time." I eased open the outer door and blinked at the light of day, unseen for so long. Other than the service van the street was empty. "Here we go."

We shuffled out and I sealed the door behind us. The air was sweet and fresh and filled with lovely pollution. Even I had had my fill of cooking odors. As The Bishop hurried to the van I slipped the two wedges into the outer door to our chamber of culinary horrors. If the mechanic tried to get out before his appointed time, these would slow him down. We only needed about fifteen minutes.

The Bishop was a dab hand with a lockpick and had the van open and the door swinging wide even as I turned about. He dived into the back among the machine parts as I started the engine.

It was just that easy. I dropped him close to the marina, where he sat on a bench in the sunshine, keeping an eye on our possessions. After that it was simplicity itself to leave the purloined van in the parking lot of the nearest liquor store. Then I strolled, not ran, back to the riverside to rejoin him.

"It's the white boat, that one there," I pointed it out, pressing on my moustache with my other hand at the same time to make sure that it was securely in place. "The entire marina is fully automated. I'll get the boat and bring it back here."

"Our cruise is about to begin," he said, and there was a merry twinkle in his eye.

I left him there in the sunlight and went to the marina to insert the boat's identification into the operations robot.

"Good morning," it said in a tinny voice. "You wish to take out the cabin cruiser *Lucky Bucks*. The batteries have been recharged at a cost of twelve bucks. Storage charges . . ."

It went on like that, reading aloud all the charges that could be clearly seen on the screen—presumably for customers who couldn't read—and there was nothing that could be done about it. I stood on one foot and then the other until it was finished, then pumped in the coins. The machine gurgled and spat out my receipt. Still strolling, I went to the boat, inserted the receipt, then waited for the welcome click when the chain unlocked. Seconds later I was out on the river and heading for the solitary figure on the bank.

Solitary no more. A girl sat beside him.

I circled out and around and she was still there. The Bishop sat slumped and gave me no sign what to do. I circled once more, then the sight of a patrolling police car sent me burbling to the bank. The girl stood and waved, then called out.

"Why little Jimmy diGriz, as I live and breathe. What a lovely surprise."

CHAPTER SIXTEEN

Life had had far too many moments like this lately. I looked at the girl more closely as I eased the boat against the bank. She knew me, I should know her; smashingly good-looking, her blouse filled to perfection. Those tulip lips, her!—object of my wildest dreams.

"Is that you Beth? Beth Naratin?"

"How *sweet* of you to remember me!"

I was ready to jump ashore with the mooring line, but she took it from my hand and tied it to the bollard there. Over her shoulder I saw the police cruiser go past and keep on cruising. Then glanced at The Bishop, who simply raised his eyes to heaven as she spoke.

"I said to myself, Beth, I said, that can't be Jimmy diGriz climbing out of that old Macswineys van and wearing a cute little moustache. Not Jimmy who has been in the news so much lately. If it is, why don't I just mosey after him, for old times' sake. Then I saw you talk to this nice gentleman here, before you went off to the marina, so I just made up my mind to wait for you to come back. Going on a trip, are you?"

"No, no trip, just a little day excursion up the river and back. Nice seeing you again, Beth."

That was the only nice part about this. Seeing her, I mean. The object of my childish worship. She had left school soon after I had entered—but she was hard to forget. Four years older than me, a real mature woman. That would make her twenty-one now. She had been head of her class, winner of the Beauty Queen of the Year.

A STAINLESS STEEL RAT IS BORN 111

With good reason. Now, old as she was, she was still a smasher. Her voice sliced through my memories.

"I don't think that you are being exactly truthful, Jimmy. Why with all these bags and things I bet that you are going on a long cruise. If I were you I would consider a long cruise a really good idea."

Was there a different tenor to her voice with these last words? What did she want? We couldn't hang around here much longer. She made her wants clear when she jumped aboard, rocking the boat at its mooring.

"Always room for one more!" she called out cheerfully, then went to sit in the bow. I stepped ashore and grabbed up the bags. Then whispered to The Bishop.

"She knows me. What do we do?"

He sighed in answer. "Very little that we can do. For the present we have a passenger. I suggest that we consider this problem once we are under way. After all—we have no choice."

Too true. I passed our belongings over to him, then struggled to untie the black knot that she had tied in the line. Gave the *Lucky Bucks* a kick out with my foot, jumped aboard, and took the wheel. The Bishop carried the cases below as I switched on the power and headed downstream. Away from Billville, Macswineys and the law.

But not from Beth. She lay stretched out on the deck before me, skirt hiked up so I could admire those gorgeous lengths of leg. I did this. Then she turned about and smiled, clearly able to read my mind. I forgot about my planned female disguise at this moment—imagining the jeering that would greet my sex change. I was getting angry.

"All right, Beth, why don't you just spell it out," I said, hauling my gaze bodily out to the clear waters of the river.

"Whatever do you mean?"

"Stop the games. You have been watching the news, that's what you said. So you know about me."

"Sure do. Know you hold up banks and escape from jail. That doesn't bother me though. I had a bitsy bit of difficulty myself. So when I saw you, then this boat, I knew you must have some money. Maybe a lot of money. So I just jumped at the chance to take this trip with you. Isn't that nice?"

"No." I kept my thoughts on the law and not the legs. She was trouble. "And I do have a bit of money put aside. If I get you some, put you ashore . . ."

"The money, yes. The shore, no. I've seen the last of *him* and Billville. I'm going to see the world now. And you are going to pay my way."

She snuggled down, with her arms for a pillow, smiling as she enjoyed the sunshine. I looked on gloomily and thought of three or four blows that would snap that delicate neck. . . .

Not even as a joke. This problem could be solved— and without deadly violence. We hummed along, the water parting in white foam at our bow, Billville behind us and green fields opening up ahead at the bend in the river. The Bishop came on deck and sat next to me. With her third presence there was nothing much we could say.

We continued in silence this way for the better part of an hour, until a dock beside a general store appeared ahead. Beth stirred and sat up, running her fingers through that gorgeous blond hair.

"You know what—I'm hungry. Bet you are too. Why don't you pull up over there and I'll jump ashore and get us some food and some beer. Isn't that a good idea?"

"Great!" I agreed. She goes into the store, we go into high gear and away.

"I am skint," she smiled. "Stone broke. If you give me a few bucks I'll buy lunch. I think a thousand will do."

Her sweet-little-girl expression never changed while she said this and I wondered just what kind of trouble she was in. Extortion and blackmail maybe; she certainly had the qualifications for that. I dug deep into my wallet.

"That's nice," she said, thumbing through the bundle with glowing eyes. "I won't be long. And I *know* you will be here, Jimmy, along with your friend. Haven't I seen him in the news broadcasts too?"

I glowered after the lovely rotations of her rump as she trotted towards the store.

"Got our hides nailed to the wall," The Bishop said gloomily.

"Nailed, flayed, and tanned. What do we do?"

"Exactly what she says for the time being. Short of killing her, we have very little choice. But I do not believe in killing."

"Nor do I. Although this is the first time that I have understood the temptation."

"What do you know about her?"

"Nothing—since I last saw her in school. She says she is in trouble, but I have no idea what she means."

He nodded in thought. "When we are well away from her I'll get close to a terminal. If she is in the police records I can dig her out."

"Will that do us any good?"

"I have no idea, dear boy. We can only try. Meanwhile we must make the best of the situation. We are well away from the terrors of the pork palace, safely away from our pursuers as well. As long as this creature gets money from us we are safe. For the moment. And you must admit that she is decorative."

I had no answer to that and could only sit glumly until our uninvited passenger returned.

After lunch we continued our voyage downstream. Exhausted by the morning of sunbathing, Beth went below for a beauty nap. The Bishop wanted a turn at the wheel so I showed him the simple controls and pointed out the navigation markers. We had very little to say to each other. But we were thinking a lot. In midafternoon the object of our fierce cogitation trotted up from below.

"Such a cute little ship," she gushed. "The cutest little girls' room, little kitchen, and everything. But only two little beds. How in the world will we all sleep?"

"In shifts," I growled, the sound of her voice already getting to me.

"You always were a card, Jimmy. I think it best if I sleep below. You and your friend can make do."

"Make do, young lady, make do? How does one my age make do on deck when the chill mists of night descend?" The Bishop's anger was under control, barely, but her bright smile seemed to be unaware of it.

"I'm sure that you will find a way," she said. "Now I would like to stop at the next town we come to, that one there. I left in such a hurry I forgot all my things. Clothes and makeup, you know."

"You wouldn't need a bit of money to buy those things?" I asked facetiously. She ignored my feeble humor and nodded.

"Another thousand will do."

"I'm going below," The Bishop said, and did not emerge again until I had tied up and she was gone. He carried two beers and I took one and drank deep.

"Murder is out," he said firmly.

"Murder is out," I agreed. "But that doesn't mean we can't enjoy thinking about it. What do we do?"

"We don't just heave anchor and go. She'll have the police after us in minutes, then will pocket the reward. We must take that into consideration, then think faster than she can. Coming with us was an impulse, obviously. She is greedy for money and we must keep giving it to her. But sooner or later she will decide that she has had enough of ours and will turn us in for the reward. Is there such a thing as a map aboard?"

That mighty brain was at work, I could tell that. I asked no questions but rooted out the map as quickly as I could. He traced it with his finger.

"We are here, I imagine, yes, here is the very place. While downstream, here, is the bustling city of Val's Halla. When will we get there?"

I squinted at the scale and marked the distance with my thumb. "Could be there by midafternoon tomorrow, if we get an early start."

His face broke into a smile so wide that his eyes were

crinkled half shut. "Splendid, absolutely splendid. That will do very nicely indeed."

"What will?"

"My plans. Which I shall keep to myself for the moment since there are details still to be worked out. When she returns you must agree with me, whatever I say; that is all you have to do. Now, next order of business. Where do we sleep tonight?"

"On the river's bank," I said, heading below. "Our friend has all the money that I was carrying, so I must get more from our stock. Then I'm going ashore to buy a tent, sleeping bags, all the gear for comfortable camping out."

"Capital. I shall man the fort and hone my plans until you return."

I bought some steaks too, along with a collection of fancy bottles of wine. We needed a major change from the Macswineys cuisine. When the sun was close to the horizon I tied the boat to the trees on the banks of a green meadow, where we could pitch our tent. The Bishop, after smacking his lips over the meat, announced that he would prepare dinner. While he did this, and Beth did her nails, I hammered stakes and got our beds ready. The sun was a ball of orange on the horizon when we tucked into the meal. It was tremendous. No one talked until we were done. When the last morsel was gone The Bishop sighed, raised his glass and sipped, then sighed with repletion.

"Though I cooked it myself, I must say that meal was a triumph."

"It does take the taste of porcuswine out of the mouth," I agreed.

"I didn't like the wine. Nasty." Only her outline was visible in the darkness. Lacking the usual glorious physical accompaniment her voice, as well as her words, left a very lot to be desired. Yet The Bishop's deep basso was free of rancor when he spoke again.

"Beth—I may call you Beth, mayn't I? Thank you. Beth, we shall be in the city of Val's Halla tomorrow, where I must go ashore and call into my bank. Our funds are running low. You wouldn't like our money to run out, would you?"

"No, I wouldn't."

"Thought not. But would you like me to go to the bank and bring you back one-hundred thousand bucks in small buck bills?"

I heard her gasp. Then she fumbled for the switch and the riding lights above the cockpit came on. She was frowning at The Bishop and, for the very first time, lost her cool.

"Are you trying to play games with me, old man?"

"Not at all, young lady. I am simply paying for our safety. You know certain facts that are, shall we say, best left unspoken aloud. I think that sum is a reasonable amount to pay for your continuing silence. Don't you?"

She hesitated—then burst out laughing. "I sure do. Just let me see the color of those bucks and I may even consider letting you boys continue your journey without poor little me."

"Whatever you say, my dear, whatever you say."

Nor would he speak another word on the subject. We retired soon after that, for it had been a busy day for all of us. Beth took possession of the boat and we had the tent. When I returned from setting the alarms to make sure that the boat would still be there in the morning, The Bishop was already in full snore. Before I slept myself I realized that, whatever he was planning, we had at least one more day of freedom before Beth would think of contacting the police. The lure of that money would ensure her silence. As I dozed off I realized that The Bishop had undoubtedly planned it that way.

We were humming down the river an hour after dawn, despite Beth's protests. She emerged later, but her anger soon vanished beneath The Bishop's monetary ministrations. He described the interest her invested bucks could earn without her spending any of her capital, touched lightly on the consumer goods she would soon purchase, and generally charmed her like a snake with a rabbit. I had no idea what his plans were but I enjoyed every moment of it.

By midafternoon I had tied up at the marina on the canal that bisected Val's Halla. The city center was close to hand and The Bishop, beard combed and moustache twirled, was neatly turned out and businesslike.

"This will not take long," he said, then left. Beth looked after him, already atwitch with anticipation.

"He's really the one they call The Bishop," she said when he had gone.

"I wouldn't know about that."

"Don't give me that old booshwah. I saw the films on 3V, how somebody got him out. A small guy with a moustache. It had to be you."

"Lot of moustaches in this world."

"I never thought, when I saw you around the school, you would ever end up like this."

"I thought the same about you. I admired you from afar."

"So did every other pubescent boy in the school. Don't think I didn't know it. We used to laugh about it, him being a teacher and all that. . . ."

She shut up and glowered at me and I smiled sweetly and went below to wash the dinner and breakfast dishes that she had so carefully ignored. I was just finishing up when there was a hail from the shore.

"Boat ahoy! Permission to come aboard?"

The Bishop stood on the dockside, beaming and splendid. His new suit must have cost a small fortune. The suitcase that he held up appeared to be made of real animal skin of some kind, with fittings of glowing gold. Beth's eyes were as wide as saucers. The Bishop climbed aboard and treated us to a conspiratorial wink.

"Best to get below before I show you what's in this case. It is not for the world to see."

Beth led the way and he held the case to his chest until I had closed and locked the door. Then he swept the papers from the table to the deck, placed the case in its center, and with tantalizing precision unlocked and opened the case.

Even I was impressed. There was far more than the hundred-thousand here. Beth stared at it—then reached out and tugged a bundle of thousand buck bills free.

"Real? Is it real?" she asked.

"Guaranteed right from the mint. I saw to that myself." With her attention on the money he turned to me. "Now, Jim, would you mind doing me a favor? Would you find some rope or twine, I'm sure that you will know what you will need. I want absolute silence as well when you tie this girl up so she cannot move."

I was expecting something—she was not. Her mouth was just opening to scream when I seized that precious neck and pressed hard just below the ears.

CHAPTER SEVENTEEN

With savage glee I cut one of the blankets into strips and bound those delicate wrists and trim ankles. I was just putting sticking tape over her mouth when she came to and tried to scream. It came out as a muffled mewl.

"Can she breathe all right like that?" The Bishop asked.

"Perfectly. See the glare in her eye and the angry heaving of that magnificent chest? She is breathing through her nostrils just fine. Now—will you tell me what this is all about?"

"On deck, if you please."

He waited until the door was closed behind us before he spoke, rubbing his hands together with joy.

"Our troubles are over, my boy. I knew that as soon as I looked at the map. There are two things about this fine city that assure me of that. One was the bank, a branch of Galactic Trust with which I have an account—sizeable as you have seen. The second fact of interest is that there is a spaceport here."

I puzzled over this for a few seconds as my sluggish brain slowly added two and two. Then my jaw gaped so hard I could barely speak.

"You mean that, us, we . . . we are going offplanet?"

He nodded and grinned. "Precisely. This little world has become, shall we say, a little too warm for us. It will be even warmer when our female friend is freed. By that time we shall have shaken the dust of Bit O' Heaven from our boots and we will be lightyears away. You did tell me that you wanted to travel?"

"I did, of course, but aren't there controls, inspections, police, things like that?"

"There are. But customs and immigration can be circumvented if you know how. I know how. And I did check on which ships were here before taking this drastic step. I am sorry that I had no opportunity to warn you— but I was certain that your magnificent reflexes would resolve the matter with ease. When I left here I did not know that this would be the day to put the plan into operation. I intended just to get the money to string the girl along. While keeping track of spacer operations. But the fates are on our side. There is a freighter here from Venia taking on cargo—and leaving in the early hours of the morning. Isn't that wonderful!"

"I'm sure that it is. But I would be a lot surer if I knew why."

"Jim, your education has been sorely neglected. I thought every schoolboy knew how venal the Venians were. They are the despair of the League polimetricians. Incorrigible. The motto on Venia is *La regloj ĉiam ŝansiliĝas*. Which may be freely translated as There are no Fixed Rules. That is to say, there are laws about everything— but bribery can change anything. It is not so much that they are a world of criminals, but rather a planet of twisters."

"Sounds nice," I agreed. "Then what have you arranged?"

"Nothing yet. But I am positive that opportunity will arrive at the spaceport."

"Yes, sure." I was far from enthusiastic. The plan had all the earmarks of improvisation and crossed fingers. But I had little choice. "What about the girl?"

"We'll leave a message for the police with the electronic post, to be delivered after we are gone. Telling them the place where she can be found."

"That place can't be here—too public. There is an automated marina farther downstream. I could tie up there, one of the outer berths."

"The perfect solution. If you will give me instructions

how to find it I will hie myself to the spaceport to make the arrangements. Shall we meet there at 2300 hours?"

"Fine by me."

I watched his impressive form move off in the growing darkness, then started the engine and made a slow turn in the canal. It was dark by the time I reached the marina. But it was brightly lit and the channel was well marked. Most of the boats had tied up close to shore, which was fine by me. I took the outermost berth, well away from the others. Then went below, turned on the lights, and faced the poisonous glare from those lovely eyes. I locked the cabin door behind me, then sat down on the bunk across from Beth.

"I want to talk to you. If I take off the tape do you promise not to scream? We are well away from the city and there is no one here to hear you in any case. Deal?"

The hatred was still there as she nodded reluctantly. I peeled off the tape—then jerked my fingers away just in time as those perfect teeth snapped at my hand.

"I could kill you, murder you, butcher you, slaughter you . . ."

"Enough," I said. "I'm the one who could do all those things, not you. So shut up."

She shut. Perhaps realizing what her position really was; there was more fear than anger in her eyes now. I didn't want to terrorize a helpless girl—but the murder talk had been her idea. She was ready to listen.

"You can't be comfortable. So lie still while I untie you."

She waited until her wrists were free, then raked her nails towards my face while I was untying her ankles. I had expected this, so she ended up back on the bunk with the breath knocked out of her.

"Act reasonable," I told her. "You can be tied and gagged again just as easily. And please don't forget that you brought this on yourself."

"You are a criminal, a thief. Wait until the police get their hands on you. . . ."

"And you are a blackmailer. Can we stop the names and

games now? Here is what is going to happen. We are going to leave you on this boat and when we are well away the police will be told where to find you. I'm sure that you will tell them a good story. There are express linears from here, as well as the highways. You'll never see us again, nor will they." A little misdirection never hurt.

"I'm thirsty."

"I'll get you something."

Of course she made a break for the door when I had my back turned, then tried for my eyes again when I pulled her away. I could understand her feelings—I just wished that she wouldn't.

Time dragged very slowly after that. She had nothing to say that I wanted to hear—and the reverse was obviously true as well. Hours passed in this way before the boat rocked as someone stepped aboard. I dived towards the bunk but she got out one good scream before I could silence her. The door handle rattled and turned.

"Who is it?" I called out, crouched and ready for battle.

"Not a stranger, I assure you," the familiar voice said. I unlocked and opened the door with a feeling of great relief.

"Can she hear me?" he asked, looking at the silent figure on the bunk.

"Possibly. Let me secure her again and we'll go on deck."

He went ahead of me and as I closed the door a sudden flare of light lit up the night sky, then climbed in a burning arc up to the zenith.

"A good omen," The Bishop said. "A deep spacer. All is arranged. And time is of the essence, so I suggest that we grab up our things and leave at once."

"Transportation?"

"A rented groundcar."

"Can it be traced?"

"I hope so. The rental return is located at the linear station. I've purchased tickets, for both of us you will be happy to hear."

"I mentioned linears to our friend inside."

"Two great minds that work as one. I think I shall manage to drop the tickets where she can see them while we are packing."

We were in and out quite quickly—and I did enjoy the way the unmistakable blue linear tickets dropped on the blankets for an instant. Fell from his pocket while both his hands were engaged elsewhere. Masterful! As I closed the door I could not resist the temptation to blow a kiss towards Beth. I received a glower and a muffled snarl in return, which I surely deserved. She still had a few thousand of our money so she should not complain.

After turning in the groundcar we took the levitrain to the linear station. Where we waited until we were alone and unobserved before continuing on to the spaceport. Up until this moment it had been all rush and plan and the reality of what I was doing struck home only when I saw the floodlit flank of a deep spacer looming up ahead.

I was going offplanet! It is one thing to watch the spaceoperas—but another thing completely to venture into space. I felt the goosebumps swell on my arm, the hair stir on my neck. This new life was going to be a good one!

"Into the bar," The Bishop ordered. "Our man is already here!"

A thin man in grease-stained spacer gear was just leaving, but dropped back into the booth when he saw The Bishop.

"*Vi estas malfrua!*" he said angrily.

"*Vere—sed me havas la monon,*" The Bishop answered, flashing a large wad of bills which soothed the other immeasurably. The money changed hands, and after some more conversation another bundle of bills went the way of the first. Greed satisfied, the spaceman led the way to a service van and we climbed into the back. The door was slammed and in the darkness we sped off.

What an adventure! Unseen vehicles passed us, then there were strange hammering sounds that came and went, followed by a loud hissing like a giant serpent. We stopped soon after this and our guide came around and opened the rear door. I stepped out first and found myself at the foot of a ramp leading up into what could only be the battered hull of a deep spacer.

Next to the ramp stood an armed guard, staring at me.

It was all over, the adventure ended before it even began. What could I do? Run, no I couldn't leave The Bishop. He pushed past me while I was still rushing about in circles inside my head, strolled casually over to the guard.

And passed him a wad of bills.

The guard was still counting them when we hurried up the ramp behind our bribed spaceman, struggling to stay close with all the baggage we carried.

"*Eniru, rapide!*" the spaceman ordered, opening the door of a compartment. We pushed through into the darkness as the door closed and locked behind us.

"Safe harbor!" The Bishop sighed with relief as he fumbled at the wall until he found the switch, and the lights came on. We were in a small, cramped cabin. There were two narrow bunks and an even smaller bathroom beyond. Pretty grim.

"Home sweet home," The Bishop said, smiling benevolently as he looked around. "We'll have to stay in here at least two days. So let us stow our gear well out of sight. Otherwise the captain will threaten to return and the bribe will be higher. I'm sure we can last it out."

"I'm not sure I understand all of that. Haven't you paid the bribe already?"

"Only the first installments. Bribes are never shared, that is your first lesson in the gentle art. The spaceman got paid to sneak us aboard, and arranged that a friendly guard would be there to take his cut. Those arrangements are in the past. Our presence aboard this ship is unknown to the officers—and particularly the captain who will need a very large payment indeed. You will see."

"I certainly intend to. Bribery is indeed an exacting science."

"It is."

"It's a good thing you speak their language so you can do a deal."

His eyebrows shot up at this and he leaned close. "You did not understand us?" he asked.

"I didn't take foreign languages in school."

"Foreign!" He looked shocked. "What a backward part of that porcuswine-rearing planet you must have come from. That was not a *foreign* language, dear boy. That was Esperanto, the galactic language, the simple, second language that everyone learns early and speaks like a native. Your education has been neglected, but that is easily repaired. Before our next planetfall you shall be speaking it as well. To begin with, all present tense verbs in all persons end in *as*. Simplicity itself. . . ."

He stopped as someone tried the handle on the cabin door. His finger touched his lips as he pointed to the adjoining bath. I dived that way and turned on the light there just as he turned off the one in the cabin. He joined me in a rush and jammed in beside me as I flicked off the light. He eased the door shut just as the corridor door opened.

Footsteps thudded across the cabin and there was the sound of thin whistling. A routine inspection, nothing to be seen, he would go away in an instant . . .

Then the bathroom door opened and the light came on. The gold-braided officer looked at The Bishop cramped into the tiny shower, at me crouching on the commode, as he smiled a singularly dirty smile.

"I thought there was too much activity belowdecks. Stowaways." A small gun appeared in his hand. "Out. You two are going ashore and I am calling the local police."

CHAPTER EIGHTEEN

I leaned forward, getting my weight on my legs, muscles tense. Ready to attack the instant that The Bishop distracted the officer's attention. I really did not want to go against that gun with my bare hands—but I wanted even less to go back to jail. The Bishop must surely have been aware of this. He reached out a restraining hand.

"Now, let us not be hasty, James. Relax while I talk to this kind officer."

His hand went slowly to his pocket, the gun following his every move, the fingers dipped deep—and came up with a thin wad of credits.

"This is advance payment for a small favor," he said, handing them over to the officer, who took the credits in both hands. Which was easy enough to do now that the gun had vanished just as quickly as it had appeared. He counted while The Bishop talked.

"The favor we so humbly request is that you do not find us for two days. You will be paid this same sum tomorrow, and again the day after when you discover us and take us to the captain."

The money vanished and the gun reappeared—and I never saw his hands move. He was so good he should have been on the stage.

"I think not," he said. "I think I will take all the money you have concealed on your person and in your bags. Take it and bring you to the captain now."

"Not very wise," The Bishop said sternly. "I will tell the captain exactly how much you took and he will relieve you of it and you will have nothing. I will also tell him which

126

crewmen were bribed and they will be deprived of their money and you will not be a popular officer on this ship. Will you?"

"There is a certain element of truth in what you say," he mused, rubbing his jaw in thought, hands empty again. "If the payments were increased perhaps . . ."

"Ten percent, no more," said The Bishop, and the payment was made. "See you tomorrow. Please relock the door behind you."

"Of course. Have a pleasant journey."

Then he was gone and I climbed down from the pot and seized and shook The Bishop's hand. "Congratulations, sir. A masterful demonstration of a science I scarcely knew existed."

"Thank you, my boy. But it helps to know the ground rules. He never had any intention of turning us out of this ship. That was just his bid. I called it, he raised, I matched and closed. He knew he couldn't squeeze higher because I need a large sum in reserve for the captain. Unspoken, but agreed nevertheless, is my silence about the bribe to him. All done by the rules. . . ."

His words were cut off by the loud sound of a hooter in the corridor outside, while a red light began blinking rapidly over the door.

"Is something wrong?" I called out.

"Something is very right. We are ready for takeoff. I suggest that we recline on the bunks because some of these old clunkers put on the Gs when they blast free. A few minutes more and we shake the dust of Bit O' Heaven from our shoes. Preferably forever. That prison, simply terrible, the food . . ."

A growing roar drowned out his words and the bunk began to tremble. Then the acceleration of takeoff jumped on my chest. Just like in the films—but far more exciting in reality. This was it! Offplanet! What joys lay ahead.

Pretty far ahead still. The mattress was thin and my back hurt from the pressure. Then we went in and out of null-G a few times before they got the artificial gravity right. Or almost right. Every once in awhile it would give a little hiccup. So would my stomach. This happened often enough so that during the next days I didn't miss the meals that I would normally have eaten. At least we had all the rusty, flat water we needed to drink. The officer stayed bribed, I stayed in my bunk most of the time and concentrated on the Esperanto lessons to forget my miseries. After two days of this the gravity finally straightened out and my appetite returned. I looked forward to our release, some more bribery—and some food.

"Stowaways!" the officer said when he unlocked the door, staggered, hand over heart. For the benefit of the crewgirl who accompanied him. "Terrible, unheard of! On your feet, you two, and come with me. Captain Garth will want to know about this."

It was a very convincing performance, spoiled only by his ready hand for the money as soon as the crewgirl's back was turned. She seemed bored by the whole thing and was probably in on the deal herself. We tramped the corridor and up three flights of metal stairs to the bridge. The captain, at least, was shocked to see us. Probably the only one on the ship who didn't know we were aboard.

"Damn and blast—where did these come from?"

"In one of the empty cabins on C deck."

"You were supposed to check those cabins."

"I did, my captain, it is in the log. One hour before takeoff. After that I was on the bridge with you. They must have come aboard after that."

"Who did you bribe?" Captain Garth said, turning to us, a grizzled old spacedog with a mean look in his eye.

"No one, captain," The Bishop said, sincerity ringing in his voice. "I know these old Reptile class freighters very well. Just before takeoff the guard at the gangway entered the ship. We came in behind him, unseen, and hid in the cabin. That is all there is to it."

"I don't believe a word of it. Tell me who you bribed or you'll be in the brig and in big trouble."

"My dear captain, your honest crewmen would never take bribes!" He ignored the unbelieving snort. "I have proof. All of my not inconsiderable fortune is intact and in my pocket."

"Out," the captain instantly ordered all the men in the control room. "All of you. I'll take this watch. I want to question these two more thoroughly."

The officer and the crewmembers shuffled out, their faces expressionless under his gaze. When they were gone the captain sealed the door and spun about. "Let's have it," he ordered. The Bishop passed over a very tidy sum and the captain riffled through it, then shook his head. "Not enough."

"Of course," The Bishop agreed. "That is the opening payment. The balance after landfall on some agreeable planet with lax custom officers."

"You ask a lot. I have no desire to risk trouble with planetary authorities by smuggling in illegal immigrants. It will be far easier to relieve you of the money right now and dispose of you as I will."

The Bishop was not impressed at all by this ploy. He tapped his pocket and shook his head. "Not possible. Final payment is with this registered check for two-hundred thousand credits drawn on Galactic Credit and Exchange. It is not legal tender until I countersign it with a second signature. You may torture me, but I will never sign! Until we are standing on firm ground."

The captain shrugged meaningfully and turned to the controls, making a minor adjustment before he turned back. "There is a matter of paying for your meals," he said calmly. "Charity does not pay my fuel bills."

"Absolutely. Let us fix a rate."

That appeared to be all there was to it—but The Bishop whispered a warning as we went back down the corridor. "The cabin is undoubtedly bugged. Our luggage searched. I have all our funds on me. Stay close so there are no accidents. That officer, for one, would make an excellent professional pickpocket. Now—what do you say to a little food? Since we have paid we can end our enforced fast with a splendid feast."

My stomach rumbled loud agreement with this suggestion, and we made for the galley. Since there were no passengers the fat, unshaven cook served only Venian peasant food. Fine for the natives, but it took some getting used to. Did you ever try to hold your nose and eat at the same time? I didn't ask the cook what we were eating—I was afraid he would tell me. The Bishop sighed deeply and began to fork down his ration of gunge.

"The one thing I forgot about Venia," he said gloomily, "was the food. Selective memory I am sure. Who would want to recall at any time a feast like this?"

I did not answer since I was gulping at my cup of warm water to get the taste out of my mouth.

"Small blessings," I said. "At least the water here isn't as nasty as the stuff from the tap in our cabin." The Bishop sighed again.

"That is coffee that you are drinking."

A fun cruise it was not. We both lost weight since it was often better to avoid a meal than to eat it. I continued my studies, learning the finer points of embezzling, expense-account grafting, double and treble entry bookkeeping—all done in Esperanto until I was as facile as a native in that fine language.

At our first planetfall we stayed in the ship since soldiers and customs officers were thick as sandfleas about the ship.

"Not here," the captain said, looking at the screened image of the ground with us. "Very rich planet, but they don't like strangers. The next planet in this system is one you will like, agricultural, low population, they can use immigrants, so there isn't even a customs office."

"The name?" The Baron asked.

"Amphisbionia."

"Never heard of it."

"Should you have? Out of thirty-thousand settled planets."

"True. But still . . ."

The Bishop seemed troubled and I couldn't understand why. If we didn't like this planet we could liberate enough funds to move on. But some instinct had him on edge. In the end he bribed the purser to use the ship's computer.

When we were toying with our dinner he told me about it.

"Something doesn't smell right about this—smells worse than this food." This was a horrifying thought. "I can find no record of a planet named Amphisbionia in the galactic guide. And the guide is updated automatically every time we land and hook into a planetary communication net. In addition to that, there is a lock on our next destination. Only the captain has the code to access it."

"What can we do?"

"Nothing—until after we land. We'll find out then what he is up to."

"Can't you bribe one of the officers?"

"I already did—that's how I found out that only the captain knows where we are heading. Of course he didn't tell me until after I paid. A dirty trick. I would have done the same thing myself."

I tried to cheer him up, but it was no use. I think the food had affected his morale. It would be a good thing to arrive at this planet, whatever it was. Certainly a good thief can make a living in any society. And one thing was certain. The food would *have* to be better than the sludge we were reluctantly eating now.

We stayed in our bunks until the ship touched down and the green light came on. Our meager belongings were already assembled and we carried them down to the airlock. The captain was operating the controls himself. He muttered as the automatic air analyzer ran through its test; the inner lock would not open until it was finished and satisfied with the results. It finally pinged and flashed its little message at him and he hit the override. The great hatch ground slowly open admitting a whiff of warm and pungent air. We sniffed it appreciatively.

"Here is a stylo," Captain Garth said. The Bishop merely smiled.

The captain led the way and we followed with our bags. It was night, stars were bright above, invisible creatures called from the darkness of a row of trees nearby. The only light was from the airlock.

"Here will do," the captain said, standing on the end of the ramp. The Bishop shook his head as he pointed at the metal surface.

"We are still on the ship. The ground if you please."

They agreed on a neutral patch close to the ramp—but far enough from the ship to foil any attempt to rush us. The Bishop took out the check, accepted the stylo at last, then wrote his careful signature. The captain—ever suspicious!—compared it with the signature above and finally nodded. He walked briskly up the ramp as we picked up our bags—then turned and called out.

"They're all yours now!"

As the ramp lifted up, out of our reach, powerful lights came on from the darkness, pinning us like moths. Armed men ran towards us as we turned, trapped, lost.

"I knew something was wrong," The Bishop said. He dropped his bags and grimly faced the rushing men.

CHAPTER NINETEEN

A resplendent figure in a red uniform strode out of the darkness and stood before us twisting a large and elegant set of moustaches. Like someone out of a historic flic, he actually wore a sword, which he held firmly by the hilt.

"I'll take everything you two have. Everything. Quickly!"

Two uniformed men came running up to see that we did as we were told. They were carrying strange-looking guns with large barrels and wooden stocks. Behind us I heard a creaking as the ramp came back down with Captain Garth standing on the end of it. I bent over to pick up the bags.

And kept turning—diving at the captain, grabbing him.

There was a loud bang and something whirred by my head and spanged off the ship's hull. The captain swore and swung his fist at me. Couldn't have been better. I stepped inside the blow, grabbed the arm and levered it up into the small of his back. He screeched with pain; a lovely sound.

"Let him go," a voice said, and I looked over the captain's trembling shoulder to see that The Bishop was now lying on the ground with the officer's foot on his chest. And his sword was not just for decoration—because the point of it was now pressed to The Bishop's throat.

It was going to be one of those days. I gave the captain's neck a little squeeze with my free hand before I let go. He slithered straight down and his unconscious head bonged nicely on the ramp. I stepped away from him and The Bishop climbed unsteadily to his feet, dusting himself off as he turned to our captor.

"Excuse me, kind sir, but might I humbly ask you the name of this planet on whose soil we stand?"

"Spiovente," was the grunted answer.

"Thank you. If you permit, I will help my friend Captain Garth to his feet, for I wish to apologize to him for my young friend's impetuous behavior."

No one stopped him as he turned to the captain, who had just regained consciousness.

He lost it again instantly as The Bishop kicked him in the side of the head.

"I am normally not a vindictive man," he said, turning away and digging out his wallet. He handed it to the officer and said, "But just this once I wanted to express my feelings before returning to my normal peaceful self. You understand, of course, why I did that?"

"Would have done the same thing myself," the officer said, counting the money. "But the games are over. Don't ever speak to me again or you are dead."

He turned away as another man appeared from the darkness with two black metal loops in his hands. The Bishop stood, numb and unresisting, as the man bent and snapped one onto his ankle. I didn't know what the thing was—but I didn't like it. Mine would not be put on that easily.

Yes it would. The muzzle of the gun ground into my back and I made no protest as the thing was snapped into place. The thing-snapper then stood up and looked me in the face, standing so close that his sewer breath washed over me. He was ugly to boot, with a puckered scar that added no improvement to the face. He pushed a sharp finger into my chest as he spoke.

"I am Tars Tukas, servant of our lord the mighty Capo Doccia. But you never call me by name; you always call me master."

I started to call him something, something that was quite an improvement on master, when he pressed a button a metal box slung from his belt.

Then I was on the ground, trying to shake the red fog of pain from my eyes. The first thing I saw was The Bishop lying before me, groaning in agony. I helped him to his feet; Tars Tukas needn't have done that, not to a man his age. He was grinning a lopsided scarred grin when I turned.

"Who am I?" he asked. I resisted all temptation, for The Bishop's sake if not my own.

"Master."

"Don't forget, and don't try to run away. There are neural repeaters right around the entire country. If I leave this on for long enough, all your nerves stop working. Forever. Understood?"

"Understood, master."

"Hand over everything you got on you."

I did. Money, papers, coins, keys, watch, the works. He frisked me roughly and seemed satisfied for the moment.

"Let's move."

A tropical dawn had come quickly and the lights were being turned out. We didn't look back as we followed our new master. The Bishop was having difficulty in walking and I had to help him. Tars Tukas led us to a battered wooden cart that was standing close by. We were waved into the back. We sat on the plank seat and watched while crates were lowered from the cargo hatch of the spacer.

"That was a nice dropkick on the captain," I said. "You obviously know something about his planet that I don't. What was the name?"

"Spiovente." He spat the word like a curse. "The millstone around the League's neck. That captain has sold us down the river with a vengeance. And he is a smuggler too. There is a complete embargo on contact with this stinking world. Particularly weapons—which I am sure those cases are full of. Spiovente!"

Which didn't really tell me very much other than that it was pretty bad. Which I knew already. "You couldn't possibly be a bit more informative about this millstone?"

"I blame myself completely for getting you involved in all this. But Captain Garth will pay. If we do nothing else, Jim, we will bring him to justice. We'll get word to the League, somehow."

The *somehow* depressed him even more and he dropped his head wearily onto his hands. I sat in silence, waiting for him to speak in his own good time. He did finally, sitting up, and in the reflected light I saw that the spark was back in his eye.

"Nil carborundum, Jim. Don't let the bastards wear you down. We are landed in a ripe one this time. Spiovente was first contacted by the League over ten years ago. It had been isolated since the Breakdown and had thousands of years to go bad. It is the sort of place that gives crime a bad name—since the criminals are in charge here. The madhouse has been taken over by the madmen. Anarchy rules—no, not true—Spiovente makes anarchy look like a Boy Sprout's picnic. I have made a particular study of this planet's system of government, while working out the stickier bits of my personal philosophy. Here we have something that belongs in the lost dark ages of mankind's rise. It is thoroughly despicable in every way—and there is nothing that the League can do about it, short of launching an invasion. Which would be completely against League philosophy. The strength of the League is also its weakness. No planet or planets can physically attack another planet. Any one that did would face instant destruction by all the others since war has now been declared illegal. The League can only help newly discovered planets, offer advice and aid. It is rumored that there are covert League organizations that work to subvert repulsive societies like this one—but of course this has never been revealed in public. So what we have here is trouble, bad trouble. For Spiovente is a warped mirror image of the civilized worlds. There is no rule of law here—just might. Criminal gangs are led by Capos, the swordman in the fancy uniform, Capo Doccia, he's one of them. Each Capo controls as large a capote as he can. His followers are rewarded with a portion of the loot extracted from the peasantry or from the spoils of war. At the very bottom of this pyramid of crime are the slaves. Us."

He pointed to the paincuff on his ankle and thoroughly depressed himself. Me as well.

"Well, we can still look at the bright side," I said with desperation.

"What bright side?"

I wondered about that myself as I furiously thought out loud.

"The bright side, yes, there is always a bright side. Like for instance—we are well away from Bit O' Heaven and our problems there. All set for a new start."

"At the bottom of the pile? As slaves?"

"Correct! From here the only direction we can go is up!"

His lips twitched in the slightest smile at this desperate sally and I hurried on.

"For example—they searched us and took away everything we had on us. Every item except one. I still have a little souvenir in my shoe from my trip to jail. This." I held up the lockpick and his smile widened. "And it works—see." I opened my paincuff and showed it to him, then snapped it back into place. "So when we are ready to leave—we leave!"

By this time the grin had widened into a full smile. He reached out and seized my shoulder in a grip of true comradeship. "How right you are," he beamed. "We shall be good slaves—for a time. Just long enough to learn the ropes of this society, the chain of command and how to penetrate it, what the sources of wealth are and how to acquire them. As soon as I determine where the chinks are in the structure of society here we shall become rats again. Not stainless steel ones, I am afraid, more of the furry, toothy kind."

"A rat by any other name is just as sweet. We will overcome!"

We had to leap aside then as the first of the crates was manhandled into the back of the cart, the fabric of its battered structure squeaking and groaning. When the last of the cases was aboard the loaders climbed in themselves. I was glad the light was so bad—I really did not want to look at them too closely. Three scruffy, dirty men, unshaven and dressed in rags. Unwashed too as my twitching nose quickly informed me. Then a fourth man heaved himself up, bigger and nastier than the others, although his garments were in slightly better shape. He glared down at us and I smelled trouble, in addition to the pong.

"You know who I am? I'm the Pusher. This is my bunch and you do what I say. The first thing I say is you, old man, take off that jacket. It'll look better on me than on you."

"Thank you for the suggestion, sir," The Bishop answered sweetly. "But I think I shall retain it."

I knew what he was doing and I hoped that I was up to it. There was little room to move about in and this thug was twice my size. I had time for one blow, no more, and it had to be a good one.

The brute roared in anger and started climbing over the crates. The terrified slaves scrambled out of his way. I scrambled aside too and he ignored me as he passed. Perfect. He was just clutching at The Bishop when I hit him in the back of the neck with my joined fists. There was a satisfactory thunk and he collapsed on top of the crate.

I turned to the slaves who were watching in wide-eyed silence.

"You just got a new pusher," I told them, and there were quick nods of agreement. I pointed to the nearest one. "What's my name?"

"Pusher," he answered instantly. "Just don't turn your back on that one when he comes to."

"Will you help me?"

His grin exposed blackened, broken teeth. "Won't help you fight. Warn you though if you don't beat us the way he did."

"No beating. You all help?"

All of them nodded agreement.

"Good. Then your first assignment will be to throw the old pusher out of this cart. I don't want to be too close when he comes to."

They did this with enthusiasm, and added a few kicks on their own initiative.

"Thank you, James, I appreciate the help," The Bishop said. "My thinking was that you would probably have to fight him sooner or later, so why not sooner, with myself as distraction. And our rise in this society has begun—for you have already climbed out of the basic slave category. Suffering satellites—what is that?"

I looked where he pointed and my eyes popped just as far out as his. It was a machine of some kind, that much was obvious. It was advancing slowly towards us, rattling and clanking and emitting fumes. The operator swivelled it about in front of the cart as his assistant jumped down and joined the two together. There was a jolt and we slowly got under way.

"Look closely, Jim, and remember," he said. "You are seeing something from the dawn of technology, long forgotten and lost in the midst of time. That landcar is powered by *steam*. It is a steamcar, as I live and breathe. You know, I am beginning to think that I will enjoy it here."

I was not as fascinated by neolithic machinery as he was. My thoughts were more on the deposed thug and what would happen when he came after me. I had to learn more about the ground rules—and quickly. I moved back to the other slaves, but before I could open conversation we clattered across a bridge and through a gate in a high wall. The driver of our steam chariot stopped and called out.

"Unload those here."

In my new persona as Pusher I supervised but did little to help. The last case was just dropped to the ground when one of my slaves called out to me.

"He's coming now—through the gate behind you!"

I turned quickly. He was right. The ex-pusher was there, scratched and bloody and red-faced with rage.

He bellowed as he attacked.

CHAPTER TWENTY

The first thing that I did was run away from my attacker—who roared after me in hot pursuit. This was done not through fear, though I did have a certain amount of that, but from the need to get some space around me. As soon as I was well away from the cart I turned and tripped him so he sprawled full-length in the muck.

This drew a big laugh from the onlookers; I took a quick glance around while he was climbing to his feet. There were armed guards, more slaves—and the red-garbed Capo Doccia who had cleaned us out. An idea began to form—but before it took shape I had to move to save my life.

The thug was learning. No more wild rushing about. Instead he came slowly towards me, arms spread, fingers extended. If I allowed him a sweet embrace I would not emerge from it alive. I backed slowly, turning to face Capo Doccia, moved to one side, then stepped quickly forward. Seizing one of my attacker's outstretched hands in both of mine, pulling and falling backwards at the same time. My weight was just about enough to send him flying over me to sprawl full-length again.

I was on my feet at once—with the plan clear in my mind. An exhibition.

"That was the right arm," I called out loudly.

He was stumbling when he returned to the attack so I took a chance and called my shot.

"Right knee."

I used a flying kick to get him on the kneecap. This is quite painful and he screamed as he dropped. He was slower getting to his feet this time, but the hatred was still there. He was not going to stop until he was unconscious. Good. All the better for my demonstration of the art.

"Left arm."

I seized it and twisted it up behind his back, held it there, pushing hard. He was strong—and still fighting, trying to clutch me with his right hand, struggling to trip me. I got in first.

"Left leg," I shouted as I kicked hard on the back of his calf and he went down another time. I stepped back and looked towards Capo Doccia. I had his undivided attention.

"Can you kill as well as dance?" he asked.

"I can. But I chose not to." I was aware that my opponent had stood up, was swaying from side to side. I turned slightly so I could see him out of the corner of my eye. "What I prefer is to render him unconscious. That way I win the fight—and you still have a slave."

The thug's hands closed on my neck and he bubbled viciously. I was showing off and I knew it. But I had to provide a good performance for my audience. So, without looking at all, I slammed backwards with my bent arm. Sinking my elbow hard into his gut, in the center, just below the rib cage, in line with the elbows. Right into the nerve ganglion known as the solar plexus. His hands loosened and I stepped forward. Hearing the thud as he hit the ground. Out cold.

Capo Doccia signalled me to him, spoke when I was close.

"That is a new way to fight, offworlder. We make wagers on the ruffians here who battle with their fists, striking each other until the blood flows and one of them cannot go on."

"Fighting like that is crude and wasteful. To know where to strike and how to strike, that is an art."

"But your art is of no value against sharp steel," he said, half-pulling his sword. I had to tread carefully now or he would be chopping me up just to see what I could do.

"Bare hands cannot stand against one such as you who is a master of the blade." For all I knew he only used the thing to carve his roast, but flattery always helps. "However against an unskilled swordsman or knife-wielder the art has value."

He digested that, then called to the nearest guard. "You, take your knife to this one."

This was getting out of hand—but I could see no way to avoid the encounter now. The guard smiled and pulled a shining length of dagger from its sheath and stalked towards me. I smiled in return. He raised it over his head to stab down—not holding it pointed directly out before him like an experienced knife-fighter. I let him come on, unmoving until he struck.

Standard defense. Step inside the blow, take the impact of his wrist against my forearm. Seize the knife-wrist with hands, turn and twist. All of this done very fast.

The knife went one way, he went the other. I had to end this demonstration quickly before I was taking on clubs, guns, whatever the head thug felt like. I stepped closer to Capo Doccia and spoke in a quiet voice.

"These are offworld secrets of defense—and killing—that are unknown here on Spiovente. I do not wish to reveal more here. I am sure you do not wish slaves to learn dangerous blows like these. Let me show you what can be done without this raw audience. I can train your bodyguards in these skills. There are those who want to kill you. Think of your own security first."

It sounded like a lecture on traffic safety to me, but it seemed to make sense to him. But he wasn't completely convinced.

"I do not like new things, new ways. I like things as they are."

Right, with him on top and the rest in chains below. I talked fast.

"What I do is not new—but as old as mankind. Secrets that have been passed on in secret since the dawn of time. Now these secrets can be yours. Change is on the way, you know that, and knowledge is strength. When others seek to take what you have, any weapon is useful to defeat them."

It sounded like nonsense to me—but I hoped that it

made sense to him. From what The Bishop had told me about this garbage world, the only security was in strength—paranoia paid off. At least it had him thinking, which from the narrowness of his forehead was something he probably found hard to do. He turned on his heel and walked away.

Politeness, like soap, was also unknown on this planet. No "see you later" or "let me think about that." It took me a few moments to realize that the audience was over. The disarmed guard was glaring at me and rubbing his wrist. But he had put the dagger away. Since I had talked with Capo Doccia I now had some status, so he wouldn't knife me without reason. Which left my first protagonist, the ex-Pusher. He was sitting up dizzily when I approached. He looked up at me, blinking and befuddled. I tried to look my meanest when I spoke.

"That is two times you have come at me. You will not do it a third time. Third time means out in my ball game. You will die if you try anything ever again."

The hatred was still there in his face—but there was fear as well. I stepped forward and he cringed back. Good enough. As long as I didn't turn my back on him very often. I turned it now and stalked away.

He shambled after me and joined the waiting gang of slaves. He seemed to have accepted his demotion, as had the others. There were a few black looks in his direction but no more violence. Which was fine by me. It is one thing to work out in the gym—but something totally different here mixing with these heavies really trying to kill me. The Bishop beamed his congratulations.

"Well done, Jim, well done."

"And all very tiring. What next?"

"From what I could discover this little group is off duty, so to speak, having worked during the night."

"Then rest and food are in order. Lead on."

I suppose it could be called food. About the only good thing I could say about it was that it was not as repulsive as the Venian cooking aboard the spacer. A large and exceedingly filthy pot was seething over a fire to the rear of the building. The chef—if one dared use that term for this repulsive individual, as filthy as his pot—was stirring the contents with a long wooden spoon. The slaves each took a wooden bowl from the dripping pile on the table close by and these were filled by the cook. There was no worry about lost or broken cutlery because there wasn't any. Everyone dipped and shoveled with their fingers, so I did the same. It was vegetable gruel of some kind, pretty tasteless, but filling. The Bishop sat next to me on the ground, back to the wall, and slowly ate his. I finished first and had no difficulty in restraining a desire for a second serving.

"How long do we stay slaves?" I asked.

"Until I learn more about how things operate here. You have spent your entire life on a single planet, so both consciously and unconsciously you accept the society you know as the only one. Far from it. Culture is an invention of mankind, just like the computer or the fork. There is a difference though. While we are willing to change computers or eating instruments, the inhabitants of a culture will brook no changes at all. They believe that theirs is the only and unique way to live—and anything else an aberration."

"Sounds stupid."

"It is. But as long as you know that, and they don't, you can step outside the rules or bend them for your own benefit. Right now I'm finding out what the rules are here."

"Try not to take too long."

"I promise not to since I am not that comfortable myself. I must determine if vertical mobility exists and how it is organized. If there is no vertical mobility, we will just have to manufacture it."

"You have lost me. Vertical what?"

"Mobility. In terms of class and culture. Take for example these slaves and the guards outside. Can a slave aspire to be a guard? If he can, then there is vertical mobility. If he cannot, this is a stratified society and horizontal mobility is all that can be accomplished."

"Such as becoming top slave and kicking all other slaves?"

He nodded. "You have it, Jim. We shall cease being slaves as soon as my studies show how that is possible. But first we need some rest. You will observe that the others are now asleep on the straw to the rear of this noisome building. I suggest we join them."

"Agreed. . . ."

"You, get over here."

It was Tars Tukas. And of course he was pointing at me. I had a feeling that it was going to be a very long day.

At least I was seeing more of the sights. We crossed the courtyard, scene of my triumphs, and up a flight of stone steps. There was an armed guard here and two more inside lolling about on a wooden bench. A bit more luxury too. Woven mats on the floors, chairs, and tables, a few bad portraits on the wall, some with a rough resemblance to Capo Doccia. I was hustled right along into a large room with windows that faced out over the outer wall. I could see fields and trees and little else. Capo Doccia was there, along with a small band of men, all drinking from metal cups. They were well-dressed, if multicolored leather trousers and billowing shirts and long swords is your idea of well-dressed. Capo Doccia waved me over.

"You, come here and let us look at you."

The others turned with interest and eyed me like an animal on auction.

"And he actually knocked the other one down without using his fists?" One of them said. "He is so weak and puny, not to mention ugly."

There are times when the mouth should be opened only to put in food. This was probably one of them. But I was tired, fed up with my lot, and generally in a foul temper. Something snapped.

"Not as weak, puny or ugly as you, you pig's git."

This got his attention all right. He howled with instant anger, turned bright red—then drew a long steel blade and rushed at me.

I had little time to think, less time to act. One of the other dandies was standing close by, his metal drinking mug held loosely. I grabbed it from him, turned, and threw the contents in the attacking man's face.

Most of it missed, but enough dripped down onto his clothes to infuriate him even more. He slashed down with his sword and I caught the blow on the mug, diverting it. Letting the mug slide up along the blade into his fingers, grabbing and twisting his sword arm at the same time.

He howled nicely and the sword clattered to the floor. After this he was turned sideways, nicely exposed for a finishing kick to the back.

Except someone tripped me from behind at that moment and I went sprawling.

CHAPTER TWENTY-ONE

They thought this very amusing because their laughter was all I could hear. When I scrambled for the fallen blade one of them kicked it aside. Things were not looking too good. I couldn't fight them all. I had to get out.

It was too late. Two of them knocked me to the ground from behind and another one kicked me in the side. Before I could get up my sword-wielding opponent was on top of me, kneeling on my chest and drawing an exceedingly ugly dagger with a wavery edge.

"What is this creature, Capo Doccia," he called out, holding my chin with his free hand, the dagger close to my throat.

"An offworlder," Capo Doccia said. "They threw him off the spacer."

"Is it valuable, worth anything?"

"I don't know," Capo Doccia said, looking down at me bemusedly. "Perhaps. But I don't like its fancy offplanet tricks. They don't belong here. Oh, kill it and be done."

I had not moved during this interesting exchange because I had some obvious interest in its outcome. I moved now.

The knife-wielder screamed as I twisted his arm—breaking it I hope—and grabbed the dagger as his fingers flew open. I held on to him as I jumped to my feet, then pushed him into the midst of his companions. They were behind me as well, but they fell back as I swept the dagger about in a circle. Moving after it, running before they could get their own weapons out. Running for my life.

The only direction I knew, back down the stairs. Bumping into Tars Tukas and rendering him unconscious as I passed.

Roars and shouts of anger sounded behind me and I wasted no time even glancing their way. Down the stairs, three at a time, towards the guards at the entrance. They were still scrambling to their feet when I plowed into them and we all went down. I kneed one under the chin as we fell, grabbing his gun by the barrel as I did this. The other was struggling to point his weapon at me when I caught him in the side of the head with the one I was holding.

The running feet were right behind me as I charged through the door, right at the surprised guard. He drew his sword but before he could use it he was unconscious. I dropped the dagger and seized his more lethal sword and ran on. The gate we had entered by was ahead. Wide open.

And well-guarded by armed men who were already raising their guns. I angled off towards the slave building as they fired. I don't know where their shots went but I was still alive as I turned the corner.

One knife, one gun, one very tired Jim diGriz. Who did not dare stop or even slow down. The outer wall was ahead—with scaffolding and a ladder leaning against it where masons were making repairs. I screeched and waved my weapons and the workmen dived in all directions. I went up the ladders as fast as I could. Noticing that bullets were striking the wall on all sides of me, chips of stone flying.

Then I was on top of the wall, fighting for breath, chancing a look behind me for the first time.

Dropping to my face as the massed gunmen below fired a volley that parted the air just above my head. Capo Doccia and his court had left the pursuit to the guards and were standing behind them cursing and waving their weapons. Very impressive. I pulled my head back as they fired again.

Other guards were climbing up to the wall and moving towards me. Which really did limit my choices a bit. I looked over the outside of the wall at the brown surface of the water that lay at its base. Some choice!

"Jim, you must learn to do something about your big mouth," I said, then took a deep breath and jumped.

Splashed—and stuck. The water was just up to my neck and I was stuck in the soft mud that had broken my fall. I struggled against it, pulling out one foot, then the other, struggling against its gluey embrace as I waded to the far bank. My pursuers weren't in sight yet—but they would surely be right behind me. All I could do was keep moving. Crawling up the grassy bank, still clutching my purloined weapons, then staggering into the shelter of the trees ahead. And still no sign of the armed guards. They should be across the bridge and after me by this time. I couldn't believe my good luck.

Until I fell headlong, screaming as the pain washed over me. Pain unbelievable, blotting out sight, sound, senses.

Then it stopped and I brushed the tears of agony from my eyes. The paincuff—I had forgotten all about it. Tars Tukas had regained consciousness and was thumbing the control button. What had he said? Leave it on long enough and it blocks all the nerves, kills. I grabbed at my shoe and the lockpick concealed there as the pain struck again.

When it stopped this time I was almost too weak to move my fingers. As I fumbled with the pick I realized that they were sadists and I should be grateful for the fact. With the button held down I was good as dead. But someone, undoubtedly Capo Doccia, wanted me both to suffer and know that there was no way out. The key was in the lock when pain consumed me one more time.

When it stopped I was lying on my side, the lockpick fallen from my fingers, unable to move.

But I had to move. Another wave of agony like that and it would be all over for me. I would lie in these woods until I died. My fingers trembled, moved. The pick crept towards the tiny opening of the lock, moved in, twisted feebly. . . .

It took a very long time for the red mists to clear from my vision, the agony to seep out of my body. I could not move, felt I would never stir again. I had to blink the tears away when I could see. See the most beautiful sight in the world.

The open paincuff lying on the moldy leaves.

Only my captor's knowledge that the pain machine led to certain death had saved my life. The searchers were in no hurry; I could hear them talking as they moved through the woods towards me.

". . .somewhere in here. Why don't they just leave him?"

"Leave a good blade and a shooter? No chance of that. And Capo Doccia wants to hang the body up in the courtyard until it rots. Never saw him that angry."

Life slowly returned to my paralyzed body. I moved off the animal track I had been following and pulled myself into the shelter of the low shrubbery, reaching out to straighten out the grass. And not too soon.

"Look—he came out of the water here. Went along this path."

Heavy footsteps approached and went by. I clutched my weapons and did the only thing possible. Lay quiet and waited for my strength to return.

This was, I must admit, a bit of a low point in my life. Friendless, alone, still throbbing with pain, exhausted, hunted by armed men just dying to kill me, thirsty. . . . It was quite a list. About the only thing that hadn't happened so far was to get rained on.

It started to rain.

There are high and low points in emotion when there is no room for excess. To love one so much it would be impossible to love any more. I think. Never having had any personal experience in that. But I had plenty of experience in being in the pits. Where I was now. I could sink no lower or get no more depressed. It was the rain that did it. I began to chuckle—then grabbed my mouth so I wouldn't laugh out loud. Then the laughter died away as my anger grew. This was no way to treat a mean and nasty stainless steel rat! Now in danger of getting rusty.

I moved my legs and had to stifle a groan. The pain was still there but the anger rode it down. I clutched the gun and stuck the sword into the ground, then pulled myself to my feet by grabbing the branches of the tree with my free hand. Grabbed up the sword again and stood there, swaying. But not falling. Until I was finally able to stagger

off, one step at a time, away from the searchers and Capo
Doccia's criminal establishment.

The forest was quite extensive and I moved along game
paths for an unmeasurable length of time. I had left the
searchers far behind, I was sure of that. So when the
forest thinned and ended I leaned against a tree to catch
my breath and looked out at the tilled field. It was time to
find my way back to the haunts of man. Where there were
plows there were ploughboys. They shouldn't be too hard to
find. When a certain measure of strength had returned I
staggered off along the edge of the field, ready to fall into
the forest at the sight of armed men. I was very pleased to
see the farmhouse first. It was low to the ground, thatched,
and windowless—at least on this side. It had a chimney
from which there rose a thin trickle of smoke. No need for
heating in this balmy climate—so this must be a cooking
fire. Food.

At the thought of food my neglected stomach began to
churn, rumble, and complain. I felt the same way. Food
and drink were next in order. And what better place to
find them than at this isolated farm? The question was the
answer. I stumbled across the furrows to the back of the
house, worked my way around the side to the front. No one.
But there were voices coming from the open doorway,
laughter—and the smell of cooking. Yum! I sauntered into
the open, along the front and through the front door.

"Hi, folks. Look who has come to dinner."

There were a half-dozen of them grouped around the
scrubbed wood table. Young and old, thick and thin. All
with the same expression on their faces. Jaw-dropped
astonishment. Even the baby stopped crying and aped its
elders. A grizzled oldster broke the spell, scrambling to his
feet in such a hurry his three-legged stool tumbled over.

"Welcome, your honor, welcome." He tugged his fore-
lock as he bowed to show how grateful he was for my
presence. "How may we aid you, honored sir?"

"If you could spare a bit of food . . ."

"Come! Sit! Dine! We have but humble fare but will-
ingly share it. Here!"

He straightened his stool and waved me to it. The others scampered away from the table so I wouldn't be disturbed. Either they were discerning judges of human nature and knew what a sterling fellow I was—or they had seen the sword and gun. A wooden plate was filled from the pot hung over the fire and put before me. Life here was a cut above the slavepens for I was also supplied with a wooden spoon. I tucked in with a great deal of pleasure. It was a vegetable stew, with the occasional shard of meat, garden fresh of course, and tasted wonderful. There was cool water to drink out of a clay cup and I could have asked for nothing more. While I shoveled it all into my face I was aware of low whispering from the farmers gathered at the far end of the room. I doubted if they were planning anything violent. Nevertheless I kept one eye on them, and my hand not far from the hilt of the sword laid out on the table.

When I had finished and belched loudly—they buzzed warmly at this gustatory approval—the old man detached himself from the group and shuffled forward. He pushed before him a shock-headed youth who looked to be about my age.

"Honored sir, may I speak with you?" I waved agreement and belched again. He smiled at this and nodded. "Ahh, you are kind enough to flatter the cook. Since you are obviously a man of good wit and humor, intelligent and handsome, as well as being a noted warrior, permit me to put a small matter to you."

I nodded again; flattery will get you everywhere.

"This is my third son, Dreng. He is strong and willing, a good worker. But our holding is small and there are many mouths to feed, as well as giving half of what we produce to the so-wonderful Capo Doccia for our protection."

He had his head lowered when he said this, but there were both submission and hatred in his voice. I imagine the only one that Capo Doccia protected them from was Capo Doccia. He pushed Dreng forward and squeezed his bicep.

"Like rock, sir, he is very strong. His ambition has

always been to be a mercenary, like your kind self. A man of war, armed and secure, selling his services to the gentry. A noble calling. And one which would enable him to bring a few groats home to his family."

"I'm not in the recruiting business."

"Obviously, honored sir! If he went as a pikeman with Capo Doccia, there would be no pay or honor, only an early death."

"True, true," I agreed, although I had heard this fact for the first time. The old boy's train of thought wandered a bit, which was fine by me since I was getting an education into life on Spiovente. Didn't sound nice at all. I sipped some more water and tried to summon up another burp to please the cook, but could not. Old dad was still talking.

"Every warrior, such as yourself, should have a knave to serve him. Dare I ask—we have looked outside and you are alone—what happened to your knave?"

"Killed in battle," I improvised. He looked dumbfounded at this and I realized that knaves weren't supposed to fight. "When the enemy overran our camp." That was better, nodded agreement to this. "Of course I killed the blackguard who butchered poor Smelly. But that's what war is about. A rough trade."

All of my audience murmured understandingly, so I hadn't put a foot wrong so far. I signalled to the youth.

"Step forward, Dreng, and speak for yourself. What is your age?"

He peered out from under his long hair and stammered an answer. "I'll be four, come next Wormfeast Day."

I wanted no details of this repulsive holiday. He was sure big for his age. Or this planet had a very long year. I nodded and spoke.

"A good age for a knave. Now tell me, do you know what the knavely duties are?" He better, because I certainly didn't. He nodded enthusiastically at my question.

"That I do, sir, that I do. Old Kvetchy used to be a soldier, told me all about it many a time. Polish the sword and gun, fetch the food from the fire, fill the water bottle, crack the lice with stones . . ."

"Fine, great, I can see you know it all. Down to the last repulsive detail. In exchange for your services you expect me to teach you the trade of war." He nodded quick agreement. The room was hushed as I pondered my decision.

"Right then, let us do it."

A bucolic cry of joy echoed from the thatch and old dad produced a crock of what could only be home brew. Things were looking up for me, ever so slightly, but certainly looking up.

CHAPTER TWENTY-TWO

Work appeared to have ceased for the day with the announcement of Dreng's new job. The home brew was pretty awful stuff, but obviously contained a fair measure of alcohol. Which seemed like a good idea at the time. I drank enough to kill the pain, then slacked off before I ended up drunk on the floor like the rest of them. I waited until old dad was well on the way to alcoholic extinction before I pumped him for information.

"I have traveled from afar and am ignorant of the local scene." I told him. "But I do hear that this local bully, Capo Doccia, is a little on the rough side."

"Rough!" he growled, then slurped down some more of the paint thinner. "Poisonous serpents flee in fear when he approaches, while it is well-known that the gaze of his eyes kills infants."

There was more like this, but I turned off my attention. I had waited too long in the drinking session to extract any reasonable information from him. I looked around for Dreng and found him just tucking into a great crock of the brew. I pried it away from him, then shook him until I attracted his attention.

"Let's go. We're leaving now."

"Leaving . . . ?" He blinked rapidly and tried to focus his eyes on me. With little success.

"We. Go. Out. Walkies."

"Ahh, walkies. I get my blanket." He stood swaying, then gave me some more rapid blinks. "Where's your blanket for me to carry?"

"Seized by the enemy, along with everything else I

155

possessed other than my sword and gun, which never leave my side while I have a breath in my body."

"Breath in body . . . Right. I'll get blanket. Get you blanket."

He rooted about in the rear of the room and appeared with two fuzzy blankets, despite a lot of domestic and female crying about the cold of winter. Capital goods were not easy to come by for the peasantry. I would have to get some groats for Dreng eventually.

He reappeared with the blankets draped over his shoulders along with a leather bag, a stout staff in his hand—and a wicked-looking knife in a wooden scabbard at his waist. I waited outside to avoid the tearful traditional departure scene. He eventually emerged, looking slightly more sober, and stood swaying at my side.

"Lead on, master."

"You show me the way. I want to visit Capo Doccia's keep."

"No! Can it be true that you fight for him?"

"That is the last thing I would ever do. In fact I would fight against him for a wooden groat. The truth is that the Capo has a friend of mine locked away in there. I want to get a message to him."

"There is great danger in even going close to his keep."

"I'm sure of it, but I am fearless. And I must contact my friend. You lead the way—and through the woods if you don't mind. I don't want to be seen by either Capo Doccia or his men."

Obviously neither did Dreng. He sobered up as he led me by obscure paths and hidden ways to the other side of the forest. I peered out carefully at the roadway leading to the drawbridge, to the entrance to the keep.

"Any closer and they will see us," he whispered. I looked up at the late afternoon sun and nodded agreement.

"It's been a busy day. We'll lay up in the woods here and make our move in the morning."

"No move. It's death!" His teeth chattered though the afternoon was hot. He hurried as he led the way deeper into the forest, to a grassy hollow with a stream running through it. He produced a clay cup from his bag, filled it with water and brought it to me. I slurped and realized that having a knave wasn't a bad idea after all. Once his chores were done he spread the blankets on the grass and promptly fell asleep on his. I sat down with my back to a tree and, for the first time, had a chance to examine the gun I had lifted.

It was sleek and new and did not fit this broken-down planet at all. Of course—it had to be from the Venian ship. The Bishop said that they had probably been smuggling weapons. And I was holding one of them in my hands. I looked at it more closely.

No identification, or serial number—or any other indication where it had been manufactured. And it was pretty obvious why. If the League agents succeeded in getting their hands on one of these it would be impossible to trace it back to the planet of origin. The gun was small in size, about halfway between a rifle and a pistol. I can claim some acquaintance with small arms—I am an honored member of the Pearly Gates Gun Club and Barbecue Society because I am a pretty good shot and helped them win tournaments—but I had never seen anything like this before. I looked into the muzzle. It was about .30 calibre, and unusually enough it was a smoothbore. It had open, iron sights, a trigger with safety button, one other lever on the stock. I turned this and the gun broke in half and a handful of small cartridges fell to the ground. I looked at one closely and began to understand how the gun worked.

"Neat. No lands or grooves so there is no worry about keeping the barrel clean. Instead of rotating, the bullet has fins to keep it in straight flight. And, uggh, make a nastier hole in anyone it hits. And no cartridge case either—this is solid propellent. Does away with all the worries about ejecting the brass." I peeked into the chamber. "Efficient and foolproof. Push your cartridges into the recessed stock. When it's full put one more into the chamber. Close and lock. A little solar screen here to keep a battery charged. Pull the trigger, a spot in the chamber glows hot and ignites the charge. The expanding gas shoots out the bullet—while part of the gas is diverted to ram the next bullet into the chamber. Rugged, almost foolproof, cheap to make. And deadly."

Depressed and tired, I lay the gun beside me, dropped the sword close to hand, lay back on the blanket and followed Dreng's good example.

By dawn we were slept out and slightly hungover. Dreng brought me water, then handed over a strip of what looked like smoked leather. He took one himself and began chewing on it industriously. Breakfast in bed—the greatest! I bit my piece and almost broke a tooth. It not only resembled smoked leather, but tasted exactly like it as well.

By the time that the drawbridge clanked down for the day we were lying in a copse on the hill above it, as close as we could get. It was the nearest cover that we could find since, for pretty obvious reasons, all the trees and shrubs had been cleared away from the approaches to the gate. It wasn't as near as I liked, but would have to do. But it was far too close for Dreng for I could feel him shivering at my side. The first thing to emerge from the gate was a small body of armed men, followed by four slaves dragging a cart.

"What's going on?" I asked.

"Tax collecting. Getting in their share of the crops."

"We've now seen who comes out—but do any of your farmers ever go in?"

"Madness and death! Never!"

"What about selling them food."

"They take all they want from us."

"Do you sell them firewood?"

"They steal what they need."

They had a pretty one-sided economy, I thought gloomily. But I had to come up with something—I just couldn't leave The Bishop as a slave in this dismal place. My cogitation was interrupted by a commotion inside the gate. Then, as though my thoughts had coalesced into reality, a figure burst out of the gate, knocking aside the guard there, rushing on.

The Bishop!

Running fast. But right behind him were the pursuing guards.

"Take this and follow me!" I shouted, jamming the hilt of the sword into Dreng's hand. Then I was off down the slope as fast as I could go, shouting to draw their attention. They ignored me until I fired a shot over their heads.

Things got pretty busy after that. The guards slowed, one even dived to the ground and put his hands over his head. The Bishop pelted on—but one of his pursuers was right behind him, swinging a long pike. Catching The Bishop on the back and knocking him down. I fired again as I ran, jumped over The Bishop and felled the pikeman with the butt of my gun.

"Up the hill!" I called out when I saw that The Bishop was struggling to his feet, blood all over his back. I banged off two more shots, then turned to help him. And saw that Dreng was clutching the sword—but still lying on top of the hill.

"Get down here and help him or I'll kill you myself!" I shouted, turning and firing again. I hadn't hit anyone but I was sure keeping their heads down. The Bishop stumbled on and Dreng, having plumbed some deep well of decency—or in fear that I would kill him—was coming to our aid. Shots were whistling past us now so I spun and returned their fire.

We reached the top of the low hill, went over it towards the relative safety of the woods. Dreng and I half carried the great form of The Bishop as he stumbled and staggered. I took a quick—and reassuring—look at his back. There was a shallow cut there, nothing too bad. Our pursuers were still not in sight when we crashed through the bushes and reached the safety of the trees.

"Dreng—lead us out of here. They mustn't catch us now!"

Surprisingly enough they didn't. The farm lad must have played in these woods for all of his young life because he knew every track and path. But it was hard work. We staggered on, then struggled our way along a steep grassy slope with a few miserable bushes halfway up. Dreng pulled the bushes aside to reveal the entrance to a shallow cave.

"Chased a Furry in here once. No one else knows about it."

The entrance was low and it was a labor to pull The Bishop through. But once inside, the cave opened out and there was more than enough space to sit up, although it wasn't high enough to stand. I took one of the blankets and spread it out, then rolled The Bishop onto it so that he lay on his side. He groaned. His face was filthy and bruised. He had not an easy time of it. Then he looked towards me and smiled.

"Thank you, my boy. I knew you would be there."

"You did? That's more than I knew."

"Nonsense. But, quickly please, the . . ."

He writhed and moaned and his body arched into the air with unbearable pain. The paincuff—I had forgotten about it! And it was receiving a continuous signal, certain death.

Haste makes waste. So I controlled my anxiety and slowly slipped off my right shoe, opened the compartment, and seized the lockpick firmly in my fingers. Bent over, inserted it—and the cuff sprang open. Pain lanced through my hand, numbing it, as I threw the thing aside.

The Bishop was unconscious and breathing heavily. There was nothing more I could do except sit and wait.

"Your sword," Dreng said, holding it out to me.

"You take care of it for awhile. If you think you are up to it?"

He lowered his eyes and trembled again. "I want to be a fighter, but I am so afraid. I could not move to help you."

"But you did—finally. Remember that. There isn't a person alive who has not been afraid at one time or another. It is only the brave man who can feel fear and still go forward."

"A noble thought, young man," the deep voice said. "And one that you should always remember."

The Bishop had regained consciousness and was smiling a wan smile.

"Now, Jim, as I was saying before they turned on their little machine, I was certain that you would be here this morning. You were free—and I knew that you would not leave me alone in that wicked place. There was an immense hue and cry when you escaped, with abundant to-ing and fro-ing until the gate was closed for the night. It was obvious that it would be impossible for you to come then. But with dawn the gate would be opened and I had not the slightest doubt that you were sure to be close by, trying to find a way to get to me. Simple logic. So I simplified the equation by coming to you."

"Very simple! You almost got yourself killed."

"But I didn't. And we are both safely away from them. Plus I see that you have managed to enlist an ally. A good day's work. Now the important question. What do we do next?"

What indeed?

CHAPTER TWENTY-THREE

"As to what we do next—the answer is obvious," I said. "We stay here until the excitement has died down. Which should happen fairly quickly since there is not much market value in a dead slave."

"But I feel remarkably healthy."

"You have forgotten that the paincuff will kill if used continuously. So, when our way is clear we head for the nearest habitation and dress your wound."

"It is bloody, but can't be more than a scratch."

"Sepsis and infection. We take care of the cut first." I turned to Dreng. "Any farmers you know who live close to this place?"

"No, but the widow Apfeltree is just over the hill, past the dead tree, through the end of the swamp. . . ."

"Great. Show us the way, don't tell." I turned back to The Bishop. "And after we fix your back, then what?"

"After that, Jim, we join the army. Since you are now a mercenary, that is the proper thing to do. An army will be based in a keep, and there will be a locked room in that keep where all the groats are stored. While you practice your military profession I shall, as the expression goes, case the joint. In order to further this noble work of ours I have one particular army in mind for you. The one that serves the Campo Dimonte."

"Not Capo Dimonte!" Dreng wailed, clutching his hair with both hands. "He is evil beyond measure, eats a child for breakfast every day, has all of his furniture upholstered in human skin, drinks from the skull of his first wife . . ."

"Enough," The Bishop ordered, and Dreng was stilled.

"It is obvious that he does not have a good press here in the Capote of Doccia. That is because he is the sworn enemy of Capo Doccia and goes to war against him periodically. I am sure that he is no worse—or better—than any other capo. But he does have one advantage. He is our enemy's enemy."

"So hopefully our friend. Right. I owe old Doccia one and I look forward to paying it back."

"You should not bear grudges, Jim. It dulls the vision and interferes with your career. Which should now be grabbing groats not wreaking vengeance."

I nodded agreement. "Of course. But while you are planning the heist there is no reason why I can't enjoy a bit of revenge."

I could see that he disapproved of my emotions—but I could not attain his olympian detachment. A weakness of youth, perhaps. I changed the subject.

"After we empty the treasury, then what?"

"We find out how the locals are contacting the offplanet smugglers, like the Venians. With the obvious aim of leaving this backward and deadly world as soon as possible. In order to do that we may have to get religion." He chuckled at my shocked expression. "Like you, my boy, I am a Scientific Humanist and feel no need for the aid of the supernatural. But here on Spiovente what technology there is seems to be in the hands of an order called the Black Monks. . . ."

"No, stay away!" Dreng wailed; he was certainly a source of bad news. "They know Things that Drive Men Mad. From their workshops all forms of unnatural devices pour forth. Machines that scream and grunt, that talk through the skies, the paincuffs as well. Avoid them, master, I beg of you!"

"What our young friend has decried is true," The Bishop said. "Minus the fear of the unknown, of course. Through some process that is not relevant now all of technology on this world became concentrated in the hands of this order, the Black Monks. I have no idea what their religious affiliations are—if any—but they do supply and repair the machines that we have seen. This gives them a certain protection, since if one capo were to attack them the others would rush to their defense to insure their continued access to the metallic fruits of technology. It is to them that we may have to turn for salvation and exodus."

"I second the motion and it is carried by acclamation. Join the army, whip as many groats as we can, contact the smugglers—and buy our way out."

Dreng gaped at all the long words, drooling a bit at the same time. He obviously followed little of what we discussed. Action was more his style. He made a silent exit on a scouting trip and an even more slithery return. No one was about, our way was clear. The Bishop could walk now, with a little aid from us, and the widow's house was not too distant. Even with Dreng's reassurances she was trembling with fear when she admitted us to her hovel.

"Guns and swords. Murder and death. I'm doomed, doomed."

Despite her muttering, punctuated by the smacking of her toothless gums, she followed my instructions and put a pot of water over the fire. I cut a strip of cloth from my blanket, boiled it clean, then used it to wash The Bishop's wound. It was shallow but deep. The widow was persuaded to part with some of her store of moonshine and The Bishop shuddered, but did not cry out, when I poured it into the open cut. Hoping the alcohol content was high enough to act as an antiseptic. I used more boiled blanket as a bandage—which was about all that I could do.

"Excellent, James, excellent," he said, gingerly pulling his sliced jacket over his shoulders. "Your years in the Boy Sprouts were obviously not wasted. Now let us thank the good widow and leave since it is obvious that she is upset by our presence."

Leave we did, strolling the open, rut-filled road, every footstep taking us farther away from Capo Doccia. Dreng was a good provider, drifting off into orchards for fruit, or rooting out edible tubers from the fields we passed, even digging them up under the noses of the rightful owners. Who only touched their forelocks at the sight of my weapons. It is a nasty world that only respects bullies. For the first time I began to appreciate the better qualities of the League worlds.

It was late afternoon when the walls of the keep loomed up before us. This place had a little more style than Doccia's, or at least it looked that way from a distance, because it was situated on an island in a lake. A causeway and drawbridge connected it to the mainland. Dreng was shaking with fear again and was more than happy to stay on the shore with The Bishop while I braved the dangers of the keep. I strode militarily along the stone causeway, then stamped over the bridge. The two guards eyed me with open suspicion.

"Good morn, brothers," I called out cheerfully, gun on shoulder, sword in hand, gut in and chest out. "Is this the establishment of the Capo Dimonte, known the length and breadth of the land for his charm and strength of arm?"

"Who wants to know?"

"I do. An armed and powerful soldier who wishes to enlist in his noble service."

"Your choice, brother, your choice," he said with obvious gloom. "Through the gate, across the courtyard, third door on your right, ask for Sire Srank." He leaned close and whispered. "For three groats I'll give you a tip."

"Done."

"So pay."

"Shortly. I'm a little skint right now."

"You must be—if you want to hire out to this lot. All right, five then, in five days." I nodded agreement. "He'll offer you very little, but don't settle for less than two groats a day."

"Thanks for the credit. I'll get back to you."

I swaggered through the gate and found the right door. It was open to admit the last light, and a fat man with a bald head was scratching away at some papers. He looked up when my shadow fell across the table.

"Get out here," he shouted, scratching his head so hard

that a shower of dandruff sparkled in the sunbeam. "I've told you all, no groats until morning after next."

"I've not enlisted yet—nor will I if that's the way you pay the troops."

"Sorry, good stranger, sun in my eyes. Come in, come in. Enlist? Of course. Gun and sword—and ammunition?"

"Some."

"Wonderful." His hands rustled when he dry-washed them. "Food for you and your knave and a groat a day."

"Two a day and all ammunition used to be replaced."

He scowled—then shrugged and scratched one of the sheets and pushed it over to me. "A one-year enlistment, salary open to review at end of contract. Since you can't read or write I hope you can manage to scratch your illiterate X down here."

"I can read so well I see that you have me down for four years, which I will now correct before I sign." Which I did, writing Judge Nixon's name on the line, knowing full well that I would be leaving well before my enlistment was up. "I'll get my knave who awaits without, along with my aged father."

"No extra food for poor relations!" he snarled generously. "You share yours."

"Agreed," I said. "You're all heart."

I went back to the gate and waved my companions over.

"You owe me," the guard said.

"I'll pay you—when that scrofulous toad pays me."

He grunted agreement. "If you think he's bad—wait until you meet Capo Dimonte. I wouldn't be hanging around this damp dump if it weren't for the loot bonus."

They were coming on slowly, The Bishop half dragging the reluctant Dreng.

"Loot bonus? Paying out soon?"

"Soon as the fighting is over. We march tomorrow."

"Against Capo Doccia?"

"No such luck. The word is that he is loaded with jewels and golden groats and more. Be nice to share in that haul. But not this time. All they have told us is that we are heading north. Must be a surprise attack on someone, probably a friend, and they don't want word to leak out. That's good thinking. Catch them with their drawbridge down and it's half the battle."

I pondered this bit of military wisdom as I led my small band in the indicated direction. The soldier's quarters, while not something to put in a travel brochure, were certainly a cut above the slave quarters. Wooden bunks with straw mattresses for the fighting men—some straw under the bunk for the knave. I would have to make some arrangements for The Bishop, but I was sure that bribery would take care of that. We sat together on the bunk while Dreng went to find the kitchen.

"How is the back?" I asked.

"Sore, but only a small bother. I'll take bit of a rest, then begin a survey of the layout. . . ."

"In the morning will be time enough. It has been a long couple of days."

"Agreed. And here is your knave with the food!"

It was a hot stew with fragments of some nameless bird bobbing in it. Had to be a bird; the feathers were still attached. We divided the stew into three equal portions and wolfed it down. All this fresh air and walking was certainly good for the appetite. There was also a ration of sour wine which neither I nor The Bishop could stomach. Not so Dreng, who slurped and smacked his way through it in moments. Then rolled under the bunk and began to snore raucously.

"I'm going to have a look around," I said. "Take a rest on the bunk until I get back. . . ."

I was interrupted by an off-key blare on a bugle. I looked up to see that the malevolent musician was standing in the doorway. He emitted another toneless blast. I was ready to grab him by the throat if he tried it again, but he stepped aside and bowed. A thin figure in blue uniform took his place. All of the soldiers who were watching bowed their heads slightly or shook their weapons in salute, so I did the same. It could be no other than Capo Dimonte himself.

He was lean to the point of being hollow-stomached. He

either had circulation trouble or was naturally blue of skin. His little red eyes peered out of hollow blue sockets, while he fingered his blue jaw with azure fingers. He looked around suspiciously, then spoke: for all of his leanness his voice had a deep strength to it.

"My men, I have good news for you. Prepare yourselves and your weapons for we march at midnight. This will be a forced march to enable us to reach Pinetta Woods before dawn. Fighting men only—and we travel light. Your knaves will stay here to look after your goods. We will lay up there during the day, then leave at dusk tomorrow. We will meet our allies during the night and join forces for an assault on the enemy at dawn."

"A question, Capo," one of the men called out. He was grizzled and scarred, obviously a veteran of many conflicts. "Against whom do we march?"

"You will be told before the attack. We will gain victory only by surprise."

There were murmurs on all sides as the veteran called out again.

"Our enemy a mystery—at least tell us then who are our allies."

Capo Dimonte was not pleased with the question. He scratched his chin and fiddled with the hilt of his sword while his audience waited. He obviously needed our voluntary assistance, so in the end he spoke.

"You will all be pleased to hear that we have allies of great strength and will. They also have war machines to batter the stoutest wall. With their assistance we can take any keep, defeat any army. We are lucky to serve at their side." He pressed his lips together, reluctant to go on but still knowing that he must.

"Our victory is assured since our allies are none other than . . . the order of the Black Monks."

There was a long moment of shocked silence—followed instantly by shouts of anger. The significance of all this escaped me—other than the fact that it did not sound good at all.

CHAPTER TWENTY-FOUR

As soon as he had spoken, Capo Dimonte made his exit and the door slammed shut behind him. There were shouts and cries of anger from all sides—but there was one man who bellowed louder than all the others. It was the scarred veteran. He climbed onto a table and shouted them all into silence.

"Everyone here knows me, knows old Tusker. I was cutting off heads when most of you weren't even potty trained. So I'm going to talk and you are going to listen and then you will get a chance to talk too. Anyone here don't like that idea?"

He closed one immense fist and held it out, then turned in a circle, scowling fiercely. There were some angry mutters, but none loud enough to imply disagreement.

"Good. Then listen. I know those black-frocked buggers from a long way back and I don't trust them. All they think of is their own hides. If they want us to fight for them that's only because there is big trouble ahead and they would like to see us killed rather than them. I don't like it."

"I don't like it either," another man called out. "But what kind of a choice do we have?"

"None," Tusker growled angrily. "And that's what I was going to say next. I think we have been grabbed by the short and curlies." He drew his sword and shook it at them. "Every weapon we have, outside of them new guns, comes from the Black Monks. Without their supplies we have nothing to fight with, and without nothing to fight with we have nothing to do and we can starve or go back to the farm. And that's not for me. And it better not be for any of you either. Because we are all in this together. We all fight—or none fight. And if we fight and any of you try to sneak out of here before the action starts, then he is going to find my sword stuck all the way through his liver."

He shook the shining blade at them while they glared in silence.

"A solid argument," The Bishop whispered," the logic impeccable. Too bad that it is wasted on this ignoble cause. You and your comrades have no choice but to agree."

The Bishop was right. There was more shouting and argument, but in the end they had to go along with the plans. They would march at the side of the Black Monks. None of them, myself included, were very happy about the idea. They could stay up and argue until midnight but I was tired and could use the few hours sleep. The Bishop wandered out in search of information and I rolled up on the bunk and slipped into a restless slumber.

The shouted orders woke me, feeling more tired than when I had gone to sleep. No one seemed happy about the midnight march—or our battle companions—and there were dark looks and much cursing. There were even some oaths I hadn't heard before, real nice ones, that I filed away for future use. I went out to the primitive lavabo and threw cold water on my face which seemed to help. When I returned, The Bishop was sitting on the bunk. He rose and extended his large hand.

"You must watch yourself, Jim. This is a crude and deadly world and all men's hands are turned against you."

"That is the way I prefer to live—so don't worry yourself."

"But I do." He sighed mightily. "I have nothing but contempt for superstition, astrologers, palm readers, and the like, so you will understand why I feel great disgust at myself for the black depression that possesses me. But I see nothing but darkness in the future, emptiness. We have been companions for such a brief period, I do not wish it to end. Yet, I am sorry, do excuse me, I have a sense of danger and despair that cannot be alleviated."

"With good reason!" I cried, trying to put enthusiasm into my words. "You have been torn from the security of your quasi-retirement, imprisoned, freed, fled, hid, dieted, fled again, bribed, were cheated, beaten, enslaved, wounded—and you wonder why you are depressed?"

This brought a wan smile to his lips and he grasped my hand again. "You are right, Jim, of course. Toxins in the bloodstream, depression in the cortex. Watch your back and return safely. By the time you do I'll have worked out how to relieve the capo of some of his groats."

He was looking his age—for the first time since we had met. As I left I saw him stretch out wearily on the bunk. He should be feeling better when I returned. Dreng would fetch his food and look after him. What I must do is concentrate on staying alive so I would come back.

It was a dreary and exhausting march. The day had been hot, and so was the night. We shuffled along, dripping with perspiration and slapping at the insects that rushed out of the darkness to attack us. The rutted road caught at my feet and dust rose into my nostrils. On we marched, and on, following along after the clanking and hissing conveyance that led our nightmarish parade. One of the steam cars was hauling Capo Dimonte's war wagon in which he traveled in relative comfort. His captains were in there with him, swilling down booze no doubt and generally enjoying themselves. We marched on, the cursing in the ranks growing steadily weaker.

By the time we stumbled under the sheltering trees of Pinetta Woods we were tired and mutinous. I did what most of the others did, dropped onto the bed of sweet-smelling needles under the trees and groaned in appreciation. And admiration for the sturdier warriors, with old Tusker in the van, who insisted on their ration of acid wine before retiring. I closed my eyes, groaned again, then slept.

We stayed there all day, glad to have the rest. Around noon rations were reluctantly handed out from the cart.

Warm, foul water to wash down rock-like bits of what might have been bread. After this I managed to sleep some more, until we formed ranks again at dusk and the night march continued.

After some hours we came to a crossroads and turned right. There was a murmur through the ranks at this, starting with those who knew the area well.

"What are they saying?" I asked the man who marched beside me, in silence up until now.

"Capo Dinobli. That's who we're after. Could be no one else. No other keep in this direction for one day, two day's march."

"Do you know anything about him?"

He grunted and was silent, but the man behind him spoke up. "I served with him, long time ago. Old bugger then, must be ancient now. Just one more capo."

Then it was one foot after another in a haze of fatigue. There had to be better ways to make a living. This was going to be my first and last campaign. As soon as we returned I and The Bishop would sack the treasury and flee with all the groats we could carry. Wonderful thought. I almost ran into the man in front of me and stopped just in time. We had halted where the road passed near the forest. Against the darkness of the trees even darker shadows loomed. I was trying to see what they were when one of the officers came back down the ranks.

"I need some volunteers," he whispered. "You, you, you, you."

He touched my arm and I was one of the volunteers. There seemed to be about twenty of us who were pulled out of line and herded forward towards the woods. The clouds had cleared and there was enough light from the stars now to see that the black bulks were wheeled devices of some kind. I could hear the hiss of escaping steam. A dark figure strode forward and halted us.

"Listen and I will tell you what you must do," he said.

As he spoke a metal door was opened on the machine nearest us. Light gleamed as wood was pushed into the firebox. By the brief, flickering light I could see the speaker clearly. He was dressed in a black robe, his head covered by a cowl that hid his face. He pointed to the machine.

"This must be pushed through the woods—and in absolute silence. I will put my knife into the ribs of any of you who makes a noise. A track was cut during daylight and will be easy to follow. Take up the lines and do as you are instructed."

Other dark-robed figures were handing us the ropes and pushing us into line. On the whispered signal we began hauling.

The thing rolled along easily enough and we pulled at a steady pace. There were more whispered instructions to guide us—then we halted as we approached the edge of the forest. After this we dropped the ropes and sweated as we pushed and pulled the great weight about until the guides were satisfied. There was much whispered consultation about alignment and range, and I wondered just what was going on. We had been forgotten for the moment, so I walked as quietly as I could past the thing and peered out through the shrubbery at the view beyond.

Very interesting. A field of grain stretched down a gentle slope to a keep, its dark towers clear in the starlight. There was a glimmer of reflection about its base, where the waters of the moat protected it from attack.

I stayed there until dawn began to gray the sky, then moved back to examine the object of our labors. As it emerged from the darkness its shape became clear—and I still hadn't the faintest idea of what it was. Fire and steam, I could see the white trickle of vapor clearly now. And a long boom of some kind along the top. One of the black figures was working the controls now. Steam hissed louder as the long arm sank down until the end rested on the ground. I went to look at the large metal cup there—and was rewarded for my curiosity by being drafted to help move an immense stone into place. Two of us rolled it from the pile of its fellows nearby, but it took four of us, straining, to raise it into the cup. Mystery upon mystery. I rejoined the others just as Capo Dimonte appeared with the tall, robed man at his side.

"Will it work, Brother Farvel?" Dimonte asked. "I know nothing of such devices."

"But I do, capo, you shall see. When the drawbridge is lowered my machine will destroy it, crush it."

"May it do just that! Those walls are high—and so will our losses be if we must storm the keep without being able to break through the gate."

Brother Farvel turned his back and issued quick instructions to the machine's operators. More wood was pushed into its bowels and the hissing rose in volume. It was full daylight now. The field before us was empty, the view peaceful. But behind us in the forest lurked the small army and the war machines. It was obvious that battle would be joined when the drawbridge was lowered and destroyed.

We were ordered to lie down, to conceal ourselves as the light grew. It was full daylight by this time, the sun above the horizon—and still nothing happened. I crouched near the machine, close to the cowled operator at the controls.

"It is not coming down!" Brother Farvel called out suddenly. "It is past due, always down at this time. Something is wrong."

"Do they know that we are here?" Capo Dimonte said.

"*Yes!*" an incredibly loud voice boomed out from the trees above us. "*We know you are there. Your attack is doomed—as are all of you! Prepare to face your certain death.*"

CHAPTER TWENTY-FIVE

The roaring voice was totally unexpected, shocking in the silence of the forest. I jumped, startled—nor was I the only one. The monk at the machine's controls was even more startled. His hand pulled on the control lever and there was a gigantic hissing roar. The long arm on top of the device thrashed skyward, pushed by a stubbier arm close to its hinged end. The arm rose up in a high arc and slammed into a concealed buffer that jarred and shook the entire machine. The arm may have stopped—but the stone in the cup at the end of the arm continued, high into the air, rising in a great arc. I rushed forward to see it splash into the moat just before the closed drawbridge. Good shot—it would certainly have demolished the structure had it been down.

All around me things became busy quite suddenly. Brother Farvel had knocked the monk from the controls and was now kicking him, roaring with rage. Swords had been drawn, soldiers were rushing about—some of them firing up into the trees. Capo Dimonte was bellowing orders that no one was listening to. I put my back to a tree and held my gun ready for the expected attack.

It never came. But the amplified voice thundered again.

"Go back. Return from whence you came and you will be spared. I am talking to you, Capo Dimonte, you are making a mistake. You are being used by the Black Monks. You will be destroyed for nothing. Return to your keep, for only death awaits you here."

"It is there, I see it!" Brother Farvel shouted, pointing up into the trees. He spun about and saw me, seized me by the arm in a painful grip, and pointed again. "There, on that branch, the device of the devil. Destroy it!"

Why not. I could see it now, even recognize what it was. A loudspeaker of some kind. The gun cracked and kicked my shoulder hard. I fired again and the speaker exploded, bits of plastic and metal rained down.

"Just a machine," Brother Farvel shouted, stamping the fragments into the ground. "Start the attack—send your men forward. My death-throwers will give you support. They will batter down the walls for you."

The capo had no choice. He chewed his lip a bit, then signalled the bugler at his side. Three brazen notes rang out and were echoed by other buglers to our rear and on both flanks. When the first of his troops burst from beneath the trees he drew his sword and ordered us to follow him. With great reluctance I trotted forward.

It was not quite what you would call a lightning attack. More of a stroll when you got down to it. We advanced through the field, then stopped on order to wait for the death-throwers to get into position. Steam cars pulled them forward into line and the firing began. Rocks sizzled over our heads and either bounced from the keep wall or vanished into its interior.

"Forward!" the capo shouted, and waved his sword again just as the return fire began.

The silvery spheres rose up from behind the keep walls, rose high, arced forward above us—and dropped.

Hit—and cracked open. One struck nearby and I could see it was a thin container of some kind filled with liquid that smoked and turned to vapor in the air. Poison! I threw myself away from it, running, trying not to breathe. But the things were bursting all about us now, the air thick with fumes. I ran and my lungs ached and I had to breathe, could not stop myself.

As the breath entered my lungs I fell forward and blackness fell as well.

I was lying on my back, I knew that, but was aware of very little else because of the headache that possessed me completely. If I moved my head ever so slightly it tightened down like a band of fire on my temples. When I tentatively opened one eye—red lightning struck in through my eyeball. I groaned, and heard the groan echoed from all sides. This headache was the winner, the planet-sized headache of all time, before which all other headaches paled. I thought of previous headaches I had known and sneered at their ineffectivness. Cardboard headaches. This was the real thing. Someone groaned close by and I, and many others, groaned in sympathy.

Bit by bit the pain ebbed away, enough so that I tentatively opened one eye, then the other. The blue sky was clear above, the wind rustled the grain on which I lay. With great hesitation I rose up on one elbow and looked around me at the stricken army.

The field was littered with sprawled bodies. Some of them were sitting up now, holding their heads, while one or two stronger—or stupider—soldiers were climbing unsteadily to their feet. Nearby lay the silvery, broken fragments of one of the attacking missiles, looking innocent enough now with the gas dispersed. My head throbbed but I ignored it. We were alive. The gas had not killed us—it had obviously been designed only to knock us out. Potent stuff. I looked at my shadow, not wanting to risk a glance at the sun yet, and saw how foreshortened it was. Close to noon. We had been asleep for hours.

Then why weren't we dead? Why hadn't the Capo Dinobli's men pounced on us and slit our throats? Or at least taken our weapons? My gun was at my side; I broke it and saw that it was still loaded. Mysteries, mysteries. I jumped, startled—instantly regretting it as my head throbbed—as the hoarse scream rang out. I managed to sit up and turn to look.

Interesting. It was Brother Farvel himself who was still shouting and cursing while he tore handfuls of hair from his head. This was most unusual. I had certainly never seen anything like it before. I rose hesitantly to my feet to see what he was upset about. Yes indeed, I could understand his emotions.

He was standing beside one of his death-throwers which had been thrown a little death of its own. It had burst open, exploded into a tangle of twisted pipes and fractured metal. The long arm had been neatly cut into three pieces and even the wheels had been torn from the body. It was just a mass of unrepairable junk. Brother Farvel ran off, still shouting hoarsely, wisps of hair floating in the breeze behind him.

There were more cries and shouts of pain from the other monks as Brother Farvel came staggering back, stumbling towards the Capo Dimonte, who was just sitting up.

"Destroyed, all of them!" the Black Monk roared while the capo clutched his hands tightly over his ears. "The work of years, gone, crushed, broken. All my death-throwers, the steam-powered battering ram—ruined. He did it, Capo Dinobli did it. Gather your men, attack the keep, he must be destroyed for this monstrous crime that he has committed."

The capo turned to look towards the keep. It was just as it had been at dawn, quiet and undisturbed, the drawbridge still up, as though the day's events had never occurred. Dimonte turned back to Brother Farvel, his face cold and drawn.

"No. I do not lead my men against those walls. That is suicide and suicide was not our agreement. This is your argument, not mine. I agreed to aid you in taking the keep. You were to force entrance with your devices. Then I would attack. That arrangement is now over."

"You cannot go back on your word. . . ."

"I am not. Breech the walls and I will attack. That is what you promised. Now, do it."

Brother Farvel turned red with rage, raised his fists, leaned forward. The capo stood his ground—but drew his sword and held it out.

"See this," he said. "I am still armed—all of my men are armed. It is a message that I understand quite clearly. Dinobli's men could have taken our weapons and cut our throats while we lay here. They did not. They do not war on me. Therefore I do not war on them. *You* fight them—

this is your battle." He nudged the toe of his boot into the bugler lying beside him. "Sound assembly."

We were quite happy to leave the Black Monks there in the field, surveying the wreckage of their machines and their plans. Word quickly spread through the ranks as to what had occurred and smiles replaced the pained grimaces as the headaches vanished to be replaced by relief. There would be no battle, no casualties. The Black Monks had started the trouble—and it had been finished for them. My smile was particularly broad because I had some good news for The Bishop.

I knew now how we were to get off the repellent planet of Spiovente.

Through the clear wisdom of hindsight I could understand now what had happened the night before. The approach of our troops in the darkness had been observed carefully. With advanced technology of some kind. The hidden watchers must have also seen the track being constructed through the forest for the death-thrower and understood the significance of the operation. The loudspeaker had been placed in the tree directly above the site—then activated by radio. The gas that had felled us was sophisticated and had been delivered with pinpoint accuracy. All of this was well beyond the technology of this broken-down planet. Which meant only one thing.

There were off-worlders in the keep of Capo Dinobli. They were there in force and were up to something. And whatever it was had aroused the wrath of the Black Monks, so much so that they had planned this attack. Which had backfired completely. Good. Mine enemy's enemy one more time. The monks had a stranglehold on what little technology there was on Spiovente—and from what I had seen, the technology was completely monopolized by the military. I cudgeled my brain, remembering those long sessions with The Bishop on geopolitics and economics. I was getting the glimmer of a solution to our problems when there was a wild shouting from the ranks ahead.

I pushed forward with the others to see the exhausted messenger sprawled in the grass beside the road. Capo

Dimonte was turning away from him, shaking his fists skyward in fury.

"An attack—behind my back—on the keep! It is that sun of a worm, Doccia, that's who it is! We move now, forced march. Back!"

It was a march that I never want to repeat. We rested only when exhaustion dropped us to the ground. Drank some water, staggered to our feet, went on. There was no need to beat us or encourage because we were all involved now. The capo's family, his worldly goods, they were all back in the keep. Guarded only by a skeleton force of soldiers. All of us were as concerned as he was, for what little we owned was there as well. The knaves watching our few possessions. Dreng, who I scarcely knew, yet felt responsibility for. And The Bishop. If the keep were taken what would happen to him? Nothing, he was an old man, harmless, no enemy of theirs.

Yet I knew this was a lie even as I tried to convince myself of its validity. He was an escaped slave. And I knew what they did with escaped slaves on Spiovente.

More water, a little food at sunset, then on through the night. At dawn I could see our forces straggling out in a ragged column as the stronger men pushed on ahead. I was young and fit and worried—and right up in the front. I could stop now for a rest, get my breath back. Ahead on the road I saw the two men spring from the bushes and vanish over the hill.

"There!" I shouted. "Watchers—we've been seen."

The capo jumped from the war-wagon and ran to my side. I pointed. "Two men. In hiding there. They ran towards the keep."

He ground his teeth with impotent rage. "We can't catch them, not in our condition. Doccia will be warned; he'll escape."

He looked back at his straggling troops, then waved his officers forward.

"You, Barkus, stay here and rest them, then get in formation and follow me. I'm going on with all the fit men

I can. They can take turns riding on the war-wagon. We're pushing forward."

I climbed onto the roof of the cart as it started ahead. Men ran alongside, holding on, letting it pull them. The steam car wheezed and puffed smoke at a great rate as we clanked up the hill and onto the downslope beyond.

There were the towers of the keep in the distance, smoke rising from it. When we rattled around the next bend we found a line of men across the road, weapons raised, firing.

We did not slow down. The steam-whistle screeched loudly and we roared in answer, our anger taking us forward. The enemy fled. It had just been a holding party. We could see them joining the rest of the attackers who were now streaming away from the lake. When we reached the causeway it was empty of life. Beyond it was the broken gate of the keep with smoke rising slowly above it. I was right behind the capo when we stumbled forward. Long boards were still in place bridging the gap before the splintered and broken drawbridge, half raised and hanging from its chains. A soldier pushed out between the broken fragments and raised his sword in weary salute.

"We held them, capo," he said, then slumped back against the splintered wood. "They broke through into the yard but we held them at the tower. They were firing the outer door when they left."

"The Lady Dimonte, the children . . .?"

"All safe. The treasury untouched."

But the troops quarters were off the yard and not in the tower. I pushed ahead with the others, who had realized this, climbing through the ruined gate. There were bodies here, many of them. Unarmed knaves chopped down in the attack. The defenders were coming out of the tower now—and Dreng was among them, coming forward slowly. His clothing was spattered with blood, as was the ax he carried, but he seemed sound.

Then I looked into his face and read the sorrow there. He did not need to speak, I knew. The words came from a distance.

"I am sorry. I could not stop them. He is dead, the old man. Dead."

CHAPTER TWENTY-SIX

He lay on the bunk, eyes closed as though he were sleeping. But never that still, never. Dreng had drawn my blanket over him, up to his chin, combed his hair and cleaned his face.

"I could not move him when the attack came," Dreng said. "He was too heavy, too ill. The wound in his back was bad, black, his skin hot. He told me to leave him, that he was dead in any case. He said if they didn't kill him the 'fection would. They didn't have to stab him though. . . ."

My friend and my teacher. Murdered by these animals. He was worth more than the entire filthy population of this world gathered together. Dreng took me by the arm and I shook him off, turned on him angrily. He was holding out a small packet.

"I stole the piece of paper for him," Dreng said. "He wanted to write to you. I stole it."

There was nothing to be said. I unwrapped it and a carved wooden key fell to the floor. I picked it up, then looked at the paper. There was a floor plan of the keep drawn on it, with an arrow pointing to a room carefully labled STRONGROOM. Below it was the message, and I read what was written there in a tight, clear hand.

I have been a bit poorly so I may not be able to give you this in person. Make a metal copy of the key—it opens the strongroom. Good luck, Jim, it has been my pleasure to know you. Be a good rat.

His signature was carefully written below. I read the

name—then read it again. It wasn't The Bishop—or any of the other aliases he had ever used. He had left me a legacy of trust—knowing that I was probably the only person in the universe who would value this confidence. His real name.

I went and sat down outside in the sun, suddenly very weary. Dreng brought me a cup of water. I had not realized how thirsty I was; I drained it and sent him for more.

This was it, the end. He had felt the approach of darkness—but had worried about me. Thought of me when it was really his own death that was looming so close.

What next? What should I do now?

Fatigue, pain, remorse—all overwhelmed me. Not realizing what was happening I fell asleep, sitting there in the sun, toppled over on my side. When I awoke it was late in the afternoon. Dreng had wadded his blanket and put it under my head, sat now at my side.

There was nothing more to be said. We put The Bishop's body on one of the little carts and wheeled it along the causeway to the shore. We were not the only ones doing this. There was a small hill beside the road, a slope of grass with trees above it, a pleasant view across the water to the keep. We buried him there, tamping the soil down solidly and leaving no marker. Not on this disgusting world. They had his body, that was enough. Any memorial I erected in his honor would be lightyears away. I would take care of that one day when the proper moment came.

"But right now, Dreng, we take care of Capo Doccia and his hoodlums. My good friend did not believe in revenge, so I cannot either. So we shall call it simple justice. Those criminals need straightening out. But how shall we do it?"

"I can help, master. I can fight now. I was afraid, then I got angry and I used the ax. I am ready to be a warrior like you."

I shook my head at him. I was thinking more clearly now. "This is no job for a farmer with a future. But you must always remember that you faced your fear and won. That will do you well for the rest of your life. But Jim diGriz pays his debts—so you are going back to the farm. How many groats does a farm cost?"

He gaped at that one and shuffled through his memory. "I never bought a farm."

"I'm sure of that. But somebody must have that you know."

"Old Kvetchy came back from the wars and paid Widow Roslair two-hundred and twelve groats for her share of her farm."

"Great. Allowing for inflation five-hundred should see you clear. Stick with me, kid, and you'll be wearing plowshares. Now get to the kitchen and pack up some food while I put part one of the plan into operation."

It was like a chess game that you played in your head. I could see the opening moves quite clearly, all laid out. If they were played correctly, middle game and endgame would follow with an inevitable win. I made the first move.

Capo Dimonte was slumped on his throne, red-eyed and as tired as the rest of us, a flagon of wine in his hand. I pushed through his officers and stood before him. He scowled at me and flapped his hand.

"Away, soldier. You'll get your bonus. You did your work well today, I saw that. But leave us, I have plans to make. . . ."

"That is why I am here, capo. To tell you how to defeat Capo Doccia. I was in his service and know his secrets."

"Speak!"

"In private. Send the others away."

He considered a moment—then waved his hands. They left, grumbling, and he sipped his wine until the door slammed shut.

"What do you know," he ordered. "Speak quickly for I am in a foul humor."

"As are we all. What I wanted to tell you in private does not concern Doccia—yet. You will attack, I am sure of that. But in order to assure success I am going to enlist

Capo Dinobli and his secrets on your side. Wouldn't the attack be more better if they were all asleep when we came over the wall."

"Dinobli knows no more of these matters than I do—so don't lie to me. He is tottering and has been bedridden for a year."

"I know that," I lied with conviction. "But it is those who use his keep for their own ends, who cause the Black Monks to make war on them, these are the ones who will help you."

He sat up at this and there was more than a glint of the old schemer in his eyes. "Go to them then. Promise them a share of the spoils—and you will share as well if you can do this. Go in my name and promise what you will. Before this month is out Doccia's head will be roasting on a spit over my fire, his body will be torn by red-hot spikes and . . ."

There was more like this but I wasn't too interested. This was a pawn move in the opening. I now had to bring a major piece forward to the attack. I bowed myself out, leaving him muttering on the throne, splashing wine around as he waved his arms. These people had very quick tempers.

Dreng had packed our few belongings and we left at once. I led the way until we were well clear of the keep, then turned off towards a stream that ran close by. It had a grassy field at its bank and I pointed towards it.

"We stay here until morning. I have plans to make and we need the rest. I want to be sharp when I knock on old Dinobli's door."

With a night's rest to refresh my brain everything became quite clear. "Dreng," I said, "this will have to be a one-man operation. I don't know what kind of reception I will get and I may be busy enough worrying about myself, without having you to care for. Back to the keep and wait for me."

There was really no door to knock on, just two heavily armed guards at the gate. I came down through the field, past the mounds of junked machines already smeared with a red patina of rust, and crossed the drawbridge. I stopped before I reached the guards and carefully kept my gun lowered.

"I have an important message for the one in charge here."

"Turn about and quick march," the taller guard said, pointing his gun at me. "Capo Dinobli sees no one."

"It's not the capo I care about," I said, looking past him into the courtyard. A tall man in rough clothes was passing. But beneath the ragged cuffs of his trousers I saw the gleam of plasteel boots.

"I wish the capo only good health," I called out loudly. "So I hope that he is seeing a good gereontologist and takes his synapsilstims regularly."

The guard growled in puzzlement at this—but my words were not for his edification. The man I was looking at in the courtyard stopped suddenly, still. Then slowly turned about. I saw keen blue eyes in a long face. Staring at me in silence. Then he came forward and talked to the guard— though still looking at me.

"What is the disturbance?"

"Nothing, your honor. Just sending this one on his way."

"Let him in. I want to question him."

The pointed gun was raised in salute and I marched through the gate. When we were out of earshot of the gate the tall man turned to face me, looking me up and down with frank curiosity.

"Follow me," he said. "I want to talk with you in private." He did not speak until we were in the keep and inside a room with the door closed behind us.

"Who are you?" he asked.

"You know—I was about to ask you the very same question. Does the League know what you are doing here?"

"Of course they do! This is a legitimate . . ." He caught himself, then smiled. "At least that proves you're from offplanet. No one can think that fast here—or knows what you know. Here, sit, then tell me who you are. After that I will judge how much I can tell you of our work."

"Fair enough," I said, dropping into the chair and lying my gun on the floor. "My name is Jim. I was a crewman on a Venian freighter—until I got into difficulties with the captain. He dumped me on this planet. That is all there is to it."

He pulled up a pad and began to make notes. "Your name is Jim. Your last name is . . ." I was silent. He scowled. "All right, let that go for the moment. What is the captain's name."

"I think that I will save that information for later. After you have told me who you are."

He pushed the pad aside and sat back in his chair. "I'm not satisfied. Without your identity I can tell you nothing. Where do you come from on Venia? What is the capital city of your planet, the name of the chairman of the global consul?"

"It's been a long time, I forgot."

"You are lying. You are no more Venian than I am. Until I know more . . ."

"What exactly do you have to know? I am a citizen of the League, not one of the dismal natives here. I watch tri-D, eat at Macswineys—a branch on every known world, forty-two billion sold—I studied molecular electronics, and have a black Belt in Judo. Does that satisfy you?"

"Perhaps. But you told me that you were dumped on this planet from a Venian freighter, which cannot be true. All unapproved contact with Spiovente is forbidden."

"My contact was unapproved. The ship was smuggling in guns like this one."

That got his attention all right. He grabbed the pad. "The captain's name is . . ."

I shook my head in a silent *no*. "You'll have that information only if you arrange to get me off this planet. You can do that because you as much as told me you were here with League approval. So let us do a little trading. You arrange for my ticket—I have plenty of silver groats to pay for it." Or I would have, which was the same thing. "You will also give me some small help in a local matter—then I'll tell you the captain's name."

He didn't like this. He thought hard and wriggled on the hook, but could not get off it.

"While you are making your mind up," I said, "you might tell me who you are and what you are doing here."

"You must promise not to reveal our identity to the natives. Our presence is well-known offplanet, but we can only succeed here if our operation remains covert."

"I promise, I promise. I owe nothing to any of the locals."

He steepled his fingers and leaned back as though beginning a lecture. I had guessed right—as his first words revealed.

"I am Professor Lustig of the University of Ellenbogen, where I hold the chair of applied socioeconomics. I am head of my department and I must say that I founded the department, since applied socioeconomics is a fairly new discipline, an outgrowth, obviously, of theoretical socioeconomics . . ."

I blinked rapidly to keep my eyes from glazing over and forced myself to keep listening. It was teachers like Lustig who made me run away from school.

". . . years of correspondence and labor to attain our fondest ambition. Practical application of our theories. Dealing with the bureaucrats of the League was the most difficult because of the League non-intervention policy. In the end they were convinced that with the proper controls we be permitted to operate a pilot project here on Spiovente. Or as someone said with crude humor, we certainly couldn't make things worse. We keep our operation at the current level of planetary technology so it will be self-sustaining when we leave."

"What exactly are you trying to do?" I asked.

He blinked rapidly. "That should be obvious—that is the only thing I have been talking about."

"You have been telling me theory, professor. Would you mind being specific about what you hope to accomplish."

"If you insist, on *layman's* terms, we are attempting to do no less than change the very fabric of society itself. We intend to bring this planet, kicking and screaming if necessary, out of the dark ages. After the Breakdown Spiovente sank into a rather repulsive form of feudalism. More warlordism, in fact. Normally a feudalistic society performs a great service during an age of disintegration. It maintains a general framework of government as various localities protect and care for themselves."

"I haven't seen much caring or protecting."

"Correct. Which is why these warlords will have to go."

"I'll help shoot a few."

"Violence is *not* our way! In addition to being distasteful, it is forbidden to League members. Our aim is to bring into existence government independent of the capos. In order to do that we are encouraging the rise of a professional class. This will bring about increased circulation of money and the end of barter. With increased funds the government will be able to institute taxation to purchase public services. To reinforce this a judiciary will need to be formed. This will encourage communication, centralization, and the growth of common ideas."

Sounded great—although I wasn't wild about the taxes bit, or the judiciary. Still, anything would be better than the capos.

"That all sounds fine in theory," I said. "But how do you put it into practice?"

"By providing better services at a lower price. Which is why the Black Monks tried to attack us. They are no more religious than my hat—the order is just a front for their monopoly of technology. We are breaking that monopoly and they don't like it."

"Very good. Yours sounds a fine plan and I wish you the best of luck. But I have a few things to do myself before I leave this sinkhole. To help you in your task of breaking the technological monopoly I would like to purchase some of your sleeping gas."

"Impossible. In fact it is impossible for us to aid you in any way. Nor are you leaving here. I've signalled for the guards. You will be held until the next League ship arrives. You know far too much about our operation to be permitted your freedom."

CHAPTER TWENTY-SEVEN

Even as this unacceptable bit of information was sinking into my brain, my body was launched across the desk. He should have remembered the bit about the Black Belt. My thumbs bit deep and he slumped. Even before his head bounced off the desk I had bounced off the floor and dived for the door. And none too soon—as I pushed the locking bolt home I saw that the handle above it was starting to turn.

"Now Jim, move fast," I advised myself, "before the alarm is spread. But first let me see what this two-faced academic has in his possession that may be of use."

There were files, papers, and books in the desk, nothing that would be of any value to me now. I sprayed it all about me on the floor as the banging started on the door. I didn't have much time. Next the prof. I tore his cloak open and ransacked his pockets. There was even less of interest here—other than a ring of keys. I shoved them into my own pocket; they would have to do for loot. Seizing up the gun I dived for the window just as something heavy hit the door with a shuddering thud. Two stories up and the courtyard below was paved with evil-looking cobblestones. I would break my legs if I jumped. I leaned out and was grateful for the second-rate Spiovente masons. There were large gaps between the stones of the outer wall. The door crashed and splintered as I climbed out of the window, thrust the gun through my belt in the small of my back—and began to climb down.

It was easy enough. I jumped the last bit, did a shoulder roll, which jammed the gun painfully into my spine, retrieved it, and stumbled around the corner of the building before anyone appeared in the window above. I was free!

Or was I? Instant gloom descended. Free in the middle of the enemy keep with all men's hands turned against me. Some big free.

"Yes, free!" I ground my teeth together arrogantly, braced my shoulders, and put a bold swagger into my walk. "Free as only a Stainless Steel Rat can be free! Just press on, Jim—and see if you can't find some locks to go with those keys in your pocket."

I always get the best advice from myself. I marched on through an archway that led into the large courtyard. There were armed men lolling about here and they completely ignored me. That wouldn't last long. As soon as the alarm was raised they would all be after my hide. Eyes straight ahead I walked towards a massive building on the far side. It had a single large gate set into the wall, with a smaller one next to it. As I came closer I saw that both had very modern locks set into them. Very informative. I was most interested in what was locked away here. Now all I had to do was find the right key.

Trying to look as though I belonged here I stopped before the smaller door and flipped through the keys. There must have been twenty of them. But the lock was a Bolger, that was obvious to my trained eye, so I fingered through them, looking for the familiar diamond shape.

"Hey, you, what you doing there?"

He was a big thug, dirty and unshaven and red of eye. He also had a long dagger thrust through his belt, the hilt of which he was tapping with his fingers.

"Unlocking this door, obviously," was my firm response. "Are you the one they sent to help me? Here, take this."

I handed him my gun. This bought me a number of seconds as he looked at the weapon, enough time for me to push one key into the lock. It didn't turn.

"No one sent me," he said, examining the gun, which distracted him nicely for a few seconds more. I couldn't be doing anything wrong if I had given him my only weapon, could I? I could almost see him thinking, slowly, moving his lips as he did. I interrupted the turgid flow of his thoughts.

"Well, since you are here you can help me . . ."

Ahh, the next key did the job, turning sweetly. The door opened and I turned about just as sweetly with my fingers pointed to jab. I caught the gun as he slid to the ground.

"Hey, you, stop!"

I ignored this rude command since I had not the slightest desire to see who was calling, but slipped through the door instead and slammed it shut behind me. Turned and looked around and felt a sharp pang of despair. There was no hope here. I was in an enormous chamber, badly lit by slits high in the wall. It was a garage for the steam cars. Five of them, lined up in a neat row.

It would be fine to escape in one of these, really wonderful. I had watched them in operation. First the fire had to be lit, then wood pushed in, steam raised. This usually took at least an hour. At that point, say, I could manage to do all this undisturbed, I had to open the door and clank to freedom at a slow walking pace. No way!

Or was there a way? As my eyes adjusted to the gloom I realized that these weren't the same kind of steam cars I had seen before—with their wooden wheels and iron tires. These had soft tires of some kind! Improved technology? Could it be offplanet technology disguised as antique wrecks?

I hurried over to the closest one and climbed up to the operator's seat. There were the familiar big control levers and wheels—but invisible from the ground was a padded driver's seat and familiar groundcar controls. This was more like it!

Slipping my gun under the seat, I slipped myself into it. A safety belt hung there, wise precaution, but not at the moment. I pushed it aside as I leaned forward to examine the controls. Motor switch, gear selector, speedometer—as well as some unfamiliar dials and controls. A banging on the door convinced me I should make a detailed study later. I reached out and turned on the motor. Nothing happened.

Or rather something totally unexpected happened. The motor didn't start but a girl's voice did, speaking in my ear.

"Do not attempt to start this vehicle without wearing your seatbelt."

"Seatbelt, right, thank you." I clicked it on and turned the switch again.

"The engine will start only with the gear selector in neutral."

The banging on the door was even louder. I cursed as I pushed the selector, trying to find the right location in the dim light. The door crashed and splintered. There, now the switch again.

The motor turned over. I pushed the drive into forward. And the voice spoke.

"Do not attempt to drive with your handbrake on."

I was cursing louder now, the small door broke down and crashed to the floor, pistons began to move around me while steam spurted and hissed. Someone shouted and the men in the door started towards me.

The thing shuddered and lumbered forward.

This was more like it! Covered in steel plates and fake ironmongery, it must be incredibly heavy. There was a simple way to find out. I floored the accelerator, twisted the wheel—and pointed the hulk straight at the large door.

It was beautiful. The steam roared and spurted as I accelerated. Hitting the door dead center with a crash that deafened me. But my noble steed never slowed a fraction. Wood screeched and tore and fell away as I plowed through in a cloud of flying timber. I had a quick view of fleeing pedestrians before I had to duck down to prevent myself from being beheaded by a board. It scratched and clumped and fell away. I sat up and smiled with pleasure.

What a wonderful sight. Soldiers were fleeing in all directions, dashing for cover. I swung the wheel and spun in a tight circle looking for the way out. A bullet clanged into the steel plating and whined away. There the gate was—dead ahead. I floored the accelerator this time, then found the whistle cord. It screamed and steam spurted and I picked up speed.

And none too soon, either. Someone had kept his head and was trying to lift the drawbridge. Two men had plugged the handle into the clumsy winch and were turning it furiously; chains clanked and tightened. I headed for the center of the gate, whistle screeching, bullets beginning to spang on the steel around me. I crouched down and kept the pedal on the floor. I was going to have only one chance.

The drawbridge was rising, slowly and steadily, cutting off my escape, getting larger and larger before me. It was up ten, twenty, thirty degrees. I was not going to make it.

We hit with a jar that would have thrown me out if the safety belt hadn't been locked. Thank you, voice. The front wheels rose up onto the drawbridge, higher and higher, until the nose of the car was pointing into the air. If it climbed any higher it would be flipped onto its back.

Which was a chance that I would just have to take. The gears growled and my transport of delight bucked and chuntered—and I heard a squealing and snapping.

Then the whole thing pitched forward. The chains lifting the drawbridge had torn from their moorings under the massive weight of my car. The nose fell and we hit with a crash that almost stunned me.

But my foot was still down and the wheels were still turning. The vehicle shot forward—straight for the water. I twisted the steering wheel, straightened it, then tore across the bridge and onto the road. Faster and faster, up the hill and around the bend—then let up on the speed before we overturned on the ruts. I was safe and away.

"Jim," I advised myself, gasping for breath. "Try not to do that again if you can avoid it."

I looked back, but there was no one following me. But there would be, soon, if not on foot then in one of the other fake steam cars. I put my foot back down and kept my mouth clamped shut so it didn't clack and splinter my teeth when we hit the bumps.

There was a long hill that slowed my pace. Even with the accelerator on the floor we crawled because of the gearing and the weight of the beast. I used the opportunity to check the charge—batteries full! They had better be because I had no way of recharging them once they ran down. Above the clatter and rumble I heard a thin and distant whistle and flashed a quick look over my shoulder. There they were! Two of the machines, hot on my tail.

There was no way they were going to catch me. Off the road these things would be useless and mired down—and there was only one road leading to Dimonte's keep. I was on it and headed that way and I was going to keep them behind me all the way.

Except that if I led them there they would know who had pinched their wagon and would come after it with the gas bombs. No good. I looked back and saw that they were gaining—but they soon slowed to my pace when they reached the bottom of the hill. I went over the top and my speed picked up—as did the jarring. I hoped that they had built the thing to withstand this kind of beating. Then the crossroad loomed up ahead, with peasants leaping out of my way, and there was the left turning that would take me to Capo Dimonte. I streamed right through it. I didn't know this road at all so all I could do was go on and keep my fingers crossed.

Something had to be done—and fairly soon. Even if I stayed ahead of them all day I would run the battery flat and that would be that. Think, Jim, cudgel the old brain cells.

Opportunity presented itself around the next bend. A rough farm track led off through a field and down to a stream. Then, like all good ideas, this one appeared fullblown in my forebrain, complete in every detail.

Without hesitation I turned the wheel and trundled down into the meadow. Going slower and slower as I felt my wheels sink into the soft soil. If I got mired now it was the end. Or at least the end of my mastery of this crate—

which I would dearly like to keep for awhile. Carry on, Jim, but carefully.

At the lowest speed, in the lowest gear, I ground forward until the front wheels were in the stream. They were sinking mushily into the mud as I stopped—then carefully began to back out. Looking over my shoulder, keeping in the ruts I had made on the way down. Reversing out of the field until I was safely back on the road. As I shifted gears I permitted myself a quick glimpse of my work. Perfect! The ruts led straight down to the water and on into it.

On the road behind me I heard a not-too-distant whistle. I stood on the throttle and accelerated around the bend until I was hidden by the trees. Stopped, killed the engine, slammed on the brakes, and jumped down.

This was going to be the dangerous part. I had to convince them to follow the tracks. If they didn't believe me, I had little chance of escape. But it was a risk that had to be taken.

As I ran I pulled off my jacket, staggering as I pulled my arms free and turned it inside out. I draped it over my shoulders, tied the arms in front, then bent to roll up my trouser legs. Not much of a disguise, but it would have to do. Hopefully the drivers had not had a good look at me—if they had seen me at all.

I stood by the spot where I had turned and had just enough time to seize up some dirt and rub it into my face as the first pseudo steam car clanked around the bend.

They slowed as I stepped into the road and pointed. And shouted.

"He went that-away!"

The driver and the gunmen turned to look at the field and stared at the tracks. The vehicle slowed to a stop.

"Splashed right into the water and kept on going through the field. Feller a friend of yours?"

This was the moment of truth. It stretched taut, longer and longer as the second vehicle came up and slowed to a stop as well. What if they questioned me—even looked closely at me? I wanted to run—but if I did, that would be a giveaway.

"Follow him!" someone called out, and the driver twisted his wheel and turned towards the field.

I slipped back into the trees and watched with great interest. It was beautiful. I felt proud of myself; yes, I did. I am not ashamed to admit it. When a painter creates a masterpiece he knows it and does not attempt to diminuate its importance by false modesty.

This was a masterpiece. The first car rattled down through the field, bobbing and bouncing, and hit the water with an immense splash. It was going so fast that its rear wheels actually reached the stream before it slowed to a stop. And began to slowly sink into the soft mud. It went down to its hubs before it stopped.

There was much shouting and swearing at that—and best of all someone rooted out a chain and connected the two cars. Wonderful. The second one spun its wheels and churned the field until it too was safely mired. I clapped appreciatively and strolled back to my own car.

I shouldn't have done it, I know. But there are times when one just cannot resist showing off. I sat down, snapped on my belt, started the motor, moved the car carefully forward and back until I had turned about. Then accelerated back down the road.

And as I passed the turnoff I pulled down hard on the whistle. It screeched loudly and every head turned, every eye was on me. I waved and smiled. Then the trees were in the way and the beautiful vision vanished from sight.

CHAPTER TWENTY-EIGHT

It was a victory ride. I laughed aloud, sang, and blew the whistle with joy. When this first enthusiasm had died down I moved the queen on my mental chessboard and considered what came next. The hissing of steam and clanking of machinery was distracting and I examined the controls until I found the switch that turned the special effects off. The steam was being boiled to order and the sounds were just a recording. I threw the switch and rode on in peace towards Capo Dimonte's keep. It was late afternoon before I reached it—and by that time my plans were complete.

When I came around the last bend in the road and turned onto the causeway I had full sound and steam effects going again. I trundled slowly down in clear sight of the guards. They had the partially repaired drawbridge raised long before I reached it, and peered out suspiciously at me as I stopped before the gap.

"Don't shoot! Me friend!" I called out. "Member of your army and a close associate of the Capo Dimonte. Send for him at once for I know he wants to see his new steam cart."

He did indeed. As soon as the drawbridge was lowered he strode across it and looked up at me.

"Where did you get this?" he asked.

"Stole it. Climb aboard and let me show you some interesting things."

"Where is the sleeping gas?" he asked as he climbed the rungs.

"I didn't bother with it. With this cart I have developed an even better and more foolproof plan. This is no ordinary steam cart, as I hope you have noticed. It is a new and improved model with some interesting additions that will capture your attention. . . ."

"You idiot! What are you talking about?" He slipped his sword up and down in its scabbard; such a quick temper.

"I will demonstrate, your caponess, since one action speaks louder than a thousand words. I also suggest that you sit there and strap that belt about you as I have done. This demonstration, I guarantee, will impress you."

If not impressed already, he was at least curious. He strapped in and I backed the length of the causeway to the shore. Going slowly with all attendant wheezing and clanking. I stopped the car and turned to him.

"What about the speed of this thing? What you are used to?"

"Speed? You mean how fast it moves? This is an excellent yoke and goes with greater alacrity than my own."

"You have seen nothing yet, capo. First—notice this."

I turned off the sound and steam and he nodded with understanding. "You have banked its fires and it rests and does not move."

"Quite the opposite. I have simply silenced it so no one can hear its approach. It is raring to go—and go it will. After you answer one question. If this cart belonged to an enemy and it appeared here—would your soldiers have time to raise the drawbridge before it reached them?"

He snorted with derision. "What sort of fool do you take me for with questions like that? Before a cart could crawl its way there the drawbridge could be raised and lowered more than once."

"Really? Then hold on and see what this baby can do."

I floored the accelerator and the thing shot forward in almost perfect silence. There was the hum of the motor, the rustle of the tires on the smooth stone. Faster and faster towards the gate, which expanded before us with frightening speed. The guards who were standing there dived aside just in time as we hit the rough boards of the repaired wooden drawbridge with a crash, bounced, and rocked through the gate.

And shuddered to a halt inside the keep. The capo sat there with round eyes, gasping, then struggled to get his sword free.

"Assassin! Your attempt to kill me has failed. . . ."

"Capo, listen, it was a demonstration. Of how I am going to get you and your soldiers through the gate of Capo Doccia's keep. Right through the open gate into the courtyard where you can kill, loot, murder, torture, maim, destroy . . ."

This got his attention. The sword slid back into its scabbard and his eyes unfocused as they looked at the wonders I had summoned up for him.

"Right," he said, blinking rapidly and coming back to the present. "You have an interesting idea here, soldier, and I want to hear more about it. Over a flagon of wine—for that ride was something I have never experienced before."

"I obey. But let me first get this cart hidden and out of sight so it cannot be observed. The attack will only succeed if there is complete surprise."

"In that you are correct. Put it in the barn and I will post guards over it."

The wine he gave me was a good cut above the acid the troops were issued and I sipped it with pleasure. But not too much for I was going to need a clear head if the game were to proceed as planned. I had to find reasons that would make sense to him, to convince him to get cracking with his war plans at once. Because if we didn't move quickly Prof. Lustig would be swarming over us with his gas bombs. I am sure he was most unhappy about my pinching his buggy. And there were not that many keeps in the area where it could be hidden. It was time for action. I slid out a rook along a mental rank and spoke.

"The keep of the foul Capo Doccia is no more than a five-hour walk from here—is that correct?"

"Five hours, four-hour forced march."

"Good. Then consider this. He attacked you while you were away with the greater part of your army. His troops did great injury to the drawbridge and the fabric of the keep itself. Before you venture out to launch an attack you must have the drawbridge repaired, hire more soldiers perhaps. So when you begin your next campaign no advantage can be taken of your absence. Is that correct?"

He slurped his wine and glared at me over the rim. "Yes, damn and blast your head, I suppose it is. Prudence, my officers always consul prudence when I want to behead that creature, rip out his entrails, flay him alive . . ."

"And you shall, yes indeed, fine things lurk in your future. And unlike your other advisers I do not consul caution. I think that fiend in human guise should be attacked—and at once!"

This appealed to him all right and I could see that I had his undivided attention as I explained my plan.

"Leave the keep here just as it is—and take all your men. If everything goes as planned you will have troops back here long before anyone knows we have gone. We march at midnight, silent as vengeful spirits, to be in positions of concealment at dawn, as close to Capo Doccia's keep as is possible. I know just the spot. When the drawbridge is opened at dawn I shall use your new machine to see that it stays open. Your troops attack, take the keep by surprise—and the day is won. As soon as you have captured the keep you can send a strong force back here."

"It could happen that way. But how do you plan to stop them closing the drawbridge?"

As I told him the wicked grin spread across his face and he whooped with joy.

"Do it!" he shouted, "and I shall make you rich for life. With Doccia's groats of course, after I loot his treasury."

"You are kindness itself to your humble servant. May I then suggest that all in the keep be persuaded to rest, for it will be a long night?"

"Yes, that will be done. The orders will be issued."

After that I slipped away. Other than my natural concern for the tired bodies of my comrades I had other reasons for wishing all of them in their beds. I had a few important tasks to perform before I could get any rest myself.

"Tools," I told Dreng when I had rousted him out. "Files, hammers, anything like that. Where would I find them here?"

He shoved a finger deep into his matted hair and scratched hard in thought. I resisted the urge to reach out and shake him and waited instead until the slow processes had crawled to a finish. Perhaps the fingernail rasping on skull helped his sluggish synapses to function. It would be best not to interfere with an established practice. Eventually he spoke.

"I don't have any tools."

"I know, dear boy." I could hear my teeth grate together and forced myself to keep control. "You don't have tools, but someone here must. Who would that be?"

"Blacksmith," he said proudly. "The blacksmith always has tools."

"Good lad. Now, would you kindly lead the way to this blacksmith?"

The individual in question was sooty and hairy and in a foul mood, sour wine strong on his breath.

"Hiss off, runt. No one touches Grundge's tools, no one."

Runt indeed! I did not have to force the snarl and growl. "Listen you filthy piece of flab—those are the capo's tools, not your tools. And the capo sent me for them. Now either I take them now or my knave goes to bring the capo here. Shall I do that?"

He closed his fists and growled, then hesitated. Like everyone else, he had seen me drive the capo into the keep and knew I was his confidant. He couldn't take any chances on crossing his boss. He began to bob up and down bowing and scraping.

"Certainly, master. Grundge knows his place. Tools, sure, take tools. Over here, whatever you want."

I pushed past his sweaty form to the dismal display of primitive devices. Pathetic! I kicked through the pile until I found a file, hammer, and clumsy metal snips that would have to do. I pushed them towards Dreng.

"Take these. And you, Grundge, can crawl over in the morning to the barn and get them back."

Dreng followed after me, then gaped up in awe at the steam cart.

"Close your mouth before you catch some flies," I told him, seizing the tools. "What I'll need next is a stout bag or sack of some kind, about this big. Scout one out and bring it to me here. Then get to bed because you will not be getting much sleep tonight."

With proper tools I could have done the job in no time at all. But I had a feeling that tolerances wouldn't be that exact here and as long as I was close to the model it would be all right. The metal siding next to the driver's seat was roughly the thickness of the wooden key. I cut and filed and hacked a portion of it into shape. It would have to do.

Dreng—and hopefully everyone else—was now asleep and I could begin Operation Great-groat. With the key in my pocket, the bag tucked into my waist, silent as a shadow—I hoped—I made way into the depths of the keep. I had memorized The Bishop's map and his spirit must have been watching after me for I found the treasury without being seen. I slipped the key into the lock, crossed the fingers of my free hand, and turned.

With a metallic screech it clanked open. My heart did its usual pounding-in-chest routine while I stood rooted there. The noise must have been heard.

But it hadn't been. The door creaked slightly when I opened it and then I was inside the vault and easing it shut behind me.

It was beautiful. High, barred windows let in enough light so I could see the big chests against the far wall. I had done my fiscal research well, getting a look at a braggard's store of groats, so I knew just what to look for.

The first chest was stuffed with brass groats, my fingers could distinguish their thick forms in the darkness. In logical progression I found silver groats in the next chest and I shoveled my bag half full of them. As I did this I saw a smaller chest tucked in behind this one. I smiled into the darkness as I groped and felt the angled shapes within. Golden groats—and lots of them. This was going to be a very successful heist after all. I only stopped shoveling when the bag became too heavy. Beware of greed. With this bit of advice to myself I threw it over my shoulder and let myself out just the way I had come in.

There were guards in the courtyard but they never saw me as I slipped into the barn. I turned on the instrument lights of the car, which provided more than enough illumination for me to see by. I opened the storage locker below and put the money bag into place. As I closed it I was overwhelmed by a great sensation of relief. In my mind's eye I slid out another rook to join the first. The chess game was going as planned and mate was clearly visible ahead.

"Now, Jim," I advised. "Get your head down and get some sleep. Tomorrow is going to be an exceedingly busy day."

CHAPTER TWENTY-NINE

I muttered and slapped and rolled over but the irritation persisted. Eventually I blinked my grimy eyes open and growled up at Dreng who was shaking my shoulder. He stepped away in fear.

"Do not beat me, master—I am only doing as you instructed. It is time to waken for the troops are assembling now in the courtyard."

I growled something incoherent and this turned into a cough. When I did this a cup appeared before me and I drank deep of the cool water, then dropped back onto the bunk. Not for the first time did I approve of the knave system. But I was beat, bushed, fatigued. Even the stamina of youth can be sapped by adversity. I shook my head rapidly, then sat up on my elbows, angry at myself for the brief moment of self-pity.

"Go, good Dreng," I ordered, "and find me food to nourish my hungry cells. And some drink as well since alcohol is the only stimulant these premises seem to have."

I splashed cold water over my head in the courtyard, gasping and spluttering. As I wiped my face dry I saw in the clear starlight the ranks of soldiers being drawn up as the ammunition was being issued. The great adventure was about to begin. Dreng was waiting when I returned. I sat on my bunk and ate a pretty repellent breakfast of fried dinglebeans washed down by the destructive wine. I talked between gruesome mouthfuls because this was the last private moment I would have with my knave.

"Dreng, your military career is about to end."

"Don't kill me, master!"

"Military career, idiot—not your life. Tonight is your last night of service and in the morn you will be off home with your pay. Where does your old dad hide his money?"

"We are too poor to have any groats."

"I am sure of that. But *if* he had any—where would he put it?"

This was a complicated thought and he puzzled over it while I chewed and swallowed. He finally spoke.

"Bury it under the hearth! I remember he did that once. Everyone buries their money under the fire; that way it can't be found."

"Great. That way it certainly can be found. You have got to do better than that with your fortune."

"Dreng has no fortune."

"Dreng will have one before the sun rises. I'm paying you off. Go home and find two trees near your home. Stretch a rope between them. Then dig a hole exactly halfway along the rope. Bury the money there—where you can find it when you need it. And only take out a few coins at a time. Do you have that?"

He nodded enthusiastically. "Two trees, halfway. I never heard of anything like that before!"

"An earth-shaking concept, I know," I sighed. There certainly was a lot that he hadn't heard about. "Let's go. I want you to be stoker on my chariot of fire."

I staggered to my feet and led the way to the barn. Now that the troops were lined up and ready the officers were finally appearing, scratching and yawning, with the capo at their head. I didn't have much time. Dreng climbed into the car behind me and squealed with fear when I turned on the instrument lights.

"Demonic illumination! Spirit lights! Sure sign of death!"

He clutched at his chest and looked ready to expire until I gave him a good shaking. "Batteries!" I shouted. "The gift of science denied to this dumb world. Now, stop quaking and open your bag."

All thoughts of death vanished and his eyes stuck out like boiled eggs as I shoveled silver and gold groats into his leather bag. This was a fortune that would change his entire life for the better, so at least I was accomplishing one good deed by my presence here.

"What are you doing up there?"

It was Capo Dimonte, glaring up suspiciously from below.

"Just stoking the engines, excellency."

"Kick that knave out of the way, I'm coming up."

I waved the goggle-eyed Dreng to the back of the car as the capo climbed aboard.

"You favor me with your presence, capo."

"Damned right. I ride while the troops walk. Now, move this thing out."

The scouts had already gone on ahead when we rumbled across the drawbridge and onto the causeway. The main body of troops came behind us, a certain eagerness in their step despite the hour. All of them had lost valuables and possessions—even knaves—during the raid. All were eager for revenge and theft.

"The Capo Doccia must be taken alive," Capo Dimonte suddenly said. I started to answer until I realized that he was talking only to himself. "Tied and left helpless, brought back to the keep. First a little flaying, just enough skin to make a hatband. Then maybe blinding. No—not right away—he must see what is happening to him. . . ."

There was more like this, but I tuned it out. I had thoughts of my own—and even some regrets. When The Bishop had been killed, my anger had overwhelmed all of the clear thinking that I should have been doing. All excuses vanished now—I was embarking on this expedition solely for revenge. And I couldn't claim to be doing it in The Bishop's memory because he would have been seriously opposed to violent action of this kind. But it was too late now to turn back. The campaign had been launched and we were well on our way.

"Stop this thing!" the capo ordered suddenly, and I hit the brakes.

There was a dark knot of men waiting on the road ahead—our advanced scouts. The capo climbed to the ground and I leaned out to see what was happening. They were leading a man who had his arms bound behind him.

"What happened?" the capo asked.

"Found him watching the road, excellency. Caught him before he could get away."

"Who is he?"

"Soldier, name of Palec. I know him, served with him in the southern campaign."

The capo walked up to the prisoner and shoved his face close to the other's and snarled. "I have you, Palec. Tied and bound."

"Aye."

"Are you the Capo Doccia's man?"

"Aye, I serve under him. I took his groat."

"You've spent that on wine a long time ago. Will you serve with me and take my groat?"

"Aye."

"Release him. Barkus—a silver groat for this man."

These mercenaries fought well, but they also changed sides easily enough. Why not? They had no stakes in any of the capos' quarrels. Once Palec had accepted the coin they gave him his weapons back.

"Speak, Palec," the capo ordered. "You are my loyal servant now, who has taken my groat. But you used to serve with Capo Doccia. Tell me what he plans."

"Aye. No secret there. He knows that your army is intact and you will be coming after him as soon as you can. Some of us have been sent out to watch the roads, but he doesn't think that you will march for some time yet. He stays drunk, that's a sign he's not expecting a fight."

"I'll put a sword through his belly, let out the wine and guts!" The capo cut off his dreaming with an effort and forced himself back to the present. "What about his troops? Will they fight?"

"Aye, they've just been paid. But they have little love for him and will change sides as soon as the battle is lost."

"Better and better. Fall in with the ranks, scouts out ahead, start this machine."

The last was directed at me as he climbed back to his seat. I kicked it into gear and the advance continued again. There were no more interruptions and we proceeded, with hourly rest breaks, towards the enemy keep. It was well before dawn when we came to the scouts waiting on the road. This was the spot I had picked. The keep of Capo Doccia was around the next bend.

"I will post your lookout now," the capo said.

"Agreed. My knave here will show them the exact spot where they are to stay hidden, in sight of the gate." I waited until he was out of earshot before I whispered my instructions to Dreng.

"Take your bag and everything you possess with you—because you are not coming back."

"I do not understand, master. . . ."

"You will if you shut up and listen instead of talking. Lead the soldiers to the bushes where we hid, when we were getting ready to rescue The Bishop. You do remember the place?"

"It is past the burnt tree over the hedge and . . ."

"Great, great—but I don't need the description. Take the soldiers as I said, show them where to hide, then lie close beside them. Soon after dawn things are going to get very, very busy. At that time you will do nothing, understand that—don't speak, just nod."

He did. "Fine. You just remain there when everyone rushes off. As soon as they are gone and no one is looking at you—slip away. Back into the woods and get to your home and lay low until the excitement is over. Then count your money and live happily ever after."

"Then—I will no longer be your knave?"

"Right. Discharged from the army with honor."

He dropped to his knees and seized my hand, but before he could say anything I touched my finger to his lips.

"You were a good knave. Now be a good civilian. Move!"

I watched him leave until he was swallowed up in the darkness. Dumb—but loyal. And the only friend that I had on this rundown planet. The only one that I wanted! Now that The Bishop . . ."

This morbid turn of thought was happily interrupted by the capo who clambered back to his seat. He was followed by armed soldiers until the upperworks of the car were packed solid with them. The capo squinted up at the sky.

"There is the first light. It will be dawn soon. Then it will begin."

After that we could only wait. The tension so thick in the air that it was hard to breathe. Blurred faces began to emerge from the darkness, all of them set in the same grim expression.

I concentrated on what was happening around the bend, remembering the way it had been when Dreng and I had lain out there. Watching and waiting. The locked gate of the keep, the drawbridge up, all of it growing clearer as the sun rose. Smoke from cooking fires drifting up from behind the thick walls. Then the stirring of the soldiery, changing of the guards. At last the gate unlocked, the drawbridge lowered. Then what? Would they keep to the same routine? If they did not our force would soon be discovered. . . .

"The signal!" the capo said as he crashed his elbow hard into my ribs.

He didn't have to. I had seen the soldier wave the instant that he had appeared. My foot was already jammed down on the accelerator and we were picking up speed. Around the bend in the road, bouncing and swaying on the ruts, then straight ahead towards the entrance to the keep.

The guards looked up and gaped as we shot towards them. The slaves pulling the cart stared too, frozen and unmoving.

Then the shouting started. The drawbridge creaked as they tried to raise it, but the cart and slaves were still on it. There were kicks and screamed orders and every second of wasted time brought us that much closer. They finally started to drag the cart back through the gate—but it was too late.

We were upon them. The front wheels hit the drawbridge and we bounced into the air, coming down with a splintering crash. I stood on the brakes as we plowed into the cart. Slaves and guards were diving into the moat to escape destruction as we skidded, with locked wheels, right into the mouth of the gate.

"For Capo Dimonte, for groats, and for God!" The capo shouted as he leapt to the attack.

The others leapt with him, walking over my back as I crouched down, jumping onto the drawbridge then through the gate.

There was screaming and shouting, the banging of guns. From behind me a growing roar of voices from the rest of the attacking army. I could see that the capo and his men were fighting inside the gate and had captured the drawbridge mechanism from the soldiers who were trying to raise it. Raising it had of course been impossible because of the great weight of the car resting on it. That had been the beauty and simplicity of my plan. Once I had arrived the drawbridge had to stay down. Only now did I trundle forward so that the rest of the troops had a clear way to the gate.

The battle for the keep of Capo Doccia was joined.

CHAPTER THIRTY

This was a surprise attack that really had been a surprise. Our invading forces were pouring across the drawbridge and into the keep even as Capo Doccia's soldiers were emerging from their quarters. The guards on the wall fought fiercely, but they were outnumbered.

To add to the confusion I turned on the steamer sound effects and hung onto the whistle as I charged at the defenders who were trying to group up ahead. A few shots were fired at me, but most of the soldiers dived aside and ran. I screeched about and saw that the battle was going very well indeed.

The defenders on the walls were raising their hands in surrender. Being outnumbered from the start, and having little reason to fight for the capo as we had been told, they were eager to save their lives. Near the inner gate a group of officers were showing more spirit and a fierce battle was going on there. But one by one they were cut down or clubbed into submission. Two of them fled for the building but found the heavy door slammed in their faces.

"Bring torches!" the Capo Dimonte shouted. "We'll smoke the buggers out!"

The battle had ended as swiftly as it had begun. The gate, walls and courtyard were in our hands. Huddled corpses showed the ferocity of the brief engagement. Slaves shivered in fear against the walls while the soldiers who had surrendered were being marched off. Only the central building remained in the hands of the defenders. Capo Dimonte knew exactly what to do about this. He waved a smoking torch over his head and called out loudly.

"All right, Doccia, you fat-bellied toad, this is your end. Come out and fight like a man you worm, or I'll burn you out. And burn alive every man, woman, child, dog, rat, pigeon who stays in there with you. Come out and fight, you ugly piece of vermin—or remain and be cooked like a roast!"

A gun fired from inside and a bullet spanged from the cobbles at the capo's feet. He waved his red-drenched sword and a blast of gunfire roared out as our troops fired en masse. Bullets zinged from the stonework, thudded into the sealed door, and whistled in through the windows. When the firing stopped, shrill screaming could be heard from inside the building.

"One warning only!" Capo Dimonte called out. "I do not war on women or on good soldiers who surrender. Lay down your arms and you will go free. Resist and you will be burned alive. There is only one I want—that pig, Doccia. Hear that, Doccia, you lout, swine, worm . . ."

And more, once he warmed to the subject. The torch crackled and smoked and there was the sound of muffled shouting and scuffling from inside the building.

Then the door burst open and Capo Doccia came rolling down the steps end over end. He was barefooted, half-dressed—but he was holding his sword.

At the sight of his enemy Capo Dimonte lost whatever little remaining cool he had left. He howled with anger and rushed forward. Doccia climbed to his feet, blood on his face, and raised his sword in defense.

It was a sight to watch—and everyone did. There was an undeclared truce as the two leaders battled. The soldiers lowered their weapons and faces appeared at all of the windows above them. I climbed out of my seat and stood on the front of the car, where I had a perfect view of the combatants.

They were well-matched, both in anger and ability. Dimonte's sword crashed down on Doccia's raised blade. He did a neat parry, then thrust—but Dimonte had moved back. After that it was steel on steel, punctuated by grunted curses.

Back and forth across the cobbles they went, slashing away as if their lives depended on it. Which, of course, they did. It was pretty primitive saber work, slash and parry, but it certainly was energetic. A cry went up as Dimonte drew first blood—a cut on Doccia's side that quickly stained his shirt.

This was the beginning of the end. Dimonte was stronger and angrier, high on victory. If Doccia had been drinking as much as we had been told he was also fighting a hangover as well as his enemy. Dimonte began pressing harder and harder, slashing remorselessly, pushing the other capo relentlessly across the courtyard. Until his back was to the wall of the building and he could retreat no more. Dimonte beat down the other's guard, hammered him on the jaw with the hilt of his sword—then disarmed Capo Doccia with a savage twist of his blade.

All of his plans for sadistic torture were washed away in the passion of his anger. He drew the blade back—then slashed out.

It was not an attractive sight as the sharp steel tore across Doccia's throat. It sickened me and I turned away. Just as the shadow darkened the sun.

One person looked up, then another—and there was a gasp. I looked too. Only unlike the rest of them I knew exactly what I was looking at.

The immense shining form of a D-class spacer that was equipped with atmospheric G-lift. Tonnes of ship drifting light as a feather over the courtyard. Coming to an effortless stop. Hanging there over our heads in silent menace.

I turned and dived for the controls. There was no time to escape, no way to escape. I was scratching at the storage compartment as the first silvery spheres fell free of the ship. I gave them one horrified glance—then took a deep breath and held it as I pulled the compartment door open and plunged my arm inside. Grabbing up the leather bag as I sat back onto the driver's seat.

All around me the spheres were hitting and bursting, releasing their loads of gas. I dropped the bag onto my lap as the first soldiers crumpled and fell. My fingers fumbled at the seat belt, lengthening it, as Capo Dimonte tottered then fell forward onto his dead enemy's body.

There was a stinging in my nostrils as I snapped the belt buckle over the bag, sealing it against me. And that was all that I could possibly do.

My lungs were beginning to hurt as I took a last, long look around the courtyard. I had the strong feeling that it would also be my last sight of the fair world of Spiovente.

"Good riddance!" I shouted at the now silent forms, blasting the breath from my lungs. Then breathed in. . . .

I was conscious, I knew that. I could feel something soft under my back and there was a light burning down on my closed eyelids. I was afraid to open them—remembering the blasting headache that had accompanied the last gassing. With this thought I cringed and moved my head.

And felt nothing. Emboldened by this tiny experiment, I let one eye open a crack. Still nothing. I blinked in the strong light but there was no pain, no pain at all.

"A different gas, thank you kindly," I said to no one in particular as I opened my eyes wide.

A small room, curved metal walls, a narrow bunk under me. Even if my last sight had not been of the hovering spacer, I should have been able to figure this one out. They had taken me aboard. But where were all my groats? I looked around rapidly, but they were certainly not in sight. The rapid movements of my head had brought on an attack of dizziness so that I fell back onto the bunk and groaned in loud self-pity.

"Drink this. It will eliminate the symptoms of the gas."

I snapped my eyes open again and looked at the big man who was just closing the door behind him. He was in uniform of some kind, with plenty of gold buttons and stripes, the sort of thing much favored by the military. He was holding out a plastic beaker which I seized gingerly and sniffed.

"We had plenty of time to poison or kill you while you were unconscious," he said. A sound argument. I drained the bitter liquid and instantly felt better.

"You have stolen my money," I said just as he was beginning to speak.

"Your money is safe—"

"It will be safe only when it is in my hands. As it was when you found me, strapped to my body. Whoever took it is a thief."

"Don't talk to me of thievery!" he snapped. "You probably stole it yourself."

"Prove it! I say I worked hard for that money and I don't intend to have it stolen for the space-war widows pension scheme. . . ."

"That is enough. I did not come here to talk about your miserable groats. They will be placed on deposit in the galactic bank. . . ."

"At what rate of exchange? And what kind of interest will it earn?"

He was coldly angry now. "That's enough. You are in deep trouble—and you have a lot of explaining to do. Professor Lustig tells me that your name is Jim. What is your entire name and where do you come from?"

"My name is Jim Nixon and I am from Venia."

"We will get nowhere if you persist in lying. Your name is James diGriz and you are an escaped convict from Bit O' Heaven."

Well, as you can imagine, I did some rapid blinking at this information. Whoever this lad was he had one hell of an intelligence network. I could see that I was no longer playing the amateur team of the professors. They had called in the pros. And he had thrown me this curve ball to catch me off-balance, get me rattled, get me to talk freely. Except I did not work that way. I shifted mental gears, sat up in the bed so I could see him eye to eye, and spoke calmly.

"We have not been introduced."

The anger was gone now and he was as calm as I was. He turned and pressed a button on the wall that unfolded a metal chair. He sat down on it and crossed his legs.

"Captain Varod of the League Navy. Specializing in planetary mop-up details. Are you ready to answer questions?"

"Yes—if you will trade me one for one. Where are we?"

"About thirteen lightyears out of Spiovente, you'll be happy to hear."

"I am."

"My turn. How did you get to that planet?"

"Aboard a Venian freighter that was smuggling weapons to the now deceased Capo Doccia."

That got his attention all right. He leaned forward eagerly as he spoke. "Who was the captain of the freighter?"

"You are out of turn. What are you going to do with me?"

"You are an escaped prisoner and will be returned to Bit O' Heaven to serve out your prison sentence."

"Really?" I smiled insincerely. "Now I will be happy to answer your question—except I have completely forgotten the captain's name. Would you care to torture me?"

"Don't play games, Jim. You are in deep trouble. Cooperate and I will do what I can for you."

"Good. I remember the name and you put me down on a neutral planet and we call it quits."

"That is impossible. Records are kept and I am an officer of the law. I must return you to Bit O' Heaven."

"Thanks. I just got terminal amnesia. Before you leave would you tell me what is going to happen to Spiovente?"

He sat back in the chair with no intention at all of leaving.

"The first thing that will happen will be the termination of Lustig's disastrous intervention. We were forced into that by the Intergalactic Applied Socioeconomics Association. They manage to raise sufficient funds to put into effect some of their theories. A number of planets financed them and it was easier to let them make idiots of themselves than to try and stop them."

"And they have done that now?"

"Completely. They have all been shipped out and were very happy to go. Having political and economic theories is one thing. But applying them to harsh reality can be a traumatic experience. This has been done in the past— and always with disastrous results. We know none of the details now, they are lost in the mists of time, but there was an insane doctrine called Monetarism that is reputed to have destroyed whole cultures, entire planets. Now another experiment has gone astray, so the specialists will move in as they should have done in the first place."

"Invasion?"

"You have been watching to much tri-D. War is forbidden and you should know better than to suggest that. We have people who will work within the existing society of Spiovente. Probably with this Capo Dimonte, since he has just doubled his domain. He will be aided and encouraged to grow in power, to annex more and more territory."

"And kill more and more people!"

"No, we will see to that. Very soon he will not be able to rule without aid and our bureaucrats are waiting to help him. Centralized government . . ."

"The growth of the judiciary, taxes, I know the drill. You sound just like Lustig."

"Not quite. Our techniques are proven—and they work. Within one generation, two at the most, Spiovente will be welcomed into the family of civilized planets."

"Congratulations. Now, please leave so I can sit and brood about my future incarceration."

"And you still won't tell me the name of the gunrunner? He could continue in his smuggling operations—and you would be responsible for more deaths."

I would be too. Was I responsible for the dead in the courtyard of the keep as well? The attack had been my idea. But Dimonte would have attacked in any case and there could have been even more dead. The acceptance of responsibility was not done easily. Captain Varod must have been reading my mind.

"Do you have a sense of responsibility?" he asked.

Good question. He was a shrewd old boy.

"Yes, I do. I believe in life and the sanctity of life and I do not believe in killing. Each of us has only one go at life and I don't want to be responsible for cutting short anyone else's. I think I have made some mistakes and I hope I have learned by them. The name of the gunrunner is Captain Ga . . ."

"Garth," he said. "We know him and have been watching him. He has made his last voyage."

My thoughts spun rapidly. "Then why ask me if you knew all along?"

"For your sake, Jim, nobody else's. I told you that our job was rehabilitation. You have made an important decision and I believe that you will be a better individual for it. Good luck in the future." He stood to leave.

"Thanks a lot. I'll remember your words when I am cracking boulders on the rock pile."

He stood in the open door and smiled back at me. "I am in the justice business on a very large scale. And, in truth, I don't believe in prisons and incarceration for failed bank robbery. You are destined for better things than that. Therefore I am having you returned to prison. You will be transferred to another ship, on another planet, where you will be locked away until it arrives."

He went out, then turned back for just an instant. "Taking into consideration what you have told me, I am forgetting that you still have a lockpick in the sole of your shoe."

Then he was gone for good. I stared at the closed door and suddenly burst out laughing. It was going to be a good universe after all, filled with good things to be appropriated in a manner only possible to one who knew his trade. And I knew mine!

"Thank you, Bishop, thanks for everything. You have done it, guided me and taught me. Because of you—a Stainless Steel Rat is born!"

ABOUT THE AUTHOR

HARRY HARRISON is one of the most successful and respected authors of speculative fiction writing today. In a career that spans over three decades, Harry Harrison has written such novels as *Deathworld, To the Stars, Skyfall, Make Room! Make Room!* and bestsellers such as *West of Eden, Winter in Eden,* and the *Stainless Steel Rat* series. Harrison worked as a commercial artist, art director and editor before turning to writing full time. A past president of the World Science Fiction Association, he is also a noted anthologist, editing the acclaimed Nova series and co-editing the highly praised *Decade* and *Year's Best SF* volumes with British author Brian Aldiss. Harry Harrison was born in Stamford, Connecticut, has made his home in Mexico and in several European countries over the years, and now lives in Ireland. He is presently at work on a new Stainless Steel Rat novel.